CW01430125

LORD TRAFFORD'S FOLLY

INCONVENIENT SCANDALS

NINA JARRETT

ROGUE PRESS

To the incorrigible and energetic, Mr. Jarrett.

Never change.

PROLOGUE

*"The reader of these Memoirs will discover that I never had any
fixed aim before my eyes, and that my system, if it can be called a
system, has been to glide away unconcernedly on the stream of life,
trusting to the wind wherever it led."*

Giacomo Casanova

* * *

AUGUST 3, 1821

*L*ord Julius Trafford, heir to the Earl of Stirling,
toyed with the gold and emerald signet ring on his
finger, twisting it again and again. It had been a gift
from his maternal grandfather, a blithesome fellow whom
Julius missed with a fierce yearning. He would give most
anything to debate with the old man one last time about the
various merits of phaetons versus curricles on the streets of
London.

Recent days had been troubling. His friend, Brendan Ridley, had returned home in the early morning after the King's coronation to find his father slain on the study floor. That had been more than two weeks earlier, and the study had since been cleaned and rearranged. Yet, it was still macabre to consider he was sitting in the same room as the brutal crime.

In the aftermath of the murder, Brendan had been moments away from being arrested for patricide, but a young lady had cleared his name at the cost of her reputation. Miss Lily Abbott claimed to have spent the evening with him. It was ridiculous, of course, because she was an innocent miss. However, Miss Abbott had borne witness to both Brendan's arrival at and departure from the home of his paramour that night, so when the capricious widow would not stand as an alibi, Miss Abbott had taken her place and claimed it was the Abbotts' home where Brendan had spent the night.

All a lot of tosh, in Julius's view. Polite society's rules were cumbersome and inept, or the young woman could have simply told the truth without all the unnecessary fuss. Brendan might not have swung from a hangman's noose, but he was snared by the parson's noose—he was now encumbered with a proper wife.

Which left Julius as the last free man standing within their set.

Nevertheless, despite his pique at recent events, he had poked around in an attempt to discover who was the true perpetrator of the atrocity. Brendan was a dear friend, after all. It could not be allowed to stand that a murderous fiend had set up his chum to swing.

Nothing had yet come to light until two days earlier, when Brendan's bride was attacked by a panicking footman. The killer had hired the servant to hide his identity and to

2

search for a supposedly damning letter that the victim, the late Baron of Filminster, might have written before his untimely death.

It had been fortunate that Brendan's cantankerous butler, Michaels, had been the son of a gamekeeper. An excellent shot, by all accounts. The new baroness had been saved by a musket ball to the head of her attacker.

Julius did not appreciate fearing for his friends, which was why he was sitting in Filminster's study for the third time in as many days.

"I need your help."

Brendan's declaration punctuated the tension in the room.

Across from Julius, Lady Filminster's brother straightened in his seat, presumably eager to help resolve the danger his sister faced.

"What has happened? Is Lily safe?" Abbott looked like hell, the dark circles framing his eyes speaking to his lack of sleep.

Brendan cleared his throat. "I have discovered the letter that my ... father ... wrote. I now know what led to his murder on the night of the coronation."

Julius picked at his lapel of purple silk, repressing his annoyance. Brendan had not shared vital information with him, despite their years of friendship, and he would no longer maintain his silence.

"Your father ... or your uncle?" Julius purred, knowing full well that it would grate on Brendan's nerves.

The baron turned from the window to scowl at him. "You know of that?"

Julius arched an eyebrow in response.

Abbott interjected in a belligerent tone. "What is Trafford talking about?"

Brendan sighed. "I suppose the gossip has been circulating, so I might as well speak the truth … The late baron was my uncle who married my mother to save the family from shame. My true father, his older brother, died weeks before the wedding."

Abbott pulled a face at this unsavory disclosure. "Faugh!"

Brendan responded with a sardonic laugh. "Just so."

"May I read the letter?" Julius straightened from his lazing position, energized to find any clue to the happenings of the past two weeks.

Brendan pulled a folded page from inside his coat, walking over and handing it to Julius to read. Abbott watched on with the tension of a tuning fork while Julius digested its contents, which had been censored by dripping ink to mar key words into infinite obscurity.

Sir Robert Peel

London, July 19, 1821

Sir,

It has come - - my attention that the true heir to Lord - - - - - - - - has not been acknowledged.

I was speaking with his lordship before the coronation, and he informed me of his recent bout of ill health. He spoke fondly of his youngest brother, informing - - of his strength, intelligence, and wit at great length. There was no mention of his lordship's middle brother, Peter, who you may be aware died near twenty years - - -.

Peter and I attended Oxford together, - - - his death was tragic - - - unexp- - - - -. I have thought of him often over the years, which is why I feel the need to pass this information - - - - - -u.

Before departing England, Peter married a wom- - of Catholic descent. She convert- - - - - - - - - were married - - - - - Church of England, before leaving our shores. I maintained correspondence with him until his death. He had written just months before his death to inform me of the birth of his son.

I cannot say for certain where the boy and his mother are - - - - - all these years, but he would be the true heir and I implore you to look into th- - matter. - - - - - - - - - is the true heir to the title of - - - - - and his father's legacy cannot be ignored.

I understand the trials of being a second son, and I cann- - allow this matter to stand. Whether - - - - terrible injustice is a mistake due to ignorance of the child Peter sired, or a deliberate obfuscation of the facts, I must speak on my friend's behalf. His son is the true heir and must be found immediately. I will locate our shared correspondence when I return to Somerset and have them forwarded to - - - - - - - - - - -

J. Ridley, Baron of Filminster

Julius whistled through his teeth, looking up to shake his head in disbelief. "This provides a serious motive for murder. This is both wealth and power at stake."

Abbott held out his hand with an expectant air; Julius handed the letter to him without comment. He read intently before sagging back, the implications setting in. "Lily is in danger if the killer believes his secret might be contained within the walls of Ridley House."

Julius snorted. "And the culprit would be correct, considering the letter you are holding."

"There is insufficient information to reveal his identity!"

Julius twisted his lips at Abbott's inane protest. "There is enough. An elderly lord, suffering from a recent bout of ill health, with a younger brother named Peter who died some twenty years ago, and an even younger brother set to inherit his title. Who has likely killed the baron to conceal the knowledge of the true heir in order to secure his inheritance? It drastically reduces the number of suspects."

"Precisely," Brendan responded. "Lily and I spent last evening and this morning comparing a recent copy of Debrett's to a copy from thirty years ago to compile a list of peers. The runner, Briggs, is investigating what happened to each of the Peters to learn the circumstances of their deaths. Thus far, we have a list of six heirs who might fit the description, which is why I need your help."

Julius lowered his gaze to the ring between his agitating forefinger and thumb.

Abbott leaned forward. "What do you need?"

Brendan cleared his throat, twisting the toe of his boot on the bright Aubusson rug adorning his study floor while his dark chestnut curls fell forward over his face. "It is much to ask …"

Julius smirked. "That has not stopped you before."

"This is different, Julius. My bride is in danger." Brendan faltered before continuing. "If anything happened to Lily, I would never forgive myself."

Nor would I, since the young woman saved a dear friend.

Abbott rose to his feet, interrupting the *tête-à-tête* between Julius and Brendan.

"Whatever you need, I will do it."

Brendan's brandy eyes flickered to Abbott, and he nodded. "Thank you … Aidan."

Julius heaved a heavy sigh. Why not? Investigating this matter would fill his idle hours. It would be a lark to solve a murder, he supposed. And he could not allow harm to befall his friends.

"I am in. What is next?"

Returning to the window, Brendan leaned against the sill. "I need your help to investigate these six men. Lily and I are still considered scandalous for our supposed tryst on the night of the coronation. Although the scandal is abating now that we have wed, it is difficult to be discreet when all eyes are upon us. You two gentlemen, as single young bucks around Town, will be welcomed into the homes of polite society with high hopes you might make a match with their daughters or nieces. That access will allow you to search for information that might shed light on their involvement."

Abbott rubbed his face, mirroring Julius's horror to engage with marriageable young ladies. In the normal course of things, he would never agree to such risky interactions. If he did not keep his wits about him, he might find himself caught in the parson's trap like the rest of his friends.

But this is for Brendan and the courageous baroness.

Abbott responded first. "Where is the list?"

Brendan shot a questioning look at Julius, so he shrugged with deliberate nonchalance, extinguishing the anxiety that such a notion caused in his gut. "If we travel as a pair, we should be safe even within the perilous ballrooms of the infamous marriage mart."

CHAPTER 1

"Marriage is the tomb of love."

Giacomo Casanova

* * *

AUGUST 13, 1821

*J*ulius had enjoyed the past ten days in Abbott's company. The heir to the Viscount Moreland, Abbott was an athletic but academic fellow who was wound tighter than a field drum. Not unlike his own father, Lord Snarling. Which was why Julius had delighted in poking the tense young man.

If Abbott only knew I am doing him a great favor.

Abbott and Julius had been seen in public together the length and breadth of Mayfair, attending dinners and soirées, even a musicale that had been rather an earful of pitchy singing and off-key playing.

All the while, Abbott had been forced to put up with Julius's antics. The devil had taken Julius, who had been painstaking in pushing the man past his limits. Eventually, Julius reasoned, Abbott was certain to crack into uproarious laughter. He simply needed to bide his time.

Currently, Julius and Abbott stood by the corner, observing the home of Mr. Frederick Smythe amid the loud clatter of carriage wheels. Smythe was at the top of their list of suspects, but, thus far, they had not had an opportunity to enter his home or speak with him.

The night sky was adorned with silvery clouds and a large full moon. Abbott, who topped him by a couple of inches, seemed torn between taking pleasure in the view and finding a method to enter Smythe's home.

"How do you plan to get in without an invitation?"

Julius waved his hand in dismissal, contemplating the arriving guests with a devoted gaze. There was no time for conversation. He must find someone they could accompany into the illustrious ball. Abbott growled in irritation, causing Julius to clamp his lips together to prevent a smirk. His conspirator considered him a dandified fool, but appearances were deceiving. Julius knew his elaborate sartorial elegance tricked many into underestimating him. A complicated deception he wove, like those he had observed Lord Snarling engage in when negotiating on behalf of the Crown.

Not to mention, it is entertaining to discern others' reactions to the facade.

Abbott stepped back to provide the space Julius had requested, and Julius returned his attentions to the parade of guests. Someone had done wrong by his good chum, and he was committed to securing the safety of Brendan and his bride.

Abbott cracked his knuckles, pacing while he awaited direction with obvious impatience. Julius ignored him.

Inevitably the other heir would grow accustomed to Julius's methods and, thus, realize he was not the bacon-brains Abbott believed he was.

A few minutes later, Julius was rewarded. "I see my great-aunt Gertrude, with her husband." Without a backward glance, he strode swiftly toward the Smythe home. Abbott followed hesitantly, his footsteps heavy on the trodden earth. Julius weaved through the line of carriages in the rounded drive, skipping up to an elderly couple who were descending from the carriage in front.

He grinned widely, throwing his arms up in dramatic emphasis. "Aunty!"

Aunty Gertrude, a wizened old lady with stooped shoulders in blue silk, squinted up at her great-nephew before clapping her hands in excitement. "Julius, my boy!"

Julius leaned down, and a trembling hand was extended from beneath an embroidered shawl. She pinched his cheek between arthritic fingers, beaming with pleasure. Behind her was his great-uncle, an ancient peer in old-fashioned breeches, white stockings, and buckled shoes. He had the appearance of a corpse risen from the dead to be dressed in fine clothing by an undertaker. One had to respect that the old man could still attend events such as these at his advanced years.

Aunty Gertrude squinted up at him from aging moss-colored eyes, the tiny brown motes barely visible to any but his keen vision. "What are you doing here, boy?"

Beside him, Abbott stood at attention.

"I was just walking by with my friend." Julius gestured in Abbott's direction, who visibly gritted his pearly chewers. He could read the other heir's mind as if the words were inked upon a page. They were on a small but elegant estate near the Thames—private property—which belied the notion that they happened to just be passing by.

Julius suppressed a smile. Abbott was far too direct for his own good. Obfuscation and gracious airs were excellent distractions when pursuing one's goals. Aunty Gertrude would never question his claim, stated with such confidence and charm.

"Are you attending an event?"

"It is the Smythe ball. Frederick has a daughter he has been attempting to marry off for years. She is a dear girl, but the boys do not like her, I am afraid."

"That is a pity. I was hoping to catch up, but if you are otherwise occupied …" Julius trailed off with deliberation, baiting his great-aunt to invite them in.

"Come with us, Julius! Frederick will be delighted to have such strapping young men in attendance."

Julius gladly joined arms with his beloved relation and gently assisted her up the stairs into the lit entrance hall. Abbott puffed behind him, his reluctance obvious as he trod alongside the frail great-uncle, who doddered up the steps at a snail's pace.

Soon they stood in the long receiving line, Julius chattering with his great-aunt to keep her from questioning his earlier assertions.

Abbott peered over the heads of the gathered nobles, his attention occupied. Julius wondered what had caught his eye, but remained engrossed in the discussion with Aunty Gertrude, ensuring she did not have time to think.

Julius noted when they reached a shadowed corridor leading away from the main hall. Placing Aunty Gertrude's arm with care on that of her husband, Julius murmured an excuse and stepped away.

"It is time to go."

Abbott, who was still staring toward the head of the line, was slow to comprehend that the statement was directed at him. Julius peered at him with a questioning look, wondering what had Abbott so riveted, before bobbing his head toward the dim side hall. He did not want to gaze in the same direction and attract any undue attention to their imminent disappearance.

Abbott appeared reluctant to leave the line, but followed him away. Soon they stood together in the low light of the library in silence.

"Do you have any notion how ridiculous you look in this —" Abbott threw his hand out at Julius's gold coat.

"Now, now, Little Breeches. There is no need to tell Banbury stories … I am unduly handsome in my brocade, which we both well know."

Abbott snorted in frustration.

Julius narrowed his eyes at the taller man. Not that Julius was small in stature, but Abbott and his father, Viscount Moreland, were formidable. "Did a certain young woman capture your eye out in the hall? You seemed rather bemused."

Abbott looked away, unwilling to discuss what—*or who*— had caught his attention.

"Is *Aunty* not surprised at our departure? I thought you were to catch up?" Abbott's sneer was a thin attempt to shift the subject.

Julius grinned, amused by the obvious ploy. "*Aunty* will quite forget she saw me tonight by the time she reaches the head of the line. She and Uncle are quite easily distracted these days, and I saw an opportunity to proceed with our plans."

"What is the plan?"

"I think I shall wander about and gather information while you search Smythe's office."

Julius could see Abbott wished to argue about the roles Julius had assigned. Sneaking through a gentleman's private places was not an honorable pastime, but they were both aware that Julius was better at subterfuge.

There were six men to investigate, but Smythe was the man at the top of their list. He was the heir to a baron, which made him a promising suspect because the murdered Baron of Filminster had been seated with other barons the day of his murder.

There were whispers of Smythe selling off assets in the clubs, and Filminster had pointed out that a suspect with some sort of financial difficulty could be driven to a passionate act, such as murder, if the late baron had threatened his future inheritance.

Abbott relented. "I will meet you in the ballroom when I am done."

Julius nodded. "Have fun, Little Breeches. You might learn interesting things when you search through a man's private belongings."

Abbott frowned, but before he could respond, Julius left him to his devices.

He circulated the ballroom to participate in numerous dull conversations, all the while contemplating their host. Smythe was embroiled in a discussion in the corner with several older gentlemen, not providing an opportunity for Julius to engage him in discreet discourse. Looking about, Julius examined the guests for someone who might illuminate Smythe's circumstances until he could approach the gentleman directly.

Thirty feet away, Julius spotted Lord and Lady Astley, along with other haughty members of their set, exiting to take air on the terrace. The ballroom had grown stuffy from the warm summer night.

Julius dashed after them. Lord Astley was the perfect individual to pump for information, and would be unsuspecting as an acquaintance to Lord Snarling himself.

Stepping outside behind them, Julius nearly walked straight into the now-frozen crowd of guests. He halted abruptly and lifted his head to see what had riveted their silent attention. His jaw fell open.

Bad show!

Abbott had his arms around a young woman, framed by the full moon. Worse—he had his tongue down her throat!

This is what comes of being wound so tight!

The other heir had taken leave of his senses. The embracing couple disengaged, their movements cautious, and Abbott stepped forward as if to shield her from the gaze of scandalized guests.

Assessing her unique height, Julius realized with a growing sense of horror who the young woman was. Smythe, the future lord they were here to investigate, had a daughter of marriageable age. And Abbott had compromised her—the offspring of their prime suspect!

Damned idiot!

Abbott's expression was bemused in the light spilling out from the ballroom, but he was sobering up with haste when he took in the crowd of guests who were now agog, staring at him as if he had sprouted a second head.

At the back, Julius stood appalled—dumbfounded—before casting his anxious gaze down to stroke through his mop of wheat curls. A moment later, he threw up his hands in defeat. There was nothing he could do to intercede.

"It's Moreland's heir!" The impasse was broken when Lady Astley, an older peeress with graying blonde hair and critical tendencies, shrieked. Several guests flinched at the volume.

"Is that Miss Smythe?" asked Lord Astley, whom she was holding by the arm.

Julius cleared his throat, trying to think how to assist

15

Abbott in his hour of need. "I am sure it is not what we think. Lord Abbott is a nobleman of the highest order."

Abbott stared at Julius, accomplices in their diabolical invasion of this ball to investigate the host. The thought of the innocent Miss Smythe being destroyed thus was incomprehensible. What had caper-brained Abbott been thinking?

Even as Julius's thoughts raced, he could observe Abbott considering his limited options as he held Julius's gaze over the heads of the crowd between them. Julius stared back, stricken as he comprehended what the man was about to do. He shook his head, gesturing to stay Abbott from his announcement—

"I just offered for Miss Smythe's hand in marriage ... and she accepted."

Bloody hell!

Lord Snarling was sure to give Julius grief over this.

* * *

AUGUST 14, 1821

Audrey Gideon lifted the colorful starling from the terrace paving, the bird's iridescent feathers flashing in the bright light. It was a warm afternoon; the cheerful sun shined upon the secluded garden of Lord Stirling's London townhouse.

The little bird had flown into one of the many sparkling windows facing the garden and fallen to the masonry. Wishing to assess the starling's condition, Audrey wrapped it with care in her lace handkerchief to prevent it from panic-flapping its wings into further injury. She walked over to a stone bench set close to the table upon which sat her valise.

Having taken her seat, she raised the fragile creature to eye level and released a wing from within the linen folds while using a gentle fingertip to hold the appendage in place.

It was as she had suspected. The poor bird had broken it, but the damage did not seem too drastic. Fortunately, Audrey had brought her leather valise down with her to take inventory. Between its contents and the shrubbery growing against the terrace balustrade, she ought to have all she needed to treat the creature and set its wing.

Audrey exhaled deeply, pleased to have something useful to do. Since her father, Dr. John Gideon, had died, Audrey had been living under the roof of Lord Stirling, her father's close friend. London had proved boring. All she could think of was returning home to Stirling once she reached her majority. There she would be back in the village where she had grown up and be able to return to doing what she loved —assisting the villagers with their ailments.

In the meantime, while she was stuck in the tumultuous city of the loud and unwashed, it would be a blessed respite to treat the helpless creature trembling in her hands as a reminder of better days when she had assisted her father.

Terse voices wafted out the nearby terrace doors, and Audrey winced when she realized she was seated near Lord Stirling's study.

"Lady Hays has informed me of your antics last evening with Moreland's heir."

"Tsk, tsk. So formal. *Aunty Gertrude* informed you of my antics last evening."

It was no secret that Lord Julius Trafford and the Earl of Stirling did not get along. Lord Trafford was a flippant dandy, while Lord Stirling was a solemn and traditional gentleman who paid the utmost mind to propriety. Audrey knew this because she had petitioned the earl several times to allow her to return to the village, but he insisted she remain in Town to protect her reputation. Because she was still considered a minor in the eyes of the law, she had not much choice but to concede until she reached her majority.

Audrey grimaced. Casting about, she attempted to find a new location to sit and do her work upon the starling's wing. Nobles led such privileged and impractical lives, far removed from the pragmatism of ordinary people. It was sure to be a ridiculous squabble about inconsequential issues, and it would be awkward indeed to eavesdrop on the argument between father and son.

Especially if one of them catches sight of me!

There was no other suitable location on the terrace. Looking down, Audrey considered her options. The bird was in need of assistance. Attempting to move both her things and the bird would be difficult. If her father were here to advise her, she knew what he would say.

"The needs of the patient outweigh any other considerations."

Shaking her head, Audrey reached a decision. The starling's needs superseded etiquette. Trauma would lead to further injury and a longer recovery time for the wing to mend. She must treat the bird with urgency and ignore the quarrel within.

* * *

BEING SUMMONED to Lord Snarling's study always provoked a sense of wrathful dread in the pit of Julius's stomach, but he fought the urge to twist his signet ring. Lord Snarling had sharp eyes and would note the sign of distress in Julius's demeanor, so with the careful deliberation of a jungle cat stalking his prey, he relaxed his body into a languid position and watched his father watching him.

It had been the better part of two decades since Lord Stirling had spent meaningful time with Julius. In those days, his father had possessed a ready smile and had made time for his kin. But the earl of today was a reserved man who had no time for petty considerations such as family. He had impor-

LORD TRAFFORD'S FOLLY

tant duties to the Crown to take care of, both here and on the Continent.

"Why did you attend the Smythe ball without an invitation?"

"I wished to do so, so I did."

"Why were you in the company of such a scoundrel?"

Julius nearly choked in shock. Abbott? A scoundrel? The young man was far more upstanding and honorable than any to be found in high society. The Abbotts were precious gems of whom he was becoming quite fond. Last evening had been an aberration on the other heir's part. An incident brought about by Abbott's lack of carnal relations, if Julius's inquiries were anything to judge by. Imagine a healthy young man at Abbott's age abstaining from women! It was bound to end as poorly as it had done.

"Abbott is a good man. He offered for Miss Smythe, did he not?"

Lord Snarling's visage displayed his mistrust. He and Julius were the same height, but while Julius was long and lean, his father had a solid build with no signs of surplus. Lord Snarling was the epitome of tailored elegance, the cut of his garb displaying his form to perfection. It could not be more evident that Julius took after his mother, with his lean face and form, while his father was renowned for his handsome square features.

The one thing they did share was the wheat hair.

Or some of it.

Julius tugged on the short brown locks behind his ear. Lord Snarling followed the self-conscious gesture, so Julius smirked and turned it into a condescending rub to accompany the roll of his eyes.

Never display weakness.

A lesson learned from the man gazing at him with a humorless disdain. From a time when his father had still

19

bothered to teach lessons. It was an age since Lord Snarling had made time for his family, and Julius had many years of practice in hiding his true thoughts. A matter of pride to protect himself from the harsh realities of existence.

"I fail to comprehend what you were doing there. You have persisted in your pursuit of unsuitable females, so why attend a ball with marriageable young women?"

Julius thought about his fears for Brendan Ridley, and the danger that the baron and his wife were in. He would never admit anything so personal to Lord Snarling. His father, who had abandoned his family to their solitary fates so he could do his duty to the realm? What of his duty to their household? These thoughts raised the anger that was his constant companion. Anger for what had been, but was no more because Lord Snarling was far too occupied for such trivial issues as love and family loyalty. It was why Julius appreciated his allies as he did. Brendan was a friend he could rely on who had earned his loyalty, and Julius would stand by his friends until the end at any cost. His companions were the true riches of the world.

"I was bored." Julius shrugged with pretended nonchalance.

Lord Snarling tensed his jaw, staring at Julius for several moments.

"You are willfully irresponsible," the earl finally stated in a beleaguered tone.

"And you are sufficiently priggish for both of us," Julius responded in a modulated voice that belied the fury burning in his breast.

"Do you take anything seriously?"

"Do you ever flex a smile?"

Lord Snarling's face firmed with disapproval, and Julius saw the words exiting his lips before his father could consider their content. "Your mother would be ashamed of whom you have become."

Julius had made his father react with genuine emotion. *Huzza!*

Then the words filtered through his defenses, and Julius comprehended just what his father had declared. Straightening up, Julius fired back with indignant force, dumbfounded that his father had dared to bring Lady Stirling into his withering criticism.

"My mother *is* ashamed of whom *you* have become!"

The earl scowled, turning away to stare at the empty hearth. Julius's mother smiled down from her position above the mantel. More beautiful than any woman could hope to be. More lifelike than a Da Vinci or Michelangelo. Gone but not forgotten.

They had reached yet another impasse in which neither father nor son would budge a fraction of an inch.

His father had broached the unspoken subject. All the rage Julius carried compelled him to respond. The effort to restrain his thoughts was too exhausting to bear any longer.

"When was the last time you spoke with your daughter? I have not seen Penelope since I left for my Grand Tour six years ago! She is a debutante who just enjoyed her come-out in Paris. What of your wife? My mother? When did you last exchange words with her? And Pierce remains at Oxford, or visits with his friends over the breaks, because there is no one to come home to. I had to attend a house party to even spend any time with my own brother."

Lord Snarling had his back turned, but Julius could swear he saw his father flinch with infinitesimal tension. Bravo, it was well deserved. Lady Stirling was a magnificent countess who lit every room she entered with her grace and charm. Since she was wed to Lord Snarling, then his mother must be considered Lady Smiling. Friend to all. His beloved parent.

Whom Julius had not seen since before his Grand Tour because she had departed to visit her brother, a diplomat with the British Embassy in France, prior to his return.

Even her good humor had reached its limit after years of neglect from her husband, who had been increasingly busy with important dealings. Too busy to spend time with his nearest and dearest. So it was hardly a surprise that Lady Smiling had left for Paris. And when the time had come for her to return ... she had simply remained in France along with his little sister.

Julius could not blame her. He liked to think she was enjoying herself in the city of *bonhomie* across the Channel after years of miserable attrition in London. His mother deserved to be happy, even if Julius missed her so much it made his heart ache to think of his fractured family. It was why he never wanted to marry. Julius refused to mature into the grave husk his father had become, or to be trapped in a debilitating marriage with a partner who ignored him. This place had been a home filled with laughter and joyful faces once. It was why he slept at his clubs or Aunty Gertrude's with increasing frequency—it was too depressing to return home and reflect on better times. He would not allow his soul to freeze into icy oblivion as Lord Snarling had done.

"You know not of what you speak." His father had found his tongue.

"I know you had a wife and family who loved you, but you discarded the true wealth you possessed in service to the state. All those diplomatic missions, all those deals negotiated behind closed doors on behalf of others—was it worth it? You have lost your closest. Instead of collecting your wife and daughter from Paris—apologizing for your selfish neglect—you have allowed us to grow apart in the name of duty! What of your duty to us? We were a family once."

Lord Snarling failed to reply, still facing the fireplace. Julius was shocked at his own temerity in raising these forbidden subjects. He had never allowed his true thoughts to be aired before, but it was cathartic to express the rage buried deep within. "What are we now? The answer is simple —*we* are nothing. There is no we."

Julius reached the limits of his patience. His weakness had been displayed for Lord Snarling to witness. If he allowed any more words to escape in outrage, he was certain to regret it, so he rose to his feet and exited the study through the open terrace doors, shutting them behind him with a decisive click.

The sunshine blinded him after the gloom of the study, and Julius squinted against the bright light while seeking his bearings. When his vision cleared, he was alarmed to find he was peering at Miss Gideon, his father's ward.

Silver-gray eyes stared at him with startled distress from under the rim of a straw bonnet, a quivering starling in her delicate hands and her *bric-à-brac* sprawled on the table before her. Little Audrey had grown into a lovely young woman, with curling flaxen hair that was escaping her hairpins and a little button nose that he had tweaked in his obnoxious youth. Julius instinctively noticed the swell of her full bosom with appreciation, before recollecting that Miss Gideon was a good girl and Julius had no interest in settling down. Good girls were a plague to be avoided with resolve and persistence, or he would end up like his unhappy parents.

"Miss Gideon." He gave a polite bow, aware that the young lady had overheard personal grievances being aired from within, but all he could do was pretend he had no cares.

"Lord Trafford," she responded, with a little nod of her head.

And, with that, Julius swept away with all the grace he could muster after discovering his crushing weakness had been observed not by one, but two people.

CHAPTER 2

"I have always loved truth so passionately that I have often resorted to lying as a way of introducing it into the minds which were ignorant of its charms."

Giacomo Casanova

* * *

AUGUST 26, 1821

*J*ulius arrived at Ridley House with Brendan's letter in his hand. The past weeks had been a frustrating exercise in futile intelligence gathering. The more he learned about the suspects on their list, the less he knew about the murder of the baron. It had been a kick in the gut to receive word from Brendan earlier that day.

It happened again. I have doubled the guards. - Filminster

Damn Brendan, and his vagueness. What happened again? Was anyone injured? Julius lifted the heavy brass knocker on the front door and brought it down in hard taps.

A few minutes later, the door swung open and Julius found Michaels staring back at him.

"Are they safe?"

The older man, known for his reticent attitude, shut his eyes for a moment before nodding. Julius experienced a wash of relief, stepping forward to pat the butler on his shoulder. Michaels had averted a great tragedy when the baroness had been attacked nearly a month earlier, and Julius was profoundly grateful for the retainer's sacrifice in killing her assailant.

"Good man. Where are they?"

Michaels gestured up at the large drawing room, stepping aside to allow Julius entry. Julius climbed the stairs two at a time in his haste to learn what had happened. Under normal circumstances, he would compose himself before entering, to don a mask of idle insouciance, but he did not bother this time. Sweeping into the room, he found Brendan and the baroness seated on a settee under the window.

"Ridley!"

Brendan took to his feet, his expression one of distress. As Julius approached, he noted that the baroness's face was pale and pinched.

"What happened?"

Brendan ran a hand through chestnut curls that appeared to have been raked with great vigor into disheveled disarray. "Lily was in … We had another attempt to breach Ridley House."

Lady Lily Ridley, a petite elf with chocolate brown hair, peered up at Julius, her eyes huge against her pallid features. It was obvious she was recovering from a great shock.

"I … visited the library this morning to fetch a book

before breakfast, while it was still rather gloomy outside. I was in there for several minutes before I felt a draught in the room. When I looked over to the window, I saw a ruffian climbing in and screamed for help."

Julius realized with frustration that Lily's voice was hoarse—she must have screamed with vigor if it had inflamed her throat. Anguish rose as Julius considered the brave bride who had saved his chum from the gallows. If anything happened to her ... Julius admitted the baroness had stolen into his heart as a dear friend for her courage in defending Brendan. Despite his aversion to forming bonds with women, she was one of his allies now, someone under his personal protection. This continued campaign by the killer to search Ridley House for evidence of his identity was beyond the pale.

The baroness rose to take hold of his hand. "Trafford, you must not concern yourself. I am fine. We are fine. Brendan and I have made arrangements to stay with his sister and the Duke of Halmesbury. They have ample staff and are hiring guards to protect Markham House. Please ... do not worry."

Julius stared down at her, uncertain what to say. They barely knew each other, but what he knew of Lily Ridley, he admired with his entire being. Raising his gaze to Brendan, he licked his lips as he imagined what might have happened. The baroness was so tiny, she could have been overcome with ease or stolen from them. It was fortunate she had an impressive pair of lungs to aid in her survival. Her many years as a chatterbox had served her well today.

"This is ... this is ... this has gone too far!" Julius could hear the passion in his voice, and normally he would calm himself and adopt a languid posture and pretend that none of this caused anguish.

But it does! This has gone too far!

Brendan nodded. "I agree, but there is little to be done about it. We have to press on."

Julius released the baroness and began to pace, his thoughts whirling. "Our investigations are moving far too slowly! There has to be some method of shaking this loose. We know the killer is watching the house."

Brendan cocked his head. "Well … it is more accurate to state that we know his men are watching the house."

"What of Smythe?"

"Abbott is following him. He hopes to learn something soon."

The other heir, the baroness's brother, had since married the young lady he had compromised on the night of the ball, resulting in an unusual tutoring session from Julius on Abbott's wedding day.

Their lackluster progress to date had whittled their list of six suspects down to four, including Smythe, who was now Abbott's father-in-law.

"Yet, we still have another three men on the list and I cannot learn anything new. I have gathered information, followed them around, and nothing … They attend meetings and go about their day as if nothing has occurred. A peer has been killed, his heir has been accused of murder, his bride has been attacked—there must be more that we can do! Something to draw the killer out! We know he lurks about in the shadows! What we need to do is drive him"—Julius yanked the glove off, shoving it into his pocket before twisting on his signet ring—"drive him into making a mistake!"

Julius hoped that Smythe turned out to be innocent, or Abbott would be trapped in hell when forced to accuse his own father-in-law of murder. It was one of several reasons Julius was compelled to spend so much of his time investigating the other suspects. He hoped to reveal a culprit other than Smythe.

Lady Filminster had reseated herself, and was watching Julius with curiosity. "How do you propose to do that?"

Julius paused to stare out the window above her head, thinking. If anything happened to Brendan, or the baroness, Julius would never forgive himself for allowing it to unfold. "I do not know, but I will think of something."

Brendan cleared his throat. "Thank you … for all you are doing to assist us."

Julius nodded, but his thoughts were occupied by the conundrum before him. How to draw the killer out and end this farce? "It is nothing."

He left Ridley House soon after that, a glimmer of an idea beginning to form, but he did not think the others would agree. It was a plan he would need to execute by himself, which was for the best. He worked better alone.

* * *

IT WAS EARLY EVENING, and Audrey was in the library, awaiting the announcement of dinner. Flapper, her wounded starling, was on the mend, and Audrey had found herself, yet again, with little to occupy her attentions. She was reading a fusty tome on physiology when a footman interrupted her from the door.

"Miss Gideon?"

Audrey looked up from her notes. "Yes, Howard?"

"His lordship wishes to speak with you. He is in his study."

She nodded, closing her journal and stacking her books in a neat pile for her return in the morning. Her endless days of leisure in the earl's home were driving her mad. She was bored out of her mind, so being summoned for an audience was a novelty to break the monotony of her life since her arrival in London. If she had been able to treat patients, it would have made the grief bearable, but instead she wasted away in this great London townhouse, remembering the past. Perhaps she would hear from the guild soon, and she could make plans for her future accordingly.

Dutifully, Audrey headed to the study farther down the hall, curious what the earl wished to speak with her about. Lord Stirling had been busier than usual these past two weeks. Since the quarrel with Lord Trafford, if memory served. The earl was always engaged in work, but catching sight of him had been a rare event since the argument. Considering the content of it, Audrey wondered if his son had upset him with the discussion of the earl's estranged wife.

Audrey had not been aware of why Lady Stirling and her daughter had been absent these past years. Embarrassment assailed her over the knowledge she now possessed because of her inadvertent intrusion into their private family affair. It had been worthwhile, she assured herself, because her little patient would take flight soon.

Audrey stopped in front of a gilt-framed mirror in the hall to check her hair. Re-pinning some of her wayward locks, she reflected on a simpler time when she had been considered an attractive country lass. Here in London, she was a disheveled mess by high society standards. Constant fussing with her appearance to prevent criticism had become an endless chore. Audrey longed to return to the village where she could go about her day unencumbered.

Assessing her hair from different angles, she decided it would have to do. Turning, she knocked on the study door.

"Enter."

Audrey unlatched the door and stepped inside.

Lord Stirling was an imposing peer with a warm charm

that made him likable to most. However, Lord Trafford was correct in that the earl had grown ever more grim over the years. Audrey recollected a time when he had smiled and laughed freely. And, she supposed, the shift to solemnity had been worsened after Lady Stirling's departure. Not that Audrey had spent much time in their company before Papa had died earlier in the year. But there had been dinners and gatherings in Stirling, where she had observed them from afar. Now that she was thinking on it, it was possible that Lord Trafford's attire had grown ever more colorful in approximate correlation to the earl's descent into grimness.

"Good evening, your lordship."

"Audrey, you look lovely this evening."

The earl was ever polite, but Audrey could perceive his mind was elsewhere.

"Thank you, Lord Stirling."

He was standing at the mantel, his expression bemused. He glanced up at the portrait of his wife for a second before continuing.

"I have some business to take care of on the Continent, which means I will be leaving at first light."

Audrey nodded. The earl left on Crown business from time to time, so it was not unexpected. He usually forewarned her by more than a few hours, but she supposed something urgent had arisen without warning.

"Lady Hays is not in Town, so I have arranged to have Lady Astley collect you in the morning."

Audrey's heart plummeted into her slippers. "Lady Astley?"

"That is correct."

She scrambled to think of an alternative proposal. Lady Astley was an embittered noblewoman who embodied all the worst traits of high society. She was also very proper and not to be offended. Audrey would be restricted to feminine pursuits that Lady Astley deemed suitable … which would drive her demented until she was begging to be removed to Bedlam.

"How … long … will you be gone?"

The earl took a moment to respond, as if he had not heard her. "It could be as much as two weeks."

Audrey nodded, her thoughts still scrambling. There must be something she could do. "What if I remain here? I would not want to inconvenience Lady Astley."

The earl shook his head. "You must have a chaperone. Next month, your mourning period will be over, which means we can begin the hunt for an appropriate husband. Your reputation must remain pristine."

Audrey's heart sank from her slippers into the servants' hall belowstairs. They had not discussed what would happen when her mourning period was over, but finding an appropriate husband was not in her plans. She did not wish to be disrespectful, but …

"Perhaps the maid assigned to me could act as a chaperone? She has accompanied me to the bookshop, and to the modiste?"

"It will not do for a prolonged period, I am afraid. Lady Astley is a peeress of quality who will ensure that there is no doubt of how you spent your days."

Audrey wished to stomp her feet and howl in protest. She would spend her days in a great depression if she were in the Astley household. Better to be a Bedlamite! Her ladyship was horrid beyond words. Audrey would be lucky to be allowed her books at all. She doubted Flapper would be ready to take flight in the morning. Would she be permitted to care for the starling under Lady Astley's censorious watch?

The earl had been kind and generous in taking her in, but he did not understand the life she had led in Stirling as her father's apprentice. She had treated patients, taken care of the ill and injured, been a person of consequence in their village.

In London, she was nobody. A hindrance living in the earl's household. The moment she came of age, she would take control of her inheritance and forge her own path, but in the meantime, she needed to be grateful for the assistance Lord Stirling had provided in her hour of need.

"I ... understand."

What could she say? The Season was over, and most members of high society had left Town. Lady Astley must be the last remaining noblewoman of his acquaintance whom the earl could prevail on at such short notice.

Drat! It is going to be an awful fortnight!

She could only hope that Lord Stirling was successful in his mission and returned in good time. And that the weather remained fair to facilitate a speedy journey.

* * *

JULIUS KNEW it was a terrible idea. Not one of his friends or acquaintances would support it. It was reckless. Brazen. Rash. Idiotic. Which meant Julius was in his element.

Since his friends had each irrevocably tied the knot over the past two years, he had grown dissatisfied with his idle pursuits. He had no interest in following his chums into matrimonial hell, but found himself stuck in a half-life. Too bored to carouse. Too bored to attend events. Determined to not grow up.

He had considered visiting his mother in Paris, to bury himself in the pleasures to be found there, but the notion held little appeal. If Julius were honest, Lord Snarling was not incorrect—his mother would disapprove of whom he had become. This decision had absolutely nothing to do with his last trip over the Channel when he spewed his guts into a bucket for the entire journey.

It pained him that he was rebelling against his austere father with ludicrous behavior and outlandish fashion, but it was the only escape he found from the march of time. Julius had no desire to become a humorless old goat like Lord Snarling, so he was fighting against any inclination to mature.

Which was why, despite his fears for Brendan and the baroness, or his worries over Abbott's forced marriage, Julius was chipper while inking his notes to the three remaining suspects. He was tempted to prepare one for Smythe, but Abbott was investigating his father-in-law and Julius knew it would be overstepping to insert himself.

Nay, he would focus his energies on the remaining men on the list.

Henry Montague, heir to Lord Montague. Julius had established through his investigations that Montague had a penchant for gambling. That had been a promising clue. Perhaps Montague was desperate for funds. Desperate enough to commit murder to ensure no one stood in the way of his inheritance. But, from what Julius could learn, Montague's wagers were not reckless. The man usually won more than he lost.

Then there was Simon Scott, half-brother to Lord Blackwood. A charming and handsome gentleman with aspirations. There were no indications of dubious activities. Perhaps a strong ambition to succeed, and a ruthless approach to marriage, based on his choice of bride. Scott was courting a higher-ranking debutante, and Julius did not believe it was for her scintillating personality. She had the right pedigree but with few redeeming qualities, in Julius's estimation. The sort he steered clear of and who posed no threat of luring him into marriage. Julius would rather eat his own arm than spend more than a few minutes in her company.

And, finally, the vicar Edward Stone. A jolly, well-liked priest and youngest brother of Lord Harlyn. He seemed an unlikely suspect, content to administer to his flock in a local parish. But Stone could not be ruled out as a craven killer, determined to acquire wealth and power when his older brother passed on. Perhaps he needed the funds to fix the church roof?

One of these men could very well be a stone-cold, murderous thug who had bludgeoned the late baron in his private study.

Julius scratched out his letters to each, each with the same declaration. The singular difference between them was the location and the time.

HE DID NOT SIGN his name. This was a ploy to draw out the culprit. The guilty man, or one of his minions, ought to show at the unique location and time stated in the letter, desperate to discover who had written the note.

If none showed, then Julius had cleared them of suspicion. But if one did, Julius would know whom their culprit was and then they could limit their search for information to just one individual. It would help identify which deceased Peter had wed twenty years earlier and had a son by centralizing their search to fewer parishes which might contain the needed records.

Reckless, idiotic … but effective.

Donning a cape to mask his appearance, Julius set off to deliver the letters. By morning, he would narrow the field of suspects and end the frustrating slog of intelligence gathering. Anticipation made his steps buoyant as he contemplated the thrills the next day would bring.

CHAPTER 3

"I will begin with this confession: whatever I have done in the course of my life, whether it be good or evil, has been done freely; I am a free agent."

Giacomo Casanova

* * *

AUGUST 27, 1821

The streets were still deserted except for the most intrepid of vendors, and a few citizens of London who were huddled in shop entryways while they contemplated the unrelenting rainfall. It was yet before opening time for most businesses, and with heavy showers, Julius expected the roads to remain deserted for a little while yet.

He stood in an alleyway, out of sight, to observe the coffeehouse where Stone thought to meet his mysterious blackmailer—*if* Stone was guilty of the murder of, or had committed some other heinous act against, the late Lord Filminster. If Stone arrived, it would serve as confirmation that the vicar was involved.

Julius had been up since before dawn, and this was the third location he had observed in secret this morning. If Stone did not arrive, then Julius's plan to draw the killer out had failed.

What that meant was unclear. Perhaps none of the three were involved in the murder?

Julius soughed in exasperation. The urge to whip off his glove and fiddle with his ring was stayed by the incessant drum of wet, wet rain. He kept his hands stuffed deep in his pockets where they remained—mostly—dry.

Water dripped onto Julius's hat with no sign of a truce, a chilling rivulet stealing its way down the back of his head to dampen his stock. Julius pulled a face, shivering as he huddled in his overcoat. He had failed to anticipate the torrential precipitation when he had formed his plans the night before.

Julius was damp, cold, and irritable.

Pulling on his fob, he checked the time, wiping the spatter from its dial. So much for keeping his hands tucked away from the intrusion of the unending liquid assault.

Unfortunately for his new chum Abbott, all indications pointed to the guilt of his new father-in-law, Mr. Frederick Smythe, because Stone must be innocent. As were Scott and Montague.

Julius considered his options. He had not been home in several days, but the family home was a mere three or four blocks away, and he felt miserable. And hungry. Word was Lord Snarling was to have left for the Continent this morning, so Julius could return to the townhouse and take advantage of a hearty breakfast prepared by the fine kitchen staff employed in their household. Not to mention, change into dry clothing. His current garments were decidedly limp after three or more hours in the downpour.

Julius checked the time again and shook his head in disappointment. His last suspect had failed to show. There was going to be hell to pay when Abbott eventually accused Smythe of murder. Despite Abbott's refutals, his bride would never forgive him for tearing her family apart and sending her father to the gallows. Julius did not envy the other heir's precarious position.

Spinning on his heel, Julius departed his hiding spot to head in the direction of his father's townhouse. His boots were soaked through, and his damp stockings were uncomfortable. It was as if the gods themselves were playing a joke on him, knowing he was to be out and about this morning. His good spirits of the evening before had long since dissipated. Julius was weary of being worried on behalf of his friends. Weary of his tiresome family troubles. Weary of London. This situation needed to be resolved and then … then perhaps he would return to Italy. He had enjoyed himself in Italy, though it seemed like a hundred years had passed since his Grand Tour.

His stomach growled, reminding him of his plans to eat as he squelched through puddles. Mud tugged at his boots, and Julius reflected that his valet would be most put out when the condition of his Hessians was revealed.

Leaping over a daunting puddle, Julius landed on the other side and found himself ankle-deep in mud that gave way like custard beneath his foot. Julius tugged at his boot, pushing his cane down to gain leverage and yank himself free.

"Gadzooks, this is rubbish!" he muttered. Julius had brought the cane along for protection. He was attempting to reveal a murderer this morning, and it seemed wise to arm himself even if he was to remain out of sight. Thankfully, he had it, because he needed it just to make his way down the street.

Faith! Londoners are accustomed to rain, but this is ridiculous!

With great relief, he turned in to the street where his father's home and the home of Aunty Gertrude sat across from each other. Straightening up with delight, Julius thought about the eggs and ham he would soon be offered. Picking up his pace, he strode toward his father's front door.

As he took hold of the knocker, he caught a movement from the corner of his eye. Swinging around in haste, Julius discovered a tall, cloaked figure bearing down on him. Thunking back against the door in surprise, Julius raised his cane in defense as a glinting knife slashed through the air toward his heart.

* * *

AUDREY SAT on her trunk in the lavish entry hall, surrounded by bronze sculptures and intricate displays of antique swords. Gray-green walls and white trim provided a backdrop of quiet elegance, while burnished wood banisters gleamed in the dim light, and ornate frescos upon wall panels provided an ambience of wealth and luxury.

She was battling a queasy feeling within her belly. Lord Stirling had left in his carriage at first light. She knew this because she had been sitting in the window of her room and had watched his departure in the pouring rain. Sleep had evaded her for most of the night because of her tension. Soon she would be collected by Lady Astley, a vile woman who personified the reasons that Audrey wearied of her time in London society.

She longed for long walks in the country, the whisper of

gentle breezes rustling through the oak and maple trees near her home, chitchat with the villagers at the shops, the smell of fresh baked bread wafting from Mr. Rogers's bakery. Not for stilted conversation and ladylike pursuits under the watchful eye of an embittered prig of the upper classes.

When she had worked side by side with her father, she had never thought of what might happen in the future if Papa was no longer in the world. The past five months had been a sobering reality. The moment she reached her majority, she was heading home to Stirling, hopefully with a guild membership to facilitate her future. However, if the guild refused her, Audrey would find another path to practicing the healing arts without them. Herbalism, perhaps. Or midwifery.

That was neither here nor there at the moment. She had yet a month of mourning, then several more months before she reached her majority and could finally bid farewell to Lord Stirling's empty household. London was not releasing her from its noisome grip—not yet.

Audrey was not sure if she should be happy or irritated by the downpour outside, which was delaying the peeress's arrival to collect her.

Her gaze fell on the gilded birdcage, where little Flapper frantically flapped a solitary wing, the other immobilized so that the bone could mend. She could just imagine what Lady Astley would say when she arrived.

"What is that in the cage, pray tell, Miss Gideon?"

"This is ... my pet ... starling, Flapper, your ladyship."

Even in her mental musings, the frosty gaze of her disapproving hostess intimidated Audrey.

"Your ... pet? Do you believe a starling is an appropriate pet for a young lady of the ton, *Miss Gideon?"*

Audrey had to think how she would respond to such a question.

"Lord Stirling ... had a servant capture it for me as a gift, your ladyship."

Audrey shook her head. That was an outright lie, and certain to lead to more trouble. She could not disrespect her guardian by telling such a flagrant falsehood. Perhaps she should attempt the truth?

"What is that winged creature, pray tell, Miss Gideon?"

"This is ... my patient ... Flapper, your ladyship."

The noblewoman's brows shot up in horror. "Your ... patient?"

Audrey groaned, her stomach roiling as she accepted the truth would be far worse. What the deuce was she to do when the lady's carriage drew up in front of the townhouse?

"Sweet heavens, this will be a disaster," she whispered below her breath, causing the servant in attendance to glance in her direction. Flapper chirruped, his free wing fluttering as if in sympathy for her plight.

Springing to her feet, Audrey paced the hall. Gilded mirrors reflected a little of the gloomy daylight from the fan windows above the door, and the narrow windows on either side. The starched footman on duty politely ignored her. Audrey had attempted to form relationships with the household, but had discovered that the liveried men and uniformed women belowstairs were even more committed to appropriate behavior than the nobility, if it were possible. They saw her as a guest of their lord, and the earl hired the most proper of servants.

After a few moments, the footman departed the entry to see to some household matter, leaving Audrey to the muted sound of her slippers smacking the polished marble as she walked from end to end.

She had spent half the night trying to think up a way to avoid this stay with Lady Astley without risking reputation.

Tap, tap, tap.

Reaching the far end of the hall, she turned to walk back to her trunk.

Perhaps she could claim it was a gift from her papa, a reminder of their time together. Audrey winced. She would lie about her beloved father to appease a humorless old harpy?

She should state with confidence that the starling was her pet and Lord Stirling had assured her it was acceptable to take the bird with her.

Tap, tap, tap.

Egad, she was going to be disingenuous. If she had been quicker of wit, perhaps she could have raised the subject with the earl the evening prior. Then she could have declared some sort of truth, instead of fabricating Canterbury tales this morning.

Flapper was her patient. Scrupulous care was necessary to ensure the wing mended correctly, or the little bird would be permanently grounded. She had no choice but to plant her feet and refuse to budge. Audrey did not doubt her ability to protect her helpless feathered patient—but how much uncomfortable discourse would she have to prevail through before Lady Astley relented?

Tap, tap, tap.

The thing was … she did not wish this to turn into a grand debate. Flapper needed her fastidious treatment if he was to recover his flight. It was that simple. But Lady Astley would not withdraw her objections, that was certain.

Thunk.

Audrey halted in surprise to look at the front door as the wooden panel strained against its hinges, followed by a loud cracking sound from out in the street and a muffled exclamation. Hurrying over, she peered through the foggy glass, wiping it clear to see if someone was out there. Perhaps Lady Astley's coachman—

A muted shout rang through the roar of the rain, and Audrey was startled to witness two figures struggling on the roadway. One bore a cane, which he brought down on his opponent's outstretched arm as he leapt back to avoid the slash of a shiny knife blade. He slipped in a deep puddle, landing on his buttocks before scrambling back to his feet. Audrey's jaw dropped as she watched the two men battling, wondering if she should summon the manservant back to break up the fight.

The opponent with the cane swung out to defend himself from a lunge, losing his hat to reveal a mop of wheat-colored curls with distinctive brown back and sides.

"Lord Trafford!" Audrey gasped, realizing that Lord Stirling's heir was fighting for his life. The cloaked figure lunged forward, thrusting the knife toward Lord Trafford's torso, and Audrey bit back a scream of fright as he twisted away in the nick of time.

Tossing her head around, Audrey sought some method to assist the young lord armed with only a walking stick against a lethal blade. Catching sight of an elaborate display of antique rapiers on the opposite wall, Audrey dashed across the hall to lift one off, praying she would be in time to help her guardian's son.

Racing back to fling the front door open, she burst out into the street toward the men and held the sword between her clasped hands. She was not sure how to wield it, but it was long and appeared to be sharp, so she lunged at his torso as her father had taught her to do with a stick.

"Get back, you blackguard!" she yelled, bearing toward the assailant who had drawn his elbow back, ready to stab at Lord Trafford. Both men swung their heads in surprise, and she caught sight of a flash of green and blue beneath the attacker's overcoat, perhaps a scarf or the coat's lining. Discarding the distraction, she returned to the danger of the moment. This was an important time to pay mind to what she was about.

The unknown assailant blinked, his features obscured by his brimmed hat, before spinning away to run off into the downpour. To Audrey's dismay, Lord Trafford set off in pursuit—what the blazes was he about? The other scoundrel had a lethal knife!

To Audrey's great relief, the figure had disappeared like a flash of lightning in his haste to get away, and Lord Trafford gave up the chase by the time he reached the corner.

Lord Trafford stopped to scrape back his drenched locks, gazing for several moments in the direction that the villain had run before returning to where Audrey stood. She was still holding the sword at half-mast and barely registered that her gown was soaked from the downpour.

He reached out his hand to cover hers, coaxing her to lower the weapon down before holding out his arm. She took hold of him and allowed him to lead her back inside. She appreciated the support, considering her knees had gone quite weak now that the imminent threat was over.

Realizing she was still holding the sword, she dropped it on the marble tiles with a loud clatter while Julius leaned his walking stick against the wall. Audrey perceived she was panting from the shock of the moment, her chest rising and falling in agitation as she attempted to restore her equilibrium. She was thankful she had reached the fighting men in time. The assailant had wielded his wicked blade with a sincere intent to find purchase in Lord Trafford's abdomen.

The earl's heir could have been killed!

* * *

Lord Julius Trafford, the heir to the Earl of Stirling, and the honorary Viscount of Trafford, encountered few calls to apply himself. A lamentable character flaw which he now regretted as he assessed the situation he found himself in.

Miss Gideon stood shivering in the entry, her gray mourning gown sopping wet. A fact that Julius enjoyed for a brief moment. The dress was one that did not require stays, and she was too distracted to notice that the wet fabric outlined her chilled nipples as her bosom heaved. Blinking to curtail his sinful lusting, Julius lifted his gaze away with regret.

Instead, he stared at the trunk in the middle of the hall upon which a birdcage rested. A tiny starling with a bandaged wing cocked its head about, chirruping as it fluttered the wing that was free.

Was he dreaming? Had the bloodthirsty attack merely been a nightmare? The oddity of the birdcage suggested that this might be the case.

Julius pulled off his gloves, then shoved them into his pocket and pinched himself with deliberation. It hurt as it ought to, so he supposed he was awake despite the fantastic nature of his morning activities. His heart was pounding hard enough to attest he was not in a slumber.

By Jingo, he had not even had breakfast yet!

"That dirty-dish tried to kill me," he declared in dismay.

"Was he trying to rob you?" Miss Gideon asked, still panting from her exertions and, most likely, the shock of it.

She just saved my life.

Julius frowned, trying to think through what had just occurred. He shook his head with reluctance. "No, his intent was to kill me."

"*Kill* you?" Miss Gideon's silver eyes were enormous with shock and fear. "Why would he do that?"

Julius twisted his lips, noting the rising tide of embarrassment now that he was no longer in mortal danger. His plan had been far more foolish than he had allowed himself to consider.

"I ... may have done something stupid."

Miss Gideon nodded, but her expression was bemused, as if she had not truly heard what he said. "Will he try again?"

That was a sobering thought. One of the suspects on his list must have ordered him followed. It had been dark outside, with thick black clouds obscuring the morning light, and the attacker had had a hat pulled low over his face that had concealed much of his features. Nonetheless, Julius thought he had been the wrong shape and size to be one of the men he had been investigating. Therefore, he must be a retainer or hired thug.

He had to presume the scoundrel had followed him home to discover Julius's identity. Once he had been identified, the next command must have been—

"They know where I live. It is only a matter of time before they ascertain who I am, and then ... Yes, they will try to kill me again."

Miss Gideon raised her hands to rub her bared upper arms, her teeth chattering as she responded. "They?"

"I am afraid I have involved you in a murder plot, Miss Gideon. We ought ... I need to ..." Julius clenched his hands while he tried to think what to do about the young woman. Was she in danger now that she had interceded? From the perspective of his attacker, Miss Gideon might be involved in the attempted blackmail.

He unbuttoned his damp overcoat, thinking to toss it aside and looking about for a place to set it. Across from him, Miss Gideon's gaze dropped. Her brow furrowed gently, and she bit her plump lower lip, scattering his thoughts into carnal disarray.

"I should ... take care of that."

She pointed a trembling finger toward his jacquard waistcoat. Julius looked down to find his clothing had been slashed through, a wound welling blood into his ruined garments. His nostrils filled with the metallic stench, and before another thought could enter his head, Julius dropped to the floor with a painful thud as the vestibule faded to black.

CHAPTER 4

"The man who has sufficient power over himself to wait until his nature has recovered its even balance is the truly wise man, but such beings are seldom met with."

Giacomo Casanova

* * *

*A*udrey wanted to kick herself. She should have verified if Lord Trafford was injured the moment they had entered the sanctuary of the townhouse, but she had been distracted. As a result, he had lost more blood than if she had sprung into immediate action.

"The needs of the patient outweigh any other considerations."

Audrey held a lace handkerchief she had found in Lord Trafford's pocket to the bleeding gash, while reaching over the trunk. After lifting Flapper's birdcage to set it on the floor along with her cape, she fumbled with her free hand to unlock the trunk and throw the lid open. Feeling around, she lifted her valise from its gaping interior, set it beside her, then fumbled it open with trembling fingers. She struggled to lift him so she might wind a bandage around him to hold the handkerchief in place. Then, she could get him moved.

To be fair, we had to attain security before I could begin treatment.

Lord Trafford's eyes fluttered open to her great relief, his face abnormally pale in the dim interior. "Am I to die?"

Audrey scoffed, despite her misgivings. "Of course not! The cut is not that deep, but we need to get it treated and stop the bleeding. Can you stand so we can move you, or shall I summon a footman?"

What she had stated was true, but there were other complications to be addressed.

"I can rise."

Lord Trafford clutched his side and stood, but Audrey noted he was unsteady on his feet. The injury needed to be stitched and bound urgently to stem the bleeding.

Swaying, Lord Trafford made a declaration she was not expecting. "I need … to leave."

"Leave!" Audrey's exclamation was a shriek that made both of them jump.

"Before … they … return." Trafford pointed across the street. "I shall go to Aunty Gertrude's. Rose and Patrick will be in residence to care for me."

Audrey shook her head. "You need medical attention. You are still bleeding."

"Rose will have to take care of it. I cannot remain here. It is too dangerous for the household. For me … and for you." Lord Trafford bit his lip, clutching his side and struggling to remain on his feet.

If the assailant returns, I will be in danger, regardless. The scoundrel might believe I can identify him.

It was not the time to argue. But Lord Trafford was injured, and moving him seemed ill-advised.

"This is the home of an important earl. No one would attempt to attack you within its walls, so we will remain here."

"No!"

Audrey flinched.

Lord Trafford's face contorted into immediate contrition. Dropping his voice, he continued. "These people killed a baron. And they attempted to abduct a baroness. It is not safe for me to be here."

Under normal circumstances, Audrey's head would be clear and she would know with precision what she needed to do to assist her patient. However, these were not normal circumstances. Her hands were still shaking from the earlier violence she had witnessed, and the unexpectedness of it all scrambled her thoughts. The attacker had intended to kill the lord who was currently blinking in a disoriented daze. It had been brazen and vicious.

"I shall accompany you. I must ensure that your injury is treated correctly."

It would be fine, she assured herself. She would assist him to Lady Hays's home, bind his wound, and instruct Rose how to care for the patient.

What of the fever?

Audrey shoved the thought aside. She had learned from years of assisting her father that one could not anticipate future events in an emergency. One step at a time was what was needed. Order would be restored, but it must be attained one step at a time.

"I cannot ask you to do that, Miss Gideon. You have already been so brave, but your reputation ..."

Audrey bit her lip. Lady Astley could arrive at any minute. The heavy rain must have caused considerable delay.

"The needs of the patient outweigh any other considerations."

"Never mind that. I am accompanying you because it will

set my mind at ease. It is just across the street and the rain has worsened, so no one will see."

As if to confirm the correctness of her assertion, the sound of rain had increased to a dull roar outside. It was as dark as night with the thick covering of black clouds overhead blocking any light from the heavens above. God himself agreed with her taking care of this patient. If the current deluge continued, Lady Astley would be delayed even further. And even Lord Stirling could not dispute that caring for his heir must take precedence over what society viewed to be *de rigueur*. It would create a crisis of devastating proportions for the people of Stirling if something happened to Lord Trafford. He was their future lord, after all.

Audrey bent down to grab her cape, swirling it around her shoulders and raising the hood. The time for hesitation was over. The door to Lady Hays's home was a mere thirty or forty feet away, closer than Lord Trafford's room upstairs or the drawing room on the next floor. It was time to take care of her patient.

Lord Trafford was mumbling, staring down at the bloodied handkerchief pressed to his side, his face so white in the gloom it was incandescent. "Hang it all! I just wanted sodding breakfast."

Audrey rushed forward, throwing an arm around his waist for support. Lord Trafford was near to keeling over. The news that he had not eaten since the night before was unwelcome. No wonder he was so pale! He had been stabbed and lost blood on an empty stomach. She needed to get him to Lady Hays's forthwith.

"Make sure no one sees us."

Audrey nodded as Lord Trafford and she made for the front door. She would return before Lady Astley arrived.

Truly!

But … Just in case …

"Wait!"

Lord Trafford halted, and Audrey reached down. Taking hold of the birdcage, she swung it over to Lord Trafford.

"You must take Flapper."

He frowned. "What?"

"Carry the birdcage."

He accepted it, and Audrey reached down to shut her valise and grab hold of the handle. She would need her medical supplies. Hoisting it up, she cursed under her breath. The valise was a considerable weight. Along with Lord Trafford's tall frame leaning on her, she was bearing far more weight than she was accustomed to. She squared her shoulders and coaxed the injured heir to continue their journey to the front door.

She should summon one of the servants to assist her, but Lord Trafford appeared to think it would be better if they were not involved. And … *They might inform Lady Astley where I am.*

Flapper chirruped in alarm when she clumsily pulled the door open and they were met with a drenching gust. Once outside, she wondered if she had gone mad by agreeing to cross the street. A wall of water was an apt description for the scene that met them as they stood beneath the portico.

Glancing about, Audrey could see no one in the streets. She doubted anybody was about, but they would have to risk it. If they waited any longer, the bloodthirsty scoundrel could return and observe their movements, though it seemed unlikely he would have returned this soon after being frightened off. Surely he needed time to report back to his master and gather his wits?

Setting out into the rain, they stumbled and slipped their way across the street.

"Ring at the tradesman's entrance," muttered Lord Trafford.

Audrey guided them to the gate as directed, feeling around for the bell to ring it with frantic repetition. She waited a minute or two and rang it again. With great relief, bent with Lord Trafford's increasing weight bearing down on her, Audrey heard the door opening and looked down to see Patrick, one of Lady Hays's elderly retainers, inserting his leathery face through the cracked door.

"Who's there?" the old man cried through the pouring rain.

"It is Lord Trafford," Audrey shouted back. "He needs your assistance!"

"Master Julius?"

Patrick swung open the door, then sloshed up the stairs to assist her. Flapper's cage was deposited on the top step before Lord Trafford's weight lifted off her when Patrick took hold of him from the other side. Her patient groaned in pain as they gingerly navigated the wet steps to make their way inside.

Retrieving the cage which housed a sopping Flapper, Audrey took the opportunity to look about. She saw no evidence of anyone observing them. Truth be told, it was difficult to see anything in the dark street, shrouded by a thunderous waterfall. Rain this heavy was rare, she mused. A portent, perhaps? It had been a blessing. Without the rain, Audrey would have already left before the attack on Lord Trafford. He could have been killed if she had not been home!

* * *

JULIUS WAS surprised how much the slash ached. Miss Gideon had told him earlier it was a shallow wound, but it hurt like hell. Perhaps he needed to eat?

Patrick helped him enter the kitchen, surprisingly spry

for a man of his age. There was a steely strength to the aged servant, belying his short height.

"Have him lie down on the table," commanded Miss Gideon from behind him. Rose came running forward, her broad face wreathed with alarm while Miss Gideon placed her things, including the inexplicable birdcage, on a nearby bench before discarding her cape.

"Master Julius? What has happened?"

Rose's voice quavered in alarm, and Julius felt a pang of guilt at involving the pair in his troubles. No one would be aware he was here, he assured himself. They would be safe.

He hoped it was true, but he would address it once he had received the treatment he needed. "I was attacked on the street outside. It is imperative no one knows I am here."

Julius clutched his side, heading to the table with Patrick's assistance. Rose cleared some bowls that were laid out while Julius struggled out of his overcoat. When it was off, he threw it to a bench, then pulled off his boots with Patrick's assistance. Sitting on the table edge, Julius swung his legs up to stretch out on the long worktable where the staff prepared meals.

Rose handed him the towel she had over her arm, and Julius leaned up to rub his hair dry before dropping it on the table next to him. He had lost his favorite beaver out on the road, but it was sure to be ruined by the rain and mud out there. Julius would just have to buy another like it.

"I need hot water to wash the wound." Miss Gideon's voice was confident, and Julius admitted he was relieved to have her here. Little Audrey had followed her physician father everywhere and assisted him in treating patients. It was a godsend to have her at his side.

Rose gave a vigorous nod, her gray hair loosening under her mobcap, before running to hang a large iron kettle in the hearth.

Miss Gideon was adept in an emergency, he mused, as he shut his eyes in sweet relief. "Rose, do you have something I might eat? I am ravenous."

He was hoping it would help dull the pain if he had some sustenance in his body. His stomach was hollow after being up and about for such an extended time with nothing to fuel him.

Julius could sense Miss Gideon stepping up close beside him. A slight easing of pressure on his injury indicated that she had released his makeshift bandage. She pulled his velvet coat aside before unbuttoning his waistcoat.

"If Lord Trafford has an appetite, we should feed him to keep his strength up."

The sound of metal pots clanging was a blessed relief, and he salivated in anticipation of a meal. His physician's cool fingers tugged at his bloodied linen shirt, yanking it from his buckskins to lift it away from the injury she wished to examine.

"Perhaps …" He opened his eyes to gaze up at her. Silver-gray eyes swept over in question. "Perhaps under the circumstances, it will be easier to address me as Julius … Audrey?"

There was a glimmer of a smile on her full lips before she returned her attentions to the knife wound. "Very well … Julius."

Despite his circumstances, Julius could not help but enjoy the sensation of a beautiful woman touching him as he allowed his eyes to drift shut.

Audrey pulled the bench closer to the table with a loud scraping. Rifling through her valise, she clinked some items on the table beside him before leaving his side. He could hear her washing her hands before returning to sit down. She picked up the damp towel he had dried his hair with and bundled it against his side, presumably to prevent him from bleeding on the table.

Rose deposited a bowl on the table next to Audrey.

Audrey poured something into the bowl, and Julius peered down to see what she was about.

Turning to gaze at him, she nibbled on her lower lip. "This … is going to sting."

"What is it?"

"Warm water mixed with vinegar."

Julius squinted in confusion. "Why?"

"My father had me study ancient texts on how Romans treated battle wounds. They were highly effective—far better than many of the techniques physicians practice today."

Julius grimaced, giving a slight nod in assent. Of course she could read Latin. Audrey was an unusual female.

"Once we are done, you will eat."

Audrey swabbed the gash with the tepid vinegar mixture, and Julius clenched his teeth to hold back a scream. It hurt like bloody hell, and he turned his head away from her to hide his embarrassing facial contortions as he battled to refrain from shrieking out loud.

Eventually, she was done washing the wound out. Turning back and opening one eye, he gasped in dismay when he saw she was threading a needle. It would seem that Audrey was about to stitch him.

She looked up to find him staring at the needle flashing in her hand. "Would you care for some brandy before I continue?"

Swallowing hard, Julius nodded. Even on an empty stomach, anything that would dull the searing pain would be appreciated.

Audrey arched a brow at Patrick, who was hovering with an anguished expression.

"Ah'll be back."

Soon, Patrick had returned with a tumbler containing a shot of brandy, along with the crystal decanter. Julius lifted himself on one elbow, grabbing the drink and downing it in two loud gulps. As the warmth of it burnt his throat, the scalding pain subsided a little, and he lay back to woolgather about the breakfast he could smell Rose cooking nearby.

Audrey's fingers were on him, gripping the area around his wound. She was nimble with the stitching, her precision causing a minimal amount of discomfort other than the prick of the needle and the drag of the thread.

"It is complete."

Julius opened his eyes, peering down at the sutures along the left side of his midriff.

"Good grief! A couple of inches up and that dirty-dish would have nicked my heart!"

"You were fortunate," his carer agreed. "Rose, I need honey for the wound before I bandage him. Then he can eat."

The old servant's mouth fell open in dismay. "Honey? We don't 'ave any honey, Miss Gideon."

Julius was eyeing the plate of food in Rose's hands, but realized that the room had fallen silent. Looking back at Audrey, he saw she was frowning.

"I must apply honey to the wound."

Clutching his side, Julius rose to a seated position. "What is it?"

Audrey hesitated before opening her mouth. She shut it again.

His heart skipped a beat. "Is it the wound? Is it worse than you initially thought?"

"Nay." She shook her head. "But there … will be a fever. It is imperative that I obtain a quality honey to apply as soon as possible. The vinegar should help abate it, but … there is still a risk, I am afraid."

Dread crept through his veins. Infection and fever as a result of battle wounds took countless lives, but he had not thought that far ahead. He had been focused on reaching an anonymous place to hide out. His veins ran cold as he thought of what that might mean. Surely he was too weak to lose more blood?

"Will you need to do a bloodletting?"

Audrey growled, causing Julius and the servants to pull back in surprise.

"Bloodletting is for butchers! Pompous physicians pretend they know what they are doing, but their mortalities mount up! They have no respect for thousands of years of knowledge which flies in the face of their treatments while people pay for their arrogance with their lives! Nay, I will collect the honey and return to nurse you. It might be a bad night, but I will remain by your side to see you through it."

Julius was befuddled. He dearly wanted to eat, the imminent fever was worrying, and he had a murderer pursuing him because of his ill-advised antics. Grabbing hold of one fact would lessen the confusion crowding his thoughts. "What has the honey to do with it?"

"The Chinese have used it for thousands of years to treat open wounds. And the Romans used it on the battlefields. Papa experimented with it and found it noticeably reduced infection and healing time."

Julius furrowed his brow. "You read Chinese?"

Audrey squinted at him in amazement. "Of course not. Papa had translated publications."

Patrick cleared his throat. "I could collect some from the grocer. It's two blocks away."

She mulled on this for a moment. "Nay, I will collect it. I will bandage Lord Trafford so he can eat. Then you must help him up to a bedchamber. I shall collect the honey, and return to treat the wound."

Julius twisted his signet ring, remembering the risks Audrey was taking. "Are you meant to be somewhere? Lord

Stirling left this morning, and you had a trunk in the entry hall."

She straightened her shoulders as if to steel herself. "Lady Astley is to collect me. She must have been delayed by the rain."

He stared at her, and she stared back.

"You must return."

"You need care."

"Rose and Patrick will take care of me."

Audrey shook her head. "You will need someone who is trained."

Julius twisted his ring ever faster. Scandal had forced both his chums to marry in the past few weeks. If Audrey did not return home …

"Julius?" His gaze returned to meet hers. "You will need proper care. It is the difference between life and death."

He frowned.

"You lost a lot of blood and there is a risk of fever. I am afraid it is going to be a bad night."

Her soft-spoken words penetrated the sticky thoughts clouding his mind, and Julius could not refute he was weak and he was giddy still.

"It is the brandy. I shall eat and feel better."

Audrey came over to his side, placing her cool hand over his to still the agitated toying with his ring. "The needs of the patient outweigh any other considerations. You and I must take this one step at a time, so I shall collect the honey while you eat and Patrick helps you upstairs. I will be back to take care of you."

As a wave of dizziness forced him to put an arm out to steady himself on the oak table, the wood grain of its surface beneath his fingers helping him to focus, Julius admitted he was not himself. He needed Audrey to stay. He … wanted her to stay.

"Markham House is on the way to the grocer," he finally replied in a hoarse voice.

Audrey tilted her head in question. "What of it?"

"I need you to deliver a note to a guest staying with the Duke of Halmesbury. He will want to know that I have narrowed the list of suspects in his father's murder. For the safety of the others involved, they must know this information."

Her face was reluctant as she thought about it, licking her lips. "I can deliver it, but I will need to be quick. Could I drop off the note with the servants so I can get back here in good time?"

"Agreed. Do you have paper and ink in that magic bag of yours?" Julius bobbed his head toward her valise.

"Of course."

She bent over the bench, sifting through the bag's contents until she brought out a leather notebook. Tearing a page from it with great care, she handed it to him, along with a lead pencil. Then she grabbed the birdcage and removed the starling, sitting on the bench to deftly replace the wet dressing that held its wing in place. Julius could not help but admire her resilience under pressure. Audrey was an exceptional ally to have in his corner under such circumstances.

He bent his head to scratch out his note, observing with dismay that his shirt was speckled with drops of blood, some of which made it onto the page. He wiped them away as best he could with the cuff of his bloodied shirt, but he had not the energy to start again.

It is not Smythe. 1 of the other 3. Do not inform Peel until you hear from me. - Traf....

Gadzooks! He could barely finish signing his own name.

But, when he was recovered, there was a genuine possibility he could find the killer based on this morning's events. It would be premature for Brendan to contact the Home Office to speak to Sir Robert Peel. Nay, his friends must wait.

Folding the note, he handed it to Audrey. "It is for Lord Filminster. He is the duke's brother-in-law. The duke has trustworthy servants, so you can leave it with whomever answers the door."

Audrey had been donning her cape while he was writing. Returning to his side, she took the note and stuffed it into her pocket. "You must eat and drink before you go upstairs."

He grunted, too weary to speak. Rose placed the plate in his hands, and Julius devoured his eggs with single-minded focus, sitting on the table like a barbarian. But he did not care. He would have eaten them with his bare hands if Rose had not provided the fork with such efficiency.

Food!

Stepping aside, Rose pulled a large brass key from the pocket of her apron. "This'll allow you out the door by the mews."

Audrey took the key, which looked gigantic in her delicate hand. One of the gentle hands that had treated him with professional competence.

As his unpredicted physician exited the kitchen to the garden beyond, he called out, "Be careful. No one must see you!"

She threw him a smile over her shoulder. "I shall be but a ghost in the rain."

CHAPTER 5

"I know that I have lived because I have felt, and, feeling giving me the knowledge of my existence, I know likewise that I shall exist no more when I shall have ceased to feel."

Giacomo Casanova

* * *

*D*espite her assurance, Audrey was anxious as she crossed the garden and calculated a route to Markham House, which would avoid encountering anyone who might be observing the earl's home. The rain had eased, and as Audrey exited, she decided to turn right. It would take longer to reach the duke's townhouse, and the grocer, but Julius's caution still echoed in her ears.

She took a circuitous route, stopping each time she turned a corner to peer back down the street she had left. Just to be sure. Soon she had delivered the note, visited the grocer, and found a jar of honey which was added to the earl's account. Then she bought powdered bark and herbs from the nearby apothecary, that she thought to brew for Julius. She needed to do all she could to prevent his fever.

When she returned to the mews in the back, the clouds still glowered above, but the rain had slowed to a trickle. Crossing the gardens, she walked in through the kitchen door and found that the table had been cleared up in her absence. Audrey's valise and her things remained untouched, the maid evidently reluctant to interfere.

Rose looked up from where she was ringing out a towel, which Audrey assumed was the one bloodied by Julius's injury. "It's good to see you back, Miss Gideon. We been worried about you."

"Thank you. I took my time to ensure no one was following me."

The servant pursed her lips, her broad face reflecting her anxiety over the morning's events. "It's hard to think someone would hurt Master Julius, 'e being such a good'un."

Audrey nodded as she assembled her valise back together. The black leather bag had been her father's until he had died earlier that year, and to her it was a sort of talisman, summoning the calm presence of her father to provide her guidance. He had trained her well over the years, but it was still daunting to treat such an important patient with the threat of a fever. Fortunately, Julius was a young, healthy man in good condition.

"It is outrageous. I have some herbs I need to brew for Master Julius. Could you prepare a tea tray with boiling water in a teapot?"

"Aye, Miss Gideon," Rose replied, gathering the things she would need. "Just the hot water?"

"Yes. Thank you. Where is his lordship?"

"Patrick helped 'im to 'is room on the third floor down the west hall."

Audrey knew where that was. She herself stayed on the

third floor when Lady Hays acted as her chaperone in the earl's absence.

"Could I have a teaspoon?"

Rose brought one over. Prepared for action, Audrey hoisted her valise and made for the servants' stairs.

On the second-floor landing, she set her valise down and removed her cape, which was wet through and increasingly uncomfortable. Tucking it over her arm, she shivered. Each layer of clothing was damp, and she wished she had something dry. Perhaps there would be a robe in Julius's room and she could have her things dried out. Picking up her valise, she continued up until she reached the third floor. Turning into the west hall, she walked to the door at the end and knocked.

The door swung open to reveal Patrick. His whiskered face was set with lines of worry. "Miss Gideon, you be back! Master Julius is feverish. I have 'im settled in 'is bed, but 'e needs you!"

Audrey nodded, doing her best to look confident as she swept past Patrick. Julius lay beneath the deep green and rich gold covers in the canopied bed, and Audrey shook her head. This was why she could not leave him to the servants to take care of. Crossing the room, she whipped the covers down to reveal his naked torso. Patrick must have assisted him out of his bloodied clothing, and Julius had gone straight to bed in his small clothes. Although she had seen naked bits of bodies over the years assisting her father, Audrey swallowed at the sight. Julius was a fine specimen despite the flush of fever, with a broad, muscular chest and a flat expanse of stomach.

She noted with some surprise that the light dusting of hair covering his sculpted muscles was blond. Audrey had always thought that the mop of wheat curls that topped his head were an affectation bleached by his valet. It would appear that perhaps it was the brown hair on the sides and back that was the affectation.

Removing her kid gloves, Audrey used the back of her fingers to feel his forehead, which was damp with sweat and too warm.

"Please open the windows, Patrick. We need to cool Master Julius down."

The old man crossed the room and raised the mullioned windows. The room faced the garden, so no one would see the open windows from the street.

Julius opened a bleary eye. "You are back."

Audrey nodded. "I am."

"Thank God," he mumbled, closing the eye again and shivering. A flight of gooseflesh erupted across his skin as the cooler air made contact with its heated surface. Patrick fidgeted across the room, clearly at a loss for what he should do.

Rose appeared in the open doorway with the tray that Audrey had requested. Audrey had her place it on the dressing table, where she poured out an ounce of water. Searching through her valise, she found her vial of white willow bark. She needed to do research, but meanwhile he could drink the bark to help fight the fever until she prepared a better formula. Mixing a spoonful of it into the water, she returned to Julius's side. Rose and Patrick stood together, both wringing their hands while they awaited directions. It was plain that the servants were worried about Master Julius and eager to assist.

"Rose, I will need a fresh supply of boiled water every hour. Perhaps … broth. I would like some broth brought up."

The maid nodded, looking relieved to have a specific task.

Audrey cupped Julius's head, raising him so she could help him drink his brew. His eyelids fluttered in response. "I need you to swallow, Julius." She placed the cup to his lips, and he obeyed, swallowing it down in a couple of gulps.

"'Tis foul," he murmured, falling back onto his pillow.

Straightening up, Audrey found Patrick still waiting for instruction.

"I need to raise him to remove the bandage."

The servant nodded, hurrying over to lift Julius, who mumbled in protest. Audrey unraveled the bandage, putting it aside. She collected her jar of honey and the teaspoon she had brought up from the kitchen. Returning to the patient's side, she sat in the armchair that Patrick had brought over, opened the jar, and scooped up the honey to dribble it over the reddened sutures. Then she used the back of the spoon to smear it, careful to ensure the entire wound was doused with the sticky paste.

Audrey rose to wash the sticky substance from her hands at the washstand before returning to the bed. Patrick helped lift Julius again and, after covering the wound, she reached around his firm torso to wind the bandage in place—secure, but not too tight.

"No one must be aware we are here."

The servant nodded, still waiting for something more as he gazed at the feverish patient lying in the bed. Julius was a character who left an indelible impression on all he met, and Patrick's worry was evident as he rubbed the back of his neck with a pained expression.

"Is there a robe for me to change into? My things are damp and I need to get dry." A strong breeze blew in from the gaping windows, chilling her in her damp gown. Audrey wished to prepare a new brew that she would formulate from her father's notes, but if she did not dry off, she might battle a fever of her own.

Patrick nodded, crossing to the wardrobe and pulling out

a banyan robe and loose-fitting pants. "I'll be in the 'all." He exited, closing the door behind him.

Audrey retrieved the garments, and standing behind a dressing screen, she undid her gown, contorting her arms into awkward positions and fighting with the dampened buttons, exhaling in triumph when the weight of it dropped into a pool around her feet. She pulled on the pants, rolling the top down twice to shorten their length and tying them off with the tapes. Next, she pulled the banyan on, knotting the sash around her waist. Picking up her things, she walked back to the door.

Patrick took her things to dry, along with directions to bring the broth and tray up at regular intervals. She also requested cloths and cold water to use on the patient. Audrey needed to keep Julius drinking fluids through the night and to cool him down with dampened cottons.

Propping the door open to aid with the breeze rushing in from the window, she returned to her valise and dug around for her copy of *Culpeper's Complete Herbal*. The book had her father's neat notes written throughout. Some of the printed lines were crossed out, with her father's findings written in their stead. She needed to brew a herbal tea for her patient, but first she must determine which ingredients would be best for the situation he was in.

Taking a seat in an armchair by the window, she picked up one of the books that was stacked on the mahogany table, raising her eyebrows in curiosity—*Aus den Memoiren des Venetianers* by J. Casanova. She was holding volume one.

The memoirs of the infamous Venetian adventurer seemed somehow appropriate, given the room's resident. She could envisage Julius making his escape out the second-story window of a paramour's boudoir. Not only was he handsome, he had an irrepressible air to his flippant fashion and affectations. His choice to investigate a murder to aid his friends seemed both in and out of character, but she did not know him all that well.

Putting the book back on the table, Audrey licked the tip of her finger and began to leaf through the pages of her own book to read her father's notes, with the valise on the table next to her.

On page 128, she read about oak. *"The same is singularly good in pestilential and hot burning fevers; for it resists the force of the infection, and allays the heat: It cools the heat of the liver, breaking the stone in the kidneys, and stays women's courses ..."*

Pulling the little bottle of ground-up oak bark from her valise, she continued to skim through the pages, noting that My Lady's Thistle could be of aid applied as a compress. *"The seed and distilled water is held powerful to all the purposes afore-said, and besides, it is often applied both outwardly with cloths or spunges to the region of the liver, to cool the distemper thereof, and to the region of the heart, against swoonings and the passions of it."*

Alongside the lines, her father's notes guided her as to the efficacy of the printed treatments. She could imagine his voice in her ears as she assimilated the recommended alterations based on Papa's experiences.

She pulled out My Lady's Thistle and set it down next to the oak. Methodically, she formulated a treatment plan for the coming hours until she had her ingredients for the tea she was brewing. And when the compresses arrived, she would be ready for those, too.

Collecting her bottles, Audrey prepared the mixture in the teapot and poured out a cup. Tasting it with a tentative sip, she pulled a face. It was both earthy and grassy ... not to mention bitter.

Hmm ... Perhaps adding a little honey would not go amiss.

Once the brew was ready, she returned to Julius's side and made him raise his head to drink it while she could. If he became insensate, she would have only the compresses to place over his liver while she washed him down with the cold, wet cloths. It was imperative to have him swallow as much of the medicinal concoction as possible while he was still responsive to her directions.

It was her first time treating a feverish patient without her father standing by her side, and Audrey had to fight back the nervous apprehension that this caused. There was no time for her emotions. She must remain resolute and see to her patient's needs. She had assisted her father countless times, and he might not be there to help, but his training was embedded in her very blood and she had his notes and journals to guide her through the coming hours.

Besides, what choice did she have?

She could not allow some physician to treat Julius with a barbaric bloodletting which would almost certainly result in his death, considering how much blood he had already lost.

When it came to doctors, common sense was all too often left to wither on the vine in favor of their autocratic dogma. Papa had eschewed such dogma, testing the efficacy of treatments firsthand for the benefit of his patients. Then, too, Lord Stirling had sought treatment from Papa for over three decades, so she had to believe that in the earl's absence, she was following his wishes in regard to his heir. She needed to trust herself and follow her father's fastidious notes.

Nevertheless, the weight of responsibility was a heavy mantle upon her.

* * *

JULIUS WAS HOT. So hot, he was burning. He could feel the flames licking at his heels, and the roar of the fire blasting him in the face. If it did not relent, he would be burnt to a crisp—trapped in hell, he must be.

It was payment for allowing his friends to suffer.

His new chum, Abbott, being forced into a marriage born of scandal while Julius stood by, helpless to prevent it.

The little baroness with the bruises adorning her slim throat from her attack a few weeks earlier.

The day Brendan was to be arrested for murder, and Julius could not intercede.

Julius's own cowardice for not following his mother to Paris just because he could not face the ordeal of journeying back to the Continent. Even now, he could feel the deck of the ship rolling beneath his feet to make him bilious. Which was odd because he would not have expected that the seventh circle of hell could be at once fiery and flooded with treacherous seawater.

A soft voice interrupted the howling heat and the terrifying undulation of waves beneath, a chilled cloth dampening his brow. The heat subsided, and Julius drifted into the sweet embrace of oblivion.

* * *

AUDREY SWABBED her restless patient down as he mumbled and moved about. Julius was too hot for her liking, so she rinsed the warmed-up cloth, and once it cooled down, she applied it again. She swabbed away the sweat upon his pallid face, ran it down his lean, muscled arms, which she lifted in turn to run down his sides and torso.

The sheets below him were soaked through with his perspiration. Nibbling on her lip, Audrey thought about what to do, which was when Patrick arrived with a fresh stack of cloths and a bowl of water.

"Should we change his sheets?"

"Aye. I will fetch some and return shortly." The old man placed the tray down on the table. He removed her items from the one she had been using, picked it up, and took it from the room.

Audrey returned to the task of swabbing Julius. She might as well remove as much sweat from his body as possible before they moved him. Then she raised his head to feed him more of the medicinal brew.

"Swallow, Julius."

Even in his delirious state, he must have heard her. Opening his mouth, he allowed her to pour the contents in and he swallowed weakly. She let him back down and, feeling around the wound with her fingertips, she confirmed the bandage was damp with his sweat.

Stepping back, Audrey decided she would apply fresh honey and a dry bandage with Patrick's help before they shifted Julius. Glancing at the clock on the shelf across the room, she noted it was yet a long night ahead of them. Outside, the rain had stopped, but it was still as gloomy as a funeral.

Rubbing her tired eyes, Audrey plopped back in the velvet wingback chair beside the bed, stealing a few minutes to herself while awaiting Patrick's return and before the work began anew. Perhaps she should request a meal for herself. Until that moment, she had not thought about food, but she would need to keep her strength up to take care of Julius through the night.

CHAPTER 6

"Love is three quarters curiosity."

Giacomo Casanova

* * *

AUGUST 28, 1821

*W*ith the weight of a thousand cannonballs pressing his lids shut, Julius opened his eyes. The windows were open as well as the chamber door, creating a brisk draught through the room. He shivered and, peering down, realized he was bared to the elements, his skin puckered with gooseflesh.

Across from him, on the dressing table, stood a tea tray piled with cups and used cloths, and next to his bed was an armchair in which an exhausted maiden slept. Her head was at an awkward angle, leaning against the wing of the chair, and her mouth hung open. She exhaled a snorting bleat.

Despite her disheveled blonde hair and the lamentable condition of his richly hued banyan enveloping her body, Audrey was beautiful in the morning light.

His future bride.

His wound ached in a dull rebuke and Julius sighed. He was eminently relieved to awaken, having survived the worst night of his life, but now that his fever had broken, it was time to address the muddle he had created with his ill-conceived attempt at blackmail.

Like his friends before him, Julius had entrapped himself in a scandal, and the honorable path forward was to marry the young woman who had saved his life not once, but twice. It was the least he could do.

I am forced to do the right thing. I hate doing the right thing!

Growling his disdain of all things matrimonial, he turned his head back to watch the sunrise and mourn the passing of his freedom. He supposed Audrey was a good sort. If he was required to place his head in the parson's noose, at least it was with her and not some frightful flibbertigibbet of the *beau monde*.

"You are awake!"

Audrey's tone was exuberant, shattering the silence of the morning with a finality.

Julius smiled reluctantly. "I am too obstinate to die."

"I see that," she responded with an impudent tone. "Which means it is time to drink."

Some fresh concoction was thrust in his hand. Julius's stomach flip-flopped in repulsion, but he could feel the weakness in his muscles and knew she was right. He would force himself to do so.

"Drink up!"

Julius leaned back and downed the brew, pulling a face. It tasted like embittered earth with a hint of honey. "Faugh!"

Audrey chuckled. "Now that your fever has broken, you must drink that for a few days to prevent further infection."

"I suppose foul drinks never killed anyone."

"Just so."

She moved around the room, putting her things back in the valise she seemed to never be without. In the corner sat the birdcage where the little starling was chirruping to greet the morning like an old friend being welcomed home. Audrey appeared quite cheerful, returning to flop back into the armchair she had slept in.

"I am ever so relieved," she confessed, her silver eyes bright.

"Never say you did not want my death on your hands."

"Of course not! You are my first patient since Papa died."

Julius gestured toward the starling, who was flapping its free wing. "What of the bird?"

Audrey laughed. The throaty, lyrical quality tinkled into his loins to set off an unexpected stirring. Oh well, he supposed it was fortunate that he found her attractive, what with being required to marry her and all.

He wondered if there was any way to avoid that eventual outcome, but he could not think of one.

"It is a pity you cannot be a physician. You are most competent."

Her face grew solemn, and she slumped back in her chair. "I could practice medicine officially if the Company of Apothecaries would allow me admission."

Julius blinked in surprise. "The apothecaries allow women in their ranks?"

Audrey heaved a heavy sigh. "Under special circumstances, they have permitted women into the guild since the seventeenth century. I have petitioned them several times but have been unsuccessful as yet. I await a response from my most recent request."

Julius was intrigued. "What sort of circumstances?"

"Usually, it is the widow of an apothecary, if she can prove that she apprenticed successfully at her husband's side. The Widow Wyncke was one of the first, having worked in her husband's business for decades. The guild considered he had done a great service to them and was favorable to her circumstances."

"So you wish to practice medicine?"

Audrey's nod was enthusiastic. "Once I convince the guild to accept me, I will return to Stirling to tend to the villagers."

Julius's spirits lifted at this news. He might be required to wed her, but the doctor's daughter would be quite happy to rusticate in the country. After Julius did the right thing, he would remain mostly a free man.

"Why have they rejected you? Dr. Gideon apprenticed you since you were a young child."

She appeared dejected. "It is politics. I cannot join the physicians without a university degree, and Papa was a member of the physicians' guild which is a rival to the apothecaries' guild. In my most recent petition, I provided them with documentation that he was a committed student of Nicholas Culpeper's works, and apprenticed me in the apothecary arts, but ... I am not certain that it will be well received. They might be irate that he infringed on their domain."

"Ah, yes. The competition between the guilds is not to be underestimated for the pettiness that can arise. What will you do if they reject you again?"

She fidgeted with the tie of his banyan, making him think about how her pert bosom was shielded by the single embroidered layer. Julius flickered his gaze away just as his stomach growled in hungry rebuke. He hoped Patrick appeared with his tray soon.

"I suppose I shall apply again and I will continue to apply

until they accept me. I could practice in Stirling without their permission, but as a member, I would publish my father's notes so that others can benefit from his research. Just as Nicholas Culpeper did when he published his book to encourage ordinary people to care for their own health."

His heart twisted at the heartfelt words.

Stuff! Audrey was the second female he was allowing into his circle of valued chums in a handful of weeks. Fraternal bonds were reserved for … well … brothers. But after what the new baroness had done for his chum, Brendan, destroying her reputation to save him from the gallows, she had earned a place in his loyalties. Now Audrey had claimed her place, too, with her courageous intervention in his street battle yesterday morning before providing earnest care at his bedside. Julius was … feeling things … on her behalf.

Egad! Is this … compassion?

But how could he not feel for her? The young woman had lost her only parent, and was challenging societal conventions to secure her father's legacy. It was laudable. And, if she succeeded in her quest, Audrey should be more than happy to be his estranged bride living at the Stirling estate.

This would be an excellent outcome because he had no wish to mature into a humorless adult, and certainly he had no wish to follow in the footsteps of his parents and their miserable marital situation.

How happy they had all been as a family in his youth, but when his father had become more and more encumbered with his dealings on behalf of the Crown, the happiness Julius shared with his kin had withered to ashes. He had not seen his little sister in years, his brother Pierce did not bother coming home from Oxford, and his mother's face was becoming a hazy memory. A fact that still filled him with a sense of desolate rage.

His thoughts were interrupted when Audrey crossed the room to ring the bell that summoned the servants, freeing Julius of the obligation to respond to Audrey's tale of her frustrating crusade.

* * *

AUDREY RANG the bell to order breakfast, reflecting that it had been pleasant to confess her hopes and dreams to someone. Julius had not been at all condescending to her plans, despite her being a woman, and he was respectful of her skills in medicine. He had obeyed her instructions, had he not? And, this morning, he had acknowledged her role in his recovery.

She had not been able to freely discuss her wishes since Papa's death. Most members of polite society would have scoffed in horror at the notion of engaging in work, not to mention a female doing so. Somehow, she had guessed that Julius was not one of those members, perhaps because he had followed her directions without complaint. Yesterday he had asked questions about her treatment, but not resisted except expressing worry about her reputation.

It was … nice.

She felt seen for the first time since arriving in London. For the first time since Papa had died.

For a brief instant, tears threatened at the memory of her late parent discussing her future with her over tea in his study. She missed Papa with a fierce longing for days gone by, happier times when the future had been full of possibilities.

Mourning him while remaining idle in London had been the worst of options, one she herself would have advised her patients against. But she had been biding her time and taking advantage of her proximity to the guild until she received her inheritance.

Perhaps she should inform Lord Stirling of her wishes?

Perhaps Julius or the earl would write a letter of recommendation on her behalf, if she needed to reapply?

It had been a while since she had considered her situation with optimism, but after treating Julius successfully and admitting her vision of the future, Audrey's spirits were uplifted.

She tidied the tea tray and collected the swabs from the table by the patient's bed. She hummed as she carried out the chores, feeling quite cheerful about her patient's healing while he lay dozing.

Retrieving a fresh bandage and her jar of honey, Audrey roused him to sit up with her help, then unwound his bandage before lowering him back down. She scrutinized the sutured laceration and was satisfied with what she found. Julius was healing.

Audrey swabbed the injury and had reapplied the dressing when Patrick and Rose both arrived at the door. Both servants looked pleased to find Julius awake. She requested fresh sheets and the breakfast they both required. The servants departed the room, but as soon as the door shut behind them, Audrey recollected that she needed her gown and underthings. She could hardly remain in men's garments now that her patient was awake!

She raced across the room to fling the door open, hoping to catch Patrick or Rose before they disappeared down the servants' stairs. Finding the two of them embracing in the hall startled the wits out of her!

The couple leapt apart, nonplussed to have been discovered. Rose's eyes were moist, as if she had been weeping, and Audrey realized Patrick had been comforting her.

All three of them stood in awkward silence, casting their eyes about while they considered what to say. After several ticking seconds, Audrey cleared her throat.

"Patrick, do you have my dry things?"

The servant swallowed hard, appearing relieved that Audrey was to pretend nothing had happened.

"Aye, Miss Gideon. I shall collect them along with the sheets."

"All right ... Thank you." She nodded her head and hurried back into the chamber, shutting the door behind her with a decisive click.

Julius was watching her from the bed, having plumped his pillows to raise himself and stretched out his long, lean limbs. A huge grin split his face, and he was holding back laughter. His shoulders shook with the force of it, and Audrey had to fight back the urge to explore the muscular expanse with her eyes. It had been easier to treat such a handsome patient when he had been unconscious, and she was not so aware of his virility. Julius was a potent man when he was awake and his customary humor restored. To her dismay, she felt a blush creeping up her neck as she contemplated their respective half-dressed states and realized she was all alone with an eligible gentleman.

Julius found his voice, having seized control over the threatening laughter.

"You are pondering the nature of Patrick and Rose's relationship?"

"Are they ..." Audrey made clumsy gestures, her palms connecting in a suggestive manner.

"They have been married for at least twenty years."

She considered this news with considerable surprise.

"Oh ... I thought servants in high society homes were prohibited from marrying?"

79

Julius chuckled out loud, his lean face lit like a candle. Audrey caught her breath—he was devastating now that he was awake. She was finding it hard to believe she had had the audacity to treat him, but yesterday the situation had focused her attentions as a healer.

"Aunty Gertrude is traditional. It is a secret that they are married."

Audrey frowned. "So they married, yet live apart in the men's and women's quarters?"

"No, they have a room in the attic."

She shook her head, trying to make sense of his words. "So Aunty Gertrude knows about them?"

Julius shook his head with a smile on his face. "Aunty Gertrude is a traditional peeress who would never allow such a thing."

"Then how—"

He shrugged. "It is the way of high society. If no one acknowledges it, it is not true. Rose and Patrick enjoy their marriage, while Aunty Gertrude is willfully ignorant but ensures that they share a room. She is kind, after all, and would not stand in the way of love."

Audrey groaned. "These rules make no sense!"

Julius grinned in agreement. "You might be a simple country lass from Stirling, but I believe you begin to understand."

"God help me if that is the case! I do not wish to understand this nonsense."

Julius's levity dissipated. "I could not agree more. It tries one's sanity to know how the *ton* thinks. Logic has little place in the *beau monde*."

Audrey experienced immediate regret, wishing to see him in good humor again, but she supposed this was not the time and place for that. Returning to the bedside, she sat down in the armchair and contemplated him with great solemnity, careful to keep her focus on his face despite an urge to glance down at his bared chest.

Sadly, the distance she had created between them while he was at risk had vanished and she was all too aware that this was the older boy she had been infatuated with as a young girl. From a distance, of course. They had had little reason to interact, given their age difference. Julius must be a good seven years older than her. Except for a few words at dinners and other gatherings at the earl's country seat, they had conversed more in the past twenty-four hours than they had in a lifetime of knowing each other.

"While we wait for our breakfast, could you inform me of what this is all about? You mentioned a murder?"

Julius turned away, gazing out the window. Audrey's gaze traced the line of his profile, the straight nose and firm chin that spoke to his superior lineage. Taking in his tousled curls, she yet again wondered why, for so many years, Julius had dyed part of his hair a different color. The brown part, she now knew after observing him in his semi-naked state.

"My chum, Brendan Ridley, his father was murdered a few weeks ago. On the night of the coronation."

Audrey gasped, her musings over his appearance forgotten. "I am so sorry."

The corners of his mouth lifted as he glanced her way, then turned back to the window where morning light revealed the clear sky beyond. Yesterday's storm had abated, and the day was bright with just a few puffy clouds to serve as a reminder of the merciless rain that had pummeled them the morning before.

"Brendan was not close with the baron. It was the fact that he was to be accused of the murder that was my primary concern. As a consequence, a young lady braved scandal to provide him with an alibi. Brendan and her were forced to take their vows, and the true killer is still about. Since the

81

wedding, the killer's hired men have been attempting to gain access to Brendan's home for evidence, which is how the baroness came to be attacked."

Audrey's mouth fell open. Julius had stated after the violent incident out on the street that his assailant was brazen, but hearing the details of a baron being murdered and a baroness being attacked made his claim all the more real.

"We found the evidence. It was a letter that the late baron had composed to the Home Office, but much of the words were obliterated by dripping ink. What we could read led to a list of six suspects, and over the weeks this was narrowed down to four contenders."

"What was the note I delivered?"

"It was to inform Brendan that it was one of the three men whom I was investigating who had done the deed. The attack out on the street confirmed that the fourth man must be innocent, so it was imperative I inform Brendan, in the event ..."

In the event he did not make it through the night.

Audrey breathed a sigh of deep relief that her father's training and Julius's strong physicality had led to success. What would they have done if Julius had expired?

A knock on the door announced one of the servants had returned. Audrey called for them to enter and was pleased when Rose did, bearing a tray. It was high time Julius ate, and her own stomach was rumbling.

They ate where they were, Julius sitting up in bed to gingerly fork ham and eggs into his mouth. Audrey commiserated. It was obvious he was forcing himself to eat, and she appreciated his good sense in doing so. One needed food in one's belly to heal because it took a lot of physical energy to repair a body. As inquisitive as she was to hear the rest of his story, she allowed him to eat without interruption.

* * *

JULIUS'S STOMACH rolled in protest, but he picked his way through his breakfast. Bite by bite his stomach subsided, and the strength returned to his limbs. The colors in the room were brighter, and his awareness of the beautiful young maiden at his side rose as he ate.

He might be injured, but he was still a man, after all.

Audrey finished her meal, rising to collect another cup of the awful brew. She brought it over, and he dutifully swallowed it. At least the tepid drink assuaged his thirst.

By the time they were finished eating, Patrick had returned with clean sheets and Audrey's garments. The old servant helped Julius from the bed to sit in the armchair, where he watched while the two of them changed the bedding.

When they were done, Audrey took her clothing to a room down the hall to wash up and get dressed. Patrick supported him to his washstand to do the same, helping Julius into a fresh pair of trousers and a loose shirt from the wardrobe.

The chair was returned to the table by the window, where Julius sat. His side ached, but he felt much better, and he concluded that getting some rest and a few good meals in his belly would put him back to rights.

Audrey returned, exquisite with her freshly combed hair re-pinned and the gray mourning gown, which accentuated the silver hue of her eyes. She might be one of the few women of his acquaintance who was attractive in one of those drab gowns, what with her creamy skin, blonde tresses, and those eyes! Her eyes were fascinating.

Julius reminded himself that a wedding might be unavoidable, but he was not to get any ideas of a proper marriage. The sort of marriage that started off full of hope and eventually entrapped both parties—and their children—in misery. He had hated seeing the growing distance between Lord Snarling and his mother throughout his youth.

Audrey interrupted his thoughts with the question he had been dreading.

"How do you know the fourth suspect is innocent? What was the attack about?"

Julius flushed. It was inevitable he would have to explain his stupidity to someone, and he was rather embarrassed that Audrey was the first person to hear the explanation, but he owed it to her after involving her so deeply in his plot. It was sobering to acknowledge he could have gotten himself killed with his idiotic antics!

"I thought to draw the killer out by sending blackmail notes providing different locations for a meeting. None of the men showed, but I assume that one of the suspects had his man follow me."

Horror crossed her features, and her plump lower lip dropped. "Julius! You could have been killed!"

"I freely admit it was a poorly devised plan," he grumbled, mortified, as he twisted his signet ring.

"Poorly devised! It was barely a plan at all! You are pursuing a cold-blooded killer." Under her breath, she mumbled something like daft imbecile. Julius's lips quivered despite his embarrassment. He was growing to like the tempestuous Miss Gideon. One moment she was professional competence, and the next she was waving a sword at a blackguard in the street. He would like to see her unravel when she made love for the first time.

The thought sent a tide of lust cascading to his groin as he acknowledged he would be the man to bed her, what with their impending vows. Julius tilted his head to examine his virginal temptress. Did Audrey know what fate awaited them? That their wedding was inevitable now that she had run off with him?

"Yes, but now I know it was one of the three men I attempted to blackmail, which improves my odds of discovering who it is. I shall need to follow them to learn more about them."

Audrey harrumphed. "Not today. You must rest until your strength returns. What would you do if you encountered that villain? You are as weak as a kitten."

"Tomorrow, perhaps?"

She nibbled on her lip, thinking. "Mayhap, but I would need to accompany you. And, strategy must be considered. Some sort of disguise, perhaps. Your first attempt was waving a red flag in front of a bull and racing away with the hopes it would not gore and trample you to your death."

Julius gave an exaggerated pout, drawing a reluctant giggle from his headstrong healer. The throaty tone caused a shiver to run down his spine. Mayhap a wedding night with Audrey would not be so torturous. He could think of worse companions with whom to enter the parson's trap.

"Shall we play piquet?"

His brows shot up in surprise, but Audrey was already across the room searching through her valise. She held up a pack of cards in victory.

"What does that bag not contain?"

She shrugged. "Sometimes patients are bored. The cards are in here for those occasions."

Julius grinned. "We can play, but I warn you I will not be gentle."

As soon as the words were out of his mouth, he realized the double entendre. His thoughts had been hovering in the wrong direction since he had eaten, and the flirting was inadvertent. Audrey's nostrils flared. She must have noted the train of his thought, being a worldly individual who had followed her father into all sorts of patients' rooms, but she brushed it aside as if she had not heard him.

Walking over with the cards, she shifted a chair to face the table where he sat. Her face was downcast, her blonde lashes fanning her cheeks, but Julius did not miss the reddening of her ears that spoke to her awareness of his words.

CHAPTER 7

*"I always made my food congenial to my constitution, and my
health was always excellent."*

Giacomo Casanova

* * *

AUGUST 29, 1821

*J*ulius and Audrey left by the mews after dawn. A
relaxing afternoon playing cards had given him
the rest he needed to feel more himself, and
Audrey had revealed herself to be a competitive player. She
had kept painstaking record of the complicated piquet
scores, reading them aloud with an earnest expression at
regular intervals.

Noticing that she was quick to laugh, he had used this to
his advantage by peppering their discussion with amusing
anecdotes until he had succeeded in distracting her suffi-

ciently to play the winning hand. Then they had discussed whether they should examine the street for watchers but agreed they lacked the manpower to do anything effective. Best to assume the worst and use the entrance to the alley behind the house as Audrey had done the day of the attack.

Exhaustion had claimed him shortly after, and he had fallen asleep just after dinner, which he supposed was fortunate because of their plans to rise early.

This morning, he was dressed in an overcoat, clean work boots, and a battered hat pulled down low to disguise his distinctive hair. Patrick had dug them up the day before from the room where the grooms slept, along with a hat and coat for Audrey, before heading out to purchase her a pair of lad's work boots. She swam in her bulky men's clothing, but Julius was relieved to have her covered up to maintain his focus on their objective. She must have found a way to flatten her breasts because she truly appeared to be a lad in his teens under all that gear.

Julius felt considerably stronger than the day before, although Audrey had cautioned him that they must take it easy. His knife wound still throbbed, but Audrey assured him she was satisfied with the healing process under way. With a full day of rest, and several meals in his belly, he had woken up this morning feeling almost normal.

They carefully left the neighborhood, even changing their gaits until they reached one of the main roads. Julius hailed a hackney, and soon they were on their way to watch the vicarage where Stone resided.

"This is exciting," his companion proclaimed, peering around at the streets as they drove by. "Perhaps we could visit a coffeehouse?"

Julius grinned. "Men certainly have access to far more places, but a coffeehouse? That is the top of your list?"

Audrey smiled back, her eyes glistening when she turned

to answer him. "Papa loved to visit coffeehouses. I am at a loss why we never thought to dress me as a boy so I could join him in one."

This brought back the memory of seeing her earlier that morning in trousers and a shirt, accompanied by a rush of impassioned heat that shivered down his spine at the thought of divesting the garments from her full figure. Over the last two days, it had come to light that Audrey possessed an adventuress spirit which sent his thoughts in a lascivious direction—specifically, a wedding night between the sheets to uncover just how bold she might be before she returned to Stirling to pursue her goal of practicing the healing arts.

"Perhaps we will have an opportunity to visit one. Perhaps we shall visit other domains of men."

Audrey's face lit up, evidently elated at the possibility. He wondered where he might take her. Tattersall's to witness the horse auctions? Perhaps a dancing hall to watch a show? Sharing these activities with her was unexpectedly intriguing. To watch her seeing them for the first time.

Soon they disembarked on the vicar's street. It was a block from the church where Stone presided. Of all the suspects on the list, this was the one whom Julius considered least likely. From his prior investigations over the past few weeks, Julius had been unable to learn anything of note about Stone. He was well-liked by his parishioners; he had been serving the Church of England for nearly thirty years, and most of his days appeared to be filled with good works. If anything, he seemed reluctant to one day inherit the title from his older brother.

However, in his prior attempts to uncover something incriminating, Julius had not known for certain that the killer was one of the three men on the list. Now that he did, he had a renewed interest in covering this ground again with the benefit of his new perspective. There was a one in three chance Stone was their killer, and knowing that might bring to light something Julius had not observed in his previous attempts.

To his genuine amusement, Julius peered around the street to confirm that one of his favorite coffeehouses was right on the corner.

"Et voilà!" He waved in presentation. Audrey turned to see what he was gesturing at, a grin of delight lighting her features.

"Truly?"

"I propose we sit in the window and watch Stone's home from within."

Audrey clapped her hands, skipping in the direction before realizing she was in disguise. Clearing her throat in a husky voice, she slowed to her interpretation of a masculine swagger. Julius chuckled, keeping pace with her with ease. His legs were longer, after all.

Entering the dim interior, Julius breathed in the rich aroma of coffee with joy. He noted the window seat was occupied and the tables half occupied despite the early hour, but he was determined to allow Audrey her first visit to a house of coffee. Musing for a moment that he could not simply use his status to convince the two clerks sitting at the window table, Julius considered his options.

Approaching the two studious men who must have stopped here on their way to work, Julius sidled up to stand right over them in an intimidating stance.

"Would you fellows mind if me brother an' me sit 'ere? We're to meet someone ou'side, but they ain't shown yet so we must 'ave a clear view."

The men, dressed in the neat but boring attire of cleric work, looked up at him with startled expressions. Taking in Julius's height and rough garments, a trace of fear crossed their features before both men rose with haste. "That is fine, sir. We were just done."

Throwing coin onto the table next to their half full mugs, the two men made a hasty exit. Julius turned to find Audrey staring at him in amazement.

"Do you always get what you want?" She kept her voice low and husky to avoid attracting attention to her femininity.

Julius shrugged. "Almost always."

They took their seats in the booth, Julius ensuring he had a clear view down the street to Stone's door.

"You possess many faces, Julius." Audrey's low comment implied she was not certain if this revelation should impress or disgust her.

He grinned, his attention remaining fixed out the window. "Not to mention, many personalities."

Audrey harrumphed. "I always thought you got your way because you are the son of an earl, but I am coming to realize you would find alternative methods even if you were not."

Julius shrugged again, glancing at her. "Where there is a will, there is a way."

One of the buxom women serving tables interrupted them. Julius placed their orders while Audrey sank into her coat, her hat masking her features from the server. Once they were alone once more, she continued the earlier discussion.

"I think perhaps you need to learn an ounce of moderation. Considering ..." Audrey gestured toward his injury.

"Perhaps."

"Lord, help the world if you turned your talents to something useful," she muttered.

Julius quirked an eyebrow, his gaze flickering to her for the briefest of moments before returning to his observation of Stone's front door. "A murder investigation is not useful?"

There was a pause. "I apologize if I sounded condescending. It is courageous of you to pursue justice on behalf of your friends. I meant in a general sense, not this specific situation."

Julius had the urge to remove his glove to twist his ring but, instead, he stuffed that hand into one of his ample pockets. "Ah, but if I did that, I might become Lord Snarling, and we would not want that."

"Lord Snarling ... oh! You mean your father?"

Julius gave a brusque nod. When he glanced her way after several seconds of silence, he found Audrey staring at him with a thoughtful expression. He averted his gaze back to the street, uncomfortable with the intimacy of their discussion.

The serving woman returned, planting two mugs on the table with a firm thunk which caused a few drops to spill and run down the sides. She used a towel to wipe them off and walked away to serve another table.

Audrey pulled her mug closer, lowering her face to inhale deeply. Finally, she spoke. Unfortunately, she returned to the subject of his parent.

"Why do you have to become a version of your father? Why can you not be your own man?"

Julius frowned, cocking his head at the unexpected question. He opened his mouth to reply. "Because ... because ... because ... I ... do not ... know ... why."

He supposed until that moment, he had thought that maturing meant inevitably becoming his father. But now that she had asked the question, he considered his friends and their relations. The Earl of Saunton, brother to one of his close friends, had inherited his title at eighteen, but he had retained his easy charm over the years even while expanding the wealth and influence of his estates. Saunton had a ready smile and a humorous quip under most circumstances, despite being raised by the peer who had been known as Lord Satan amongst both the nobility and servants until his untimely death. He had even married last year and was quite taken with his wife, if appearances were correct. Julius had not considered he might have a choice in the man he would become if he allowed himself to evolve.

The tension of the moment was broken, to his relief, a moment later when Audrey raised the mug to her lips and tasted coffee for the first time.

"Bah! This is horrible!"

Julius chuckled. "It is an acquired taste, young lad. The more you drink, the more you will like it."

Audrey smacked it down on the wooden surface between them. "Not likely. That is my last sip, I think."

He burst out laughing. Her down-turned lips and disgusted expression were so adorable, it wiped away the worrying sentiments she had raised in his mind, and his good humor was restored.

* * *

AUDREY AND JULIUS spent the morning and early part of the afternoon following Stone around his neighborhood. It was fun to be out and about, providing context to the difference between their genders. Julius had far more freedom than she had enjoyed since arriving in London, and in her disguise as a youthful boy, she had observed the world from a different point of view.

Stone left the vicarage midmorning, presumably after working in a study within. He had met with a women's group from the parish, and visited a young family who had a newborn in their home, before returning to the vicarage.

Julius had whispered that he wanted to see inside, so Audrey acted as a lookout on the street and, with too much time on her hands, her thoughts turned to the scandal she would face when she returned to Lord Stirling's home. Lady

Astley would have arrived to collect her two days earlier and found nothing but her trunk in the hall. Resolutely, Audrey pushed the thought aside. Hopefully she could simply return to her village, where no one would be the wiser that she had vanished with a gentleman for several days.

Julius returned. "I could see them through a window. Stone is sharing tea with his wife and the curate."

Audrey pouted in disappointment, and they took up a seat in the coffeehouse for a little while, where she eschewed tasting the coffee in her mug yet again. Eventually, they gave up their watch and returned home to share their own cup of tea, with Rose moving around them in the kitchen. The smell of baking bread made Audrey's stomach grumble in anticipation.

"I cannot see a situation in which Stone is the killer." She sighed, her elbows crudely wedged on the worktable as she sipped her tea. The vicar, the middle brother of five children, was in his fifties with a jocular manner and a round belly. He seemed satisfied in his role, providing succor to the parishioners he ministered to with frequent smiles and chuckles. The people Julius had met with all appeared to adore him. "He does not strike me as one desperate to inherit a title, or excessive wealth."

Julius exhaled heavily. "I agree. From the information I have gathered, Stone is relatively wealthy, but he lives a rather simple life. His clothes are not flashy, his wife is sensibly attired, and the vicarage looks comfortable, with no overt signs of his funds on display. The notion of him flying into a passionate rage to bludgeon a baron for wealth and power seems farfetched."

The bell to the tradesman's entrance rang, causing both of them to flinch and look toward the street out front in alarm.

"Rose?"

The maid came hurrying over from where she had been

removing baked bread from the oven. Audrey felt a stab of guilt, thinking of all the extra household work she and Julius represented for the couple, who were merely caretakers of an empty home.

"Yes, Master Julius?"

"Are we expecting anyone?"

Rose shook her head just as the bell rang again. The sound of footsteps echoed from the servants' hall as Patrick made his way to the door.

Audrey rose, hurrying after him to view who had rung, with Julius following her.

"Ahm 'fraid we ain't expecting a delivery, miss."

Audrey could hear a woman speaking, but could not make out the words. Julius nudged past Audrey, stealing up behind the door Patrick had cracked open. His jaw dropped, and Audrey saw him whispering to Patrick.

"Ah just recalled we're waiting on a delivery, miss. Ah'll let you in?" Patrick exited to climb the stairs, and Audrey heard the gate being unlocked.

Julius darted back to where Audrey stood waiting in dismay. "It is Abbott's bride."

Audrey frowned. "Who is Abbott?" she asked, but Julius was not listening. Patrick and a cloaked tradeswoman clutching a large, covered basket were entering, the old manservant shutting the door behind them.

"Lady Abbott!" Julius kept his voice low.

Audrey nibbled on her lower lip. Their visitor, too, was in disguise? Straightening to her full height, Lady Abbott pulled the hood of her cape down to reveal deep red hair. She was tall and slim, with patrician features. In fact, she would have been ethereal, too beautiful, if it were not for the wash of golden spots across her creamy skin. Audrey found them appealing, the freckles making her appear more approachable than flawless skin would have done.

Audrey put up a hand to check her hair, feeling a little daunted that she was dressed as a boy and had recently removed the battered hat she had hidden under for the better part of the day. Looking down, Audrey recalled her trousers rolled at the waist to shorten them, and the men's work boots on her feet. She winced, realizing she was hardly fit to meet peeresses of high society in her current state.

"Little Julius, I presume." Lady Abbott also spoke in a low voice, her tone warm with pleasure. Julius huffed a laugh in response.

Patrick coughed pointedly. "There be the servants' hall if you wish to sit."

He pointed at the short hall that Audrey had chosen as her vantage point. Julius nodded, and the three of them walked through a door into the room beyond to take a seat at one of the tables. She fidgeted, uncomfortably aware of her inappropriate attire, especially with the lovely Lady Abbott having gracefully swept into her place on the opposite bench after putting her basket down. Audrey resisted the urge to tug on her jerkin and shirt, forcing her hands down on the surface of the rough bench.

"Why are you here?"

"How did you recognize me?"

Julius and Lady Abbott had spoken in the same moment, both halting to allow the other to speak.

The noblewoman arched a crimson eyebrow.

"I was there the night of your father's ball. I witnessed the … um … moonlight encounter."

The redhead blushed, her freckles disappearing in the tide of red color as she focused on her folded hands. "I … see."

Julius hesitated, studying the surface of the table. "How did you find us?"

"Lady Hays has often spoken of you, regaling me with stories of your youth when you would steal into her home."

"Ah! Aunty Gertrude."

Lady Abbott smiled, her embarrassment forgotten. "Lord Filminster and your friends are most concerned, especially after seeing your note stained with blood. I persuaded them to allow me to come check Lady Hays's home to see if you were here."

Julius cocked his head. "I suppose I should be flattered. There was an incident outside my father's home and I was wounded. Fortunately, Miss Gideon is the daughter of a fine physician and a competent healer in her own right."

The young lady turned her blue eyes to Audrey, who fidgeted in place. "We appreciate your service, Miss Gideon. Lord Trafford is well-liked by his friends, and we have all been anxious to hear word."

Audrey nodded, alarmed when the redhead pulled a face.

"However, I regret to inform you that Lady Astley is quite vocal about Lord Stirling's missing ward. I am afraid scandal is brewing."

Her heart sank. It was as she feared. But surely the news would not travel as far as Stirling? Once she left London, the controversy should fade. At least she hoped so.

"We are prepared to rally in your support when you return home." Lady Abbott reached into her basket and pulled out a letter, handing it to Julius. "Lord Filminster wrote this in the hope that I would find you here. I must leave now to not raise suspicion if anyone is watching the street outside."

They all rose, Lady Abbott raising the hood of her cape. "Farewell, and I hope to reunite soon."

Their unexpected guest hesitated at the tradesman's door, turning back with a fiery blush rising over her cheeks once more to conceal her freckles. "Lord Trafford?"

Julius gave her a curt nod of encouragement to continue.

"I … wanted to express my appreciation of the instruction you provided Aidan on the day of our wedding." Lady Abbott's eyes were downcast as if her words mortified her to the core.

Audrey nibbled on her lip while she tried to figure out what sort of instruction would cause the lady so much discomfort.

Julius huffed, his lips splitting into a grin to reveal a slash of white teeth against his tanned skin. "You are most welcome. Abbott was a committed student."

The noblewoman grinned in bashful acknowledgment. Patrick let her out, leaving Julius and Audrey standing in the hall in an awkward silence.

Julius twisted on his signet ring as he stared down the hall, his reluctance to face her obvious. "We shall, you know?"

Audrey, who was still biting at her lower lip, stopped to respond. "Shall what?"

"Ensure you have the support you need when you return home."

She nodded, wondering what he could mean by his assurance. What could he, or his friends, do to mitigate the damage to her reputation?

For her part, she intended to race out of Town when they returned to the world of the living and, meanwhile, she would eke out every ounce of adventure she could. As she feared, she was ruined and could never return to London once their quest drew to an end. A thought that saddened her when she thought of the interesting places she could have visited with Julius if they had more time. Instead, they would attempt to solve the mystery of who had attacked him and had killed the baron, before she parted ways with him.

* * *

AFTER THEY FINISHED THEIR TEA, Audrey announced it was time to redress his wound. Julius followed her up the servants' stairs, thinking about what Lady Abbott had told them. He had wanted to assure Audrey that he had accepted his duty to wed her at the end of their time together, but he was reluctant to broach the subject. It would cause inevitable questions, and he wanted to savor his time with the young woman before reality set back in.

Instead, he had settled on a vague platitude, but she had appeared to find his words comforting, so he had refrained from elaborating.

Once they reached his room, where a fresh tray awaited them, Julius removed his borrowed jerkin and shirt so Audrey could unwind the bandage. He moved the armchair back to the bed for her and lay down so she could inspect the sutured slash. She hummed a pleasing tune as she washed the wound and slathered fresh honey on it. Then she wound a clean bandage around him and crossed the room to collect a fresh cup of her dreadful brew.

Returning to his side, she handed him the cup and took a seat on the bed beside him while he drank down the tepid concoction.

"Audrey …" Julius began, finding he did not have the words prepared.

She turned to look at him in query, her silver eyes huge in her worried face as she nibbled on her plump lip. Neither of them had said much since Lady Abbott had left, and he knew he must bridge the chasm that had formed when Abbott's wife had imparted that the gossip was spreading.

Moments turned into prolonged pause as they stared at each other. Julius found himself irrevocably beguiled, beginning to lean toward her to taste the lip she abused with her pearly teeth with such regularity. She looked back at him, as fascinated with him as he was with her, and he knew a kiss was inevitable. Time slowed, as did his breathing, and he leaned in to—

Audrey's lids widened in revelation. "I thought your eyes were hazel, but you have one green eye with a brown spot, and the other is brown with a green spot!"

Julius flinched away, averting his gaze. Few had noticed the flaw. They were usually too distracted by his—

"Oh! I always thought you dyed your hair, but it is two different colors! How odd!"

He grimaced, wishing to jump to his feet and stalk away. His hair had always been a source of embarrassment, a flaw he had been teased about in his youth at Eton. Fortunately, by the time he had reached Oxford, he had learned to distract, so his adult friends seldom commented on it. Julius had subsequently grown fond of dandified fashions that detracted from the defect over the years.

"Mock if you wish. Factually, both eyes are green. It is just the size of the brown spots is different," he growled in irritation, the sensual interlude with Audrey spoiled beyond redemption.

He felt her naked hand coming down on his in a gentle caress. "I think ... it makes you more interesting," she declared. His gaze flickered back to meet hers, discovering that her earnest expression was sincere.

"Truly?"

She nodded. "I do not mean to offend, but it is intriguing from a medical standpoint, and riveting from a human one."

Julius contemplated her with great attention, but her declaration appeared genuine.

"Your father was encouraging regarding the issue."

Audrey smiled in agreement. "Papa was the very best of

men. He would have known precisely what to say to a young patient with such an unusual condition."

His lips curled up in response, his ill temper eased by her charming words while his thoughts returned to the kiss he yearned to claim from her inviting mouth, but a scratch on the door announced one of the servants arriving with fresh supplies.

Their smiles widened in wry amusement while they rose to their feet in haste. Julius crossed to the wardrobe to don a fresh shirt while Audrey went to open the door.

The interruption was for the best, he assured himself, because his wound ached and his head throbbed to reveal that his body was still healing from both the injury and the loss of blood.

CHAPTER 8

"For my future I have no concern, and as a true philosopher, I never would have any, for I know not what it may be."

Giacomo Casanova

* * *

AUGUST 30, 1821

*P*atrick had brought down trunks from the attic filled with the discarded clothing of Julius's cousins. In them, they had found a pair of Hessians that almost fitted Audrey's small feet. They also found her a shirt, breeches, a waistcoat, and a cutaway coat to wear over it.

They located two beavers from Lord Hays's wardrobe, and Audrey's stockings were serviceable for their new disguises. They were to follow Henry Montague, who frequented far more fashionable districts than the vicar, so their workmen's outfits would fail to blend in if they hung about for too long.

Audrey entered his room with her coat over her arm and her waistcoat hanging loose. Julius, who had been mid pulling on his Hessians, and thankful they had dried since the day of his attack, found himself fascinated by the taut fabric stretched over her full hips. He licked his lips while he battled his thoughts into a box to shut the lid, resolute in raising his eyes, only to find her frowning.

"I cannot reach the back of this waistcoat to tie it," she announced.

"That is the least of our problems," Julius replied, averting his gaze to stare at the ceiling while he tried to gain control over his clamoring lust.

"What?"

It was early, before dawn, and Audrey was a little grumpy. Julius squared his shoulders to deliver the news.

"It … is visible that … you are a female," he croaked out.

He could see Audrey drop her head to peer down at herself, extending her arms out as she tried to determine what he had observed. Julius glanced down, then moved to the window to stare out at the darkened garden below. He was certain he was flushed with the heat that had been ignited at her entrance.

"I do not understand," cried Audrey from behind him.

Several seconds passed while Julius composed himself. "Those are not … the hips of a man, I am … afraid."

"Oh!"

"We must either find another disguise for you or—"

A booming roll of thunder sounded. Peering up, Julius realized a bank of clouds was blocking the stars to the north in an inexorable march of darkness moving in. He exhaled with relief. If he had to spend the day with Audrey dressed as she was, he would certainly not keep his hands to himself. While he understood his duty was to marry her when they returned to Lord Snarling's home, he had no desire to form an attachment.

An attachment that could lead to breakfast plagued with terse conversation, a gradual splintering of affinity, and the eventual departure of the light, such as happened when his mother had left London behind. It was imperative he maintain some distance between them, even as he admitted that he liked Audrey. He liked her a lot. What was there not to like? He could think of no one else of his acquaintance who would merrily don a disguise and follow him into one of his escapades. She was brave, competent, and—

Deuce it! I am cataloging all the reasons to grow attached!

"The weather is turning, so you can wear one of my overcoats," he proclaimed. *So, thankfully, I cannot leer at your womanly form.*

"I am still confused." Audrey's tone was plaintive as she approached him, turning so he might tighten the waistcoat from behind. Julius turned back and dropped his gaze, then swallowed hard. Her arse was round. Alluring. It filled the linen breeches in a manner that would make it difficult for her to sit, considering the unforgiving nature of the fabric. And he was forced to look at it while his bare hands assisted with the waistcoat. The overcoat was the best solution because her breasts were just as compelling—*No, Julius!*—obvious, he corrected himself, in the gentlemen's attire she was wearing.

"It requires a valet to assist," he responded in a hoarse voice as he commanded his hands to remain on the tapes of the waistcoat. *You shall not fondle that arse!*

But, ye gods, he really, really wanted to.

"What? No, not that! I fail to comprehend what your disguise is. Are you not simply dressed as Lord Trafford?"

Julius continued his chore, proud of his restraint when he only hesitated for a second to drop his gaze back down to the luscious arse inches away, before stepping away and heading toward his wardrobe for the overcoat he had mentioned. It was a fortunate happenstance that his propensity for spending his allowance on fine clothing meant he had more garments than a person of common sense ought to possess. But he had never been accused of common sense, and heaven help him if he ever was. He would have failed as a gentleman of misadventure if that day arrived.

"Julius?"

He realized he had not responded to her last question, blinking while he tried to recollect what she had said.

"This is last year's fashion. Everyone knows I would not be caught dead in anything so out of style."

Audrey groaned, causing Julius to chuckle. Taking pity, he provided a more thoughtful reply.

"It cannot be helped. The overcoats and beavers will help us blend in, and when we return, we shall be cautious to ensure we are not followed home. It has been several days since my attack, so if we are far from my father's home, that should be sufficient."

"Well, it is fortuitous that the rain is coming so we may button up the overcoats without attracting attention. I suppose if we have to follow Montague into a club, we will keep the coats on."

Julius grinned. Audrey appeared more occupied with the etiquette of wearing an overcoat indoors than with any trepidation to be shadowing a potential killer. "You are not a lady of excellent reputation this morning. Being a gentleman means you make the rules."

"Which is unfair," she grumbled back.

"Ah, but when you are weary of repressive etiquette, there is nothing to stop you from taking a respite as a man."

She glanced at him, her silver eyes sparkling in the glow of the candlelight. "Where there is a will, there is a way."

"Precisely."

* * *

AUDREY AND JULIUS arrived on Henry Montague's street at first light. Not that it differed greatly from night, with a thick bank of clouds filling the skies.

Her current disguise was much tighter than the loose-fitting workmen's outfit from the day before. Her neck was tied within the strangling embrace of a snowy cravat, and she could not lower her chin with the starched collar of her crisp shirt. It was all rather uncomfortable, but she supposed it was tolerable if she were to see more of the inner sanctums of men. Not just men—gentlemen. The truly privileged class.

Not that the gentleman at her side boasted privileged airs in private, despite the foppish airs he displayed in public. Julius treated Patrick and Rose with the same sincere interest as he did members of the *beau monde*. Friendly, irreverent, provocative, but with an underlying warmth that made him immensely popular, if the two servants at Lady Hays's were to judge by. Despite their correct behavior, Rose had been in tears after Julius's fever had broken. Which suggested that both she and her secret husband had been quite distressed about Julius's health despite their calm demeanors. Certainly, any request he put to them was met with immediate compliance, as if they were all too happy to meet his needs.

Audrey herself found she was growing fond of him. She wanted to remain on this adventure with him as long as possible. It was the most fun she had had since her father died, and she had thought that sense of happiness would never return. Yet, here she was, in her clothes of discomfort with excitement energizing her steps.

They walked about on the street, rain drops dampening their shoulders, Julius exclaiming with eagerness when he discovered a coffeehouse on the corner down the block. It was not open yet, but he assured her it should be soon, which provided them with an excuse to loiter.

At around eight o'clock, Montague exited from his front door after a loud spat of rain had receded back to a mild drizzling. Audrey and Julius sprang to their feet, Julius tossing the coin onto the table. Fortunately, Montague walked in their direction, so they waited near the door until he passed, departing to follow him down the street.

Montague walked for a couple of blocks, then turned down a street and knocked on the door of a business. They waited on the corner until he was let in, and then quickly made their way over.

"Dr. Walker," Julius read off the sign.

"It must be a surgery," Audrey responded.

"Then I shall act as lookout and allow you to lead."

Audrey experienced a rush of pleasure. Julius had deferred to her as a healer, and this was yet again confirmation that he took her calling seriously. She hoped the villagers of Stirling would accept her as easily when she returned to treat them without her father. She did not know what her reception would be, considering she was an unmarried woman. She hoped that they would recall the number of times she had been present and assisted when they had been treated, and that the London scandal would fail to reach their ears.

They hurried back down the block, turning the corner to find the alleyway that would lead past the surgery. There they cautiously entered after looking about the street to ensure they were unobserved. Audrey counted the number of buildings until she was relatively certain they stood behind the surgery.

Julius watched the area while she made her way to one of the back windows. It was high up, so she searched about and found a barrel. Beckoning him over, she asked him to move it to the window. Julius lifted her up carefully, Audrey enjoying the sensation of his hands on her waist. She was almost certain he had been thinking about kissing her the night before, and she mulled over the moment when she had gone to sleep in the room down the hall.

Did she want him to kiss her?

What would it feel like?

Was it an inevitable stop on their adventure together?

Audrey shook her head, commanding herself to focus on the task at hand. Peering in the back window, she discovered they had successfully found the treatment room. Montague lay on a table with his stockings and breeches off, his shirt and small clothes all he wore in what must be a chilly room, considering the poor weather.

He was in his forties, she estimated, and he was not in terrible condition, but neither was he in excellent shape. Although not seriously overweight, he had a rounded belly that spoke to rich meals and alcohol. His skin was pale in the dim morning light, which suggested a lack of exercise, and Audrey could hazard a guess that he suffered from gout, given his apparent habits.

The physician was mixing up powders at his desk. In a mortar, he created a paste and prepared bandages with the paste, placing them on a tray before returning to his patient's side. Audrey's stomach knotted with the knowledge of what the physician was doing.

"Butchers," she mumbled, remaining in place to confirm her suspicions.

The physician laid out strips of bandages along Montague's legs, focusing on his knees and ankles, thus confirming it was gout he was being treated for. Audrey grimaced in sympathy, all the while silently berating the bufflehead on the table for following the quack doctor's instructions without considering other options.

Montague's face contorted as the compound seeped into his skin. And it was all the confirmation she needed. Shaking her head, Audrey lowered herself from the barrel and returned to Julius's side, where he leaned against a wall in a nonchalant pose to watch the entrances to the alley.

"We can return home," she murmured in a low voice.

Julius quirked a brown eyebrow in question, but obediently followed her to the end of the alley, where they would not be overheard. Pausing where they would not be seen, Julius spoke.

"What is it?"

"They will be some hours, so it is pointless hanging about."

His expression was curious, and he waited for her to elaborate.

She shook her head in disgust. "That fool is being blistered for what appears to be gout."

Julius appeared genuinely confused, and Audrey realized that the earl's family had always been treated by her father, an intelligent physician who practiced common sense medicine. Not like the butcher whom Montague was paying to take care of him.

"Blistering is when the physician produces blisters across the patient's skin over several hours to treat conditions such as fevers or gout. It is a long and painful procedure which will take up most of the day, by my estimation. The practice should be abandoned because it has never produced a positive result to my knowledge, but the physicians' guild includes too many incompetents who follow whatever they deem to be accepted practice without question despite the empirical evidence. It is why Papa dug up articles of far more successful practices and conducted research of his own."

Julius's expression had turned to one of utter horror. "Egad! What would have happened to me if I had been forced to seek treatment for my knife wound?"

"If you summoned the wrong physician, of whom there are too many to count, bleeding or blistering for the fever despite your loss of blood. That president, Washington, over in America, was finished off by his physicians with a combination of both."

"That is awful!"

Her stomach was still tight from what she had witnessed, as she nodded. Audrey wished she could intercede and lecture the patient on being educated about his own health instead of following some quack's instruction without question. No person should relinquish autonomy over their physical form to engage in dangerous health practices without learning what was involved. There were innumerable drugs employed that were known to produce terrible side effects, even for conditions for which alternative treatments existed. The people of Stirling had been fortunate to have a responsible physician who cared for his patients.

"It is why I must publish my father's research! He wished to educate ordinary people so they could make more informed decisions. If one loses one's health, all else is meaningless, and there are far too many physicians who do not care about their patients. They wish to make coin without regard for the results. Their patients are people with families and obligations, people who need them, yet these quacks are willing to risk their patients' health with nonsensical treatments."

Julius was staring at her in amazement, and Audrey pulled a face. She had been ranting, but this was a subject near and dear to her. There were alternatives—herbalists, midwives, nurses. There were even good physicians, like her father, who were devoted to their solemn duty. Too often, patients accepted the word of the first quack they encountered and did not obtain a second opinion, which was frustrating when Papa and she had to help a patient whose treatment had harmed them far more than the illness they were suffering.

"You are an exceptional woman of integrity, Audrey Gideon. I believe I would like to assist you with your crusade when this murder investigation is over. I have never committed to a cause the way you have."

Audrey blushed, his praise washing over her to settle as a pleasant warmth in the region of her heart.

Heart? Lud!

* * *

JULIUS WAS STILL bemused by the blaze in Audrey's eyes and the passion of her convictions when they eventually reached the mews behind Aunty Gertrude's townhouse. They had taken their time to ensure they were not followed.

She had been heat and power and determination. He had never seen anyone fire off with such an unbending commitment to their principles. It was not her high emotions; it was the logic of the ideas she had presented to him. She knew her subject, and he had been convinced. He would never seek treatment without employing his judgment and would seek a second opinion if he was in any doubt about the options offered.

It was clear why Lord Snarling had favored Dr. Gideon and his daughter for treating his family and staff, and Julius was coming to realize that he had been fortunate his father had protected him from the vagaries of accepted treatments throughout his life. The blistering sounded … well … dreadful. Perhaps even worse than the bloodletting. Minimally, just as torturous.

Once they were in the door, he did not hesitate. He clasped her by the wrist to stop her. She turned in question, looking up into his face with surprise, but she had sealed her fate in the alley behind the surgery.

Ever so slowly, giving her ample opportunity to pull away, he lowered his head as they stared deep into each other's eyes until, after an infinite time, their lips met. Julius remained frozen, savoring the sensation of her plump lips against his as they breathed in unison.

Like tinder flaming, he raised his arms around her and kissed her properly. Her mouth was hot as he coaxed it open so that they might tangle their tongues in intimate contact. She tasted of honey and spearmint. Her inexperience aside, Audrey responded with a ravenous hunger, pressing herself against him as her hands found their way to comb through his hair. Their beavers fell to the ground, but neither of them paid any mind as flames kindled in his loins.

Julius drove her up against the wall of the mews, deepening their kiss even as he sought his sanity. She moaned and he growled with primal triumph as he ground his hips against hers, straying under her overcoat to clasp one of the round buttocks that had tormented and teased him this morning.

The disappointment was gutting when he felt her hands against his ribs, and she pressed him to move away. Stepping back, Julius panted as if he had run a mile at a full sprint. Audrey licked her swollen lips, her hungry gaze never looking away for even a moment until she swallowed.

"I am destined to return to Stirling and … I believe you wish to remain a free man."

She sounded reluctant, her gaze flickering to his lips and the molten desire in her eyes still very much evident. But what she had said was true. This was a temporary interlude. He wished to throw logic to the wind, forget his commitment to remaining uncommitted, and press her against the wall, but ...

Damnation ...

It was true.

CHAPTER 9

"My success and my misfortunes, the bright and the dark days I have gone through, everything has proved to me that in this world, either physical or moral, good comes out of evil just as well as evil comes out of good."

Giacomo Casanova

* * *

AUGUST 31, 1821

*T*hey left just before first light. Audrey was reasonably certain that Montague would be incapacitated for a day or two from the treatment he had received, so despite little time to learn anything about their suspect, they chose to head to Simon Scott's home instead to see what they could see.

Audrey had spent a restless night thinking about the kiss with Julius. It was her first experience, and the sensation of

Julius pressed against her, the touch of his lips on hers, caused a quivering excitement to race through her each time she had nodded off. She had awoken exhausted.

Why had she halted their embrace? It might be her single opportunity to experience such heady madness. When she returned to Stirling, she did not know if there would be any gentlemen in her future.

"I think we should hail a hackney."

Audrey traced her tongue over her lips, considering if there might be another kiss during their adventure.

"Audrey?"

Would she—should she—call a halt if he attempted to kiss her again?

"Audrey?"

Her eyes flew open, realizing that Julius and she had stopped. He was gazing at her with a quizzical expression.

You ninny! There is a murderer on the loose, and you are woolgathering!

"I apologize. My mind was elsewhere."

A grin spread over his lean face, revealing pearly teeth as his gaze flickered down to her lips. "I have thought of it, too. All night, in fact. I was thinking that there is no danger. Kissing is innocent enough."

Audrey blushed. "We should hurry if we wish to follow Scott this morning."

Julius was wrong.

I am in danger.

She was in danger of losing her heart. Which was why she needed to stop imagining the press of his firm mouth against hers and focus on who had murdered the Baron of Filminster and sent a murderous blackguard after the friend standing in front of her.

Julius could have been killed out on the street, his lifeblood washed away by the rains, and she would never have discovered his irreverent character firsthand. He brought laughter into the world, and that was what she needed to focus on.

* * *

SIMON SCOTT LEFT his home about ten in the morning. The skies were clear, the day was proving to be sunny and bright, and Julius admitted his spirits were high and he was happy to be spending the day with Audrey.

His wound was healing, and his body felt well on the way to rights, and Julius was determined to enjoy their adventure while it lasted. He had dreamed of the kiss between them several times over the course of the night, waking in a good mood despite the earliness of the hour.

Scott was tall with wide shoulders, a lean form, and a sophisticated style of dress. Much simpler than the fashions Julius favored, but the other heir did not have his specific challenges. Scott had dark brown hair, and a close-cropped beard that framed his angular jaw to perfection.

He made for a coffeehouse nearby, where he sat alone sipping from his mug while he read news sheets. Julius and Audrey watched from a corner table, her coffee untouched on the rough surface of the table upon which she leaned. He was quite satisfied to drink his coffee while he watched Audrey watching Scott. Most of her was covered up, and they both sat with their beavers on despite the breach of etiquette. But this was a quality part of Town, and no one was so crude as to pay them any mind.

She had the most fetching eyes. Silver and iridescent in the sunlit establishment. Julius had no recollection of Dr. Gideon's irises, which meant he did not know which parent had bestowed such jewels on their daughter. Suppressing a smile at the inane thought, Julius recollected that the prior year he had pretended to compose terrible poetry for his own amusement.

It had been quite humorous to recite lines to his friends, enjoying their reactions as they attempted to be complimentary. Julius had been quite aware of just how dreadful his verses were because he had acquired them from a Valentine's Day almanac intended for tradesmen, and other men who worked for a living, to send letters to their love interests.

He missed those days of *camaraderie*. One by one, his chums had married and become entangled in their new lives, and Julius had been forced to spend his time with inferior acquaintances in their stead. It was a sobering reminder that marriage ruined all the fun, and Julius found his mood dropping as he stared into his coffee, remembering better days. This time with Audrey had been an interesting respite from the ennui of recent months.

"He is leaving," announced Audrey, who rose to her feet.

Julius welcomed the interruption of thoughts that had grown dark. He supposed Audrey had made a good point two days earlier in the first coffeehouse they had visited together. He would need to consider his future perhaps and decide what course he wished to plot. She had pointed out that he could be his own man. The problem was … Julius did not know whom he wanted to be.

He pulled coin from his pocket and placed it down on the table to hurry after Audrey. They set off after Scott, who veered off at the corner to enter St. James's Street. There he weaved through the crowd to enter a gentlemen's club.

Audrey stared up at the facade in contemplation. "Should we enter?"

Julius frowned, trying to recall if he was a member. If he was not, it was possible his father would be because he maintained memberships across the city in the interests of the hundreds of connections he cultivated.

"Wait here," he commanded.

Entering the dim interior, Julius removed his overcoat and beaver. To enter the club, he would be required to reveal his identity, so there was no helping it. A member of staff approached him, and Julius announced who his father was.

Lord Snarling must have been a member because he was waved in without further fuss. Julius wandered through the paneled rooms. The fittings were luxurious and tasteful, and the air smelled like leather and brandy. He soon found Scott had taken up a seat near an unlit fireplace and was perusing a book in leisure with the air of one who had nowhere to be.

Julius departed, retrieving his beaver and coat to find Audrey leaning against a lamppost outside.

"What is he doing?"

"Reading a book."

Audrey pulled a face. "What shall we do?"

"Do you wish to enter?"

She shook her head. "I think it will be obvious we are up to something if I fail to take off my hat and coat, not so?"

Julius nodded. "Shall we go browse the market and I will check on him in half an hour?"

Audrey grinned. "That sounds wonderful."

They crossed the street to where a few vendors had set up in a line. Audrey considered colorful scarves, which had the proprietor squinting in confusion. Julius grinned. It was not every day that a gentleman examined feminine fabrics with such interest, he supposed. They next approached a food stall, and he purchased a meat pie for her. They walked up the street as she ate it, Julius glancing back at the club entrance at regular intervals.

"I must say, it is a bit warm to be wearing these overcoats."

He smiled in reply, his gaze flickering to the neglected crumbs on her lower lip as she swallowed the last of the pie.

The urge to reach out and use his thumb to brush them off the plump flesh was nearly overwhelming, and the only thing that stopped him was the attention they would attract if a gentleman touched the lips of another man in public. Especially when Audrey appeared to be a boy midway through her—his—teens.

Egad, that was a confusing muddle of thoughts!

The truth was, regardless of what she wore, Julius could just make out the curves that were hidden, as if he were attuned to the femininity of his companion. However, most were not that observant so as to pay her any mind as she walked by in elegant attire, although she was required to keep the coat on to maintain the illusion.

They had crossed the street and turned back up toward the club when Audrey's glance fell on a fruit seller walking past with a basket of strawberries, and her face lit up in interest. Julius grinned, summoning the seller back to purchase the lush berries for her. Soon, he regretted it when he watched her bite into the red flesh and had to clench his fists not to reach up and wipe the dripping juice away. He growled in frustration.

"What?" She frowned up at him, becoming aware that he was staring.

Julius indicated his own lip, handing her a handkerchief from his pocket. She wiped her mouth clean while he fought down the sensation flickering in his groin.

"I shall go check on Scott." Julius stalked away. He had not thought out the temptations of spending an uneventful day with someone as enticing as Audrey by his side.

If we are to marry because of the scandal, carnal relations are not out of the question before Audrey leaves London?

* * *

119

AUDREY FEARED she might have stained the snow-white fabric of her starched collar with the strawberries. She attempted to wipe away the juices as well as she could, watching Julius reenter the club. There was tension beneath the surface, and she suspected they were both recalling the kiss from the previous night.

A poor idea considering their current risk being seen in public with unresolved issues regarding Julius's safety. Hers, too. If high society was aware that she was missing, then the killer would be, too. They should be vigilant to their environment to ensure they remained safe.

Still, her thoughts drifted back to the kiss. What she wanted was to ignore the voice in her head that kept shouting that she was ruined. Lady Astley must be having a fit over her continued disappearance, but Audrey had no specific plans for dealing with the scandal beyond leaving London expediently with the earl's help. What she wanted was to continue this adventure. To take each day one step at a time, to eke out every second of the experience, before she had to return home.

Staring down the street, woolgathering like a fool, Audrey noticed a movement near the next corner. She narrowed her eyes, her senses finally on high alert.

Julius came out of the club, heading toward her. She turned and sauntered away, allowing Julius to catch up with her.

"I think we are being followed," she whispered.

Julius hissed. "We shall turn the corner up ahead so you can tell me what you think you saw," he responded in a low voice.

They continued side by side. When they reached the next corner, they turned and pressed up against the wall.

"I saw a man wearing an overcoat that is too heavy for the weather."

"Like the ones we are wearing?" Julius asked, the irony in his voice evident.

"Precisely."

Julius considered their attire. "You make an excellent point."

Edging up to the corner, he removed his hat to peek back to where they had been.

"You may be right."

"What do we do?"

"We will head to Covent Garden and lose him amongst the stalls. I have a tailor nearby where we can switch our overcoats and beavers."

Audrey nodded.

They strode down the block, turning down many streets until stopping to look back from their new vantage point. After several more turns, they did not spot the man again until, finally, Julius pulled them into the doorway of a boarded-up shop on a deserted street.

"There is no one."

"Was I wrong? About being followed?"

Julius rubbed his chin. "It is hard to say. It was odd, but I have not seen him since St. James's Street, so … perhaps it was nothing."

Audrey bit her lip. "I apologize for wasting our day."

He shook his head. "Not at all. It is better to be cautious, but I admit I am growing frustrated with this strategy. I wish either of us had seen more of the riffraff who attacked me. Following these three men about is not producing any results. I would prefer to focus on the attacker, but neither of us saw him well enough to identify him, or I would watch the comings and goings of the servants at the back, rather than saunter after the master of the house."

"I wish I could help, but it was so dark that morning, and

he was covered from head to toe. A generic overcoat, hat, and boots are all I saw."

Julius extended a gloved hand, chucking her under the chin to stare deep into her eyes. "You have been a wonderful asset. I may have died without your assistance. We shall figure this out."

Audrey smiled back, riveted by the unique blend of colors in his irises and the heat that flared in their depths when his gaze dropped to her lips. She knew he was thinking about their kiss, but he dropped his hand and stepped back into the street.

* * *

JULIUS WAS FIGHTING BACK his sexual frustration. He needed to get them home, where he could pull her into an embrace. They could hardly maul each other in the street where they might be arrested for deviant acts, considering she was disguised as a man. An arrest which would raise inevitable questions about why she was dressed in men's garments.

So he hurried her to Aunty Gertrude's, pausing frequently to ensure they were not followed. The journey was endless, and the moment he had the door to the mews locked behind them, he turned to face her.

Audrey was staring at him, her silver eyes ablaze. She hesitated for a second before rushing forward into his arms. Their lips met in a hungry crush of desire. Julius growled as she parted her lips, eager to find his tongue with hers. She tasted of the strawberries she had eaten, the ones that had driven him demented with lust.

Her hands worked inside his overcoat to spread over his chest, even as their kiss deepened. She moaned in the back of her throat as he caressed his hands up and down her back, wishing he could tear the coat from her body to lay her down on it.

If they were to marry, surely there was no reason to deny themselves pleasure? She was just too damn ravishing to ignore any longer. Was this how Aidan Abbott had wound up in his scandalous embrace that had forced him to wed? At the time, Julius could scarcely believe that passion for an innocent miss could overtake a bachelor to such a degree that he was compromised by his own lust. The more time Julius spent in Audrey's company, however, the more compelling the notion became.

They could enjoy passion between the sheets, and then, once their adventure was over and they returned home, he would say his vows and help her pack her trunks. Hell, he might even accompany her to Stirling and help her settle into the family estate before he left for London, just to be sure she was taken care of in her new situation.

Except ... this time ... it was he who pulled away, stepping back and releasing her with reluctance.

"What is this?"

She was panting. "I do not know."

"I am a gentleman of leisure who seeks his enjoyments. And you ... you are a gently bred woman."

Audrey nodded, still breathless from their kiss. Too breathless to nibble on that lower lip, but he would wager she wished to do so.

He continued. "We should—"

"We should collect ourselves and go inside," she finished for him. "I will redress your wound, so you can prepare for your friend to visit later."

Julius's lungs were heaving as hard as hers, and he wanted to pull her back into his embrace, but he did not wish to take advantage of her. Perhaps they could share a wedding night before she departed for Stirling, but he had not informed her of his intentions. Mostly because … he did not know what to say when he made the proposal.

When they were wed, what would he do?

Would he continue living his life as he had in the past, while she lived in the country?

Or would he remain faithful even while they lived apart?

He had never planned to be a husband who was unfaithful to his wife, but that was because he had vowed to never marry.

Marriages were the source of great unhappiness, and Julius would never lock himself in a gaol of misery as his parents had done. The way for his marriage to succeed with Audrey was if they remained apart.

Julius needed to settle his thoughts on what this new future held, and until then, until he knew what he was offering her, he must keep his hands to himself. Audrey had become a close friend, and she deserved better than a hurried bedding.

CHAPTER 10

"I have met with some of them — very honest fellows, who, with all their stupidity, had a kind of intelligence and an upright good sense, which cannot be the characteristics of fools."

Giacomo Casanova

* * *

*A*udrey bandaged Julius, both of them wordless after the kiss they had shared in the mews. The sensation of his lips was still imprinted on hers, and her mind drifted to the possibilities as her gaze ran over the defined muscles of his torso. Julius was a fine specimen of manhood, she marveled, as she followed the trail of blond, crisp hair that covered his pectorals and arrowed down to his buckskins, the bandage the singular marring of the ridged expanse.

Did the second tone of his hair, the brown, present itself anywhere else on his lean body? It was a salacious train of thought she could not help chasing. It was the physician in her that was curious, she assured herself, nibbling on her lip and trying to not imagine joining him in his bed.

"You should go," whispered Julius.

She nodded. Julius was as tempted as she was, and if she remained a moment longer, they would throw caution to the wind.

With great reluctance, she rose to gather her things before exiting his room without another word.

Down the hall, she entered the bedchamber she had been using since their second night at Lady Hays's. In a bid to keep her mind occupied while Julius rested—certainly not because she would race down the hall and fling herself into his bed to discover the pleasure between a man and a woman—she crossed to the table and put her things down.

Rummaging through her father's valise, she found the items she needed and placed them down on the surface. Focusing on what she was doing was an attempt to still her racing thoughts as she collected the birdcage from the corner and put it down next to her supplies with a distinctive clink.

She lifted Flapper from the cage and unwound the dressing on his wing. The starling was docile in her hands, fluttering his free wing from time to time.

Julius Trafford was a wild creature, like the starling which cocked his head around to look about the room while considering his path to escape. Could the tempestuous Corinthian be tamed, she mused while she worked.

When he stops resisting his future, he will settle down to some degree.

She hoped he would never be fully tamed, that his larger-than-life spirit would remain intact when he discovered his calling as a gentleman.

It was tempting to daydream about being his bride, the one who would seek out new adventures by his side long into the future. She would never be bored if such an event came to pass, but she was a fool to even hope that she would be the one to partially tame such a free spirit.

He was the epitome of the bedside memoirs. A Casanova who pursued excitement and floated upon the ebb and flow of the universe's whims.

"I think you will fly soon, little Flapper," she whispered in the quiet of the room. The thought made her eyes sting with the threat of tears. Nostalgia that the time was ending between her and the little creature was definitely not an allegory for her strange friendship with the dandy down the hall, she assured herself.

Putting the bird in the cage, Audrey went to lie upon her bed to rest. Their hours had been long, and her melancholy must be brought on by fatigue, she decided. In a couple of hours, she was to serve watch from the grooms' room above the mews, ensuring no one was following Julius's friends when they entered the property. She should take the opportunity to sleep while she could, to have her wits about her when she stood sentry later.

* * *

AT THE PREARRANGED time in the letter that Lady Abbott had delivered, Julius opened the door to the alley to find two grooms standing about, waiting for him. They rushed in through the open doorway, glancing around to ensure no one was watching them. Without a word, all three men entered the mews, Julius leading them into the tack room, which displayed neat leather straps and shining metal in the low light. Some hooks were empty of the tack that had been used when Aunty Gertrude and Lord Hays had left for the country.

All three of them were quiet, careful that their voices did

not carry, until Julius shut the door behind them to seal them into the room.

The grooms swept their coats and hats off to reveal Brendan Ridley and Lord Aidan Abbott. Brendan shook his head, his chestnut locks bouncing in disarray as he looked Julius up and down. "It is good to see you, old chap."

"I missed you, too, Ridley."

Abbott, whom Julius had met a few weeks earlier when his sister had married Brendan, narrowed his brown eyes. "Not with this again. He is Filminster, now! A baron of the realm, you … you …!"

Julius smirked with deliberation. Provoking the rather humorless laddie was a personal crusade. Abbott needed to approach life with more flippancy, and Julius was the man to see to it.

"Better a clown than a fool."

Abbott clenched his jaw.

Brendan suppressed a smile, well familiar with Julius's tactics. "What happened? How did you get injured, and how did you reach the conclusion that the killer was one of those three men?"

Julius wished to twist his ring, but he was wearing gloves, so he clasped his hands behind him. Walking away from his chums, Julius admitted to himself that his stupidity embarrassed him. He could have been killed, which was not a desire of his, and Audrey had already taken him to task for his limited planning. These friends were going to be far more vocal about their outrage than she.

"I may have sent each of the suspects a blackmail letter to learn which of them would be drawn out."

"Thunder and turf! You bird-witted chucklehead!" Brendan cursed.

Silence ensued from behind his back until Abbott exclaimed in a low bark, "So, which one did it?"

Julius pulled a face at the wall. This was the mortifying part, where his plan had fallen apart.

"I do not know. The letters pointed to three different locations, all of which I visited on the same morning. Someone followed me from one of those locations to my father's home and attacked me in the street. Fortunately, Miss Gideon came running out with a sword to frighten him off, but I was stabbed during the scuffle with the ruffian."

Silence fell again until, suddenly, Abbott exploded. "You fool! You could have been slaughtered in the street!"

Julius puffed in rejection. At the notion of being killed, not the statement which was accurate.

"Better a fool than a clown."

The inane remark was thrown out without thought, a habit of his to arouse Abbott from his proper behavior. His response was a snarl. When Julius turned back around, he found Brendan raking his hair in agitation and Abbott had stalked over to glare at the polished tack, his shoulders tense with anger.

No one spoke for several seconds, each seeking composure, until Abbott spun on his heel and came rushing forward to where Julius stood. Julius stepped back in alarm—he could scarcely credit that the very proper Abbott would punch a chap who had just been stabbed a few days earlier. He stepped back again, discovering his reaction time still slowed by his recovery, just as Abbott's arms wrapped around him in a powerful embrace, lifting him off his feet.

Ye gods—what is this?

As his feet dangled in the air, his lungs crushed against Abbott's broad chest and his sutures twinging in protest, Julius came to a realization. The other heir was strong!

He did not consider himself a weakling, perfectly able to defend himself, but no one had ever lifted him up in the air in this manner.

"I am glad you are well, Trafford," Abbott growled. Julius glanced over at Brendan, who shrugged his shoulders as if to say it was just as unexpected to him. Julius patted Abbott on the back in awkward response, his arms trapped to his sides.

"Thank … you." He was oddly touched by the sentiment, if not by the hug. He had grown rather fond of Abbott during their interactions, and he was helping Julius protect his dear chum, Brendan, after all.

Abbott lowered him back to his feet, turning away with a fierce flush blazing over his cheeks. Julius did not think the other heir made a habit of demonstrative gestures, so he appreciated the depth of sincere emotion that must have led to it.

"We were all anxious after the note. When Gwen returned with news you were alive …" Abbott shook his head, overcome.

Brendan nodded. "It is true. We had runners trying to find what happened to you, but we were afraid of putting you in danger, so our activities were limited. The blood on the note … Bloody hell, Julius, I thought I had gotten you killed!"

"I am made of resilient stuff."

His friend shook his head in disagreement. "Nay, Julius. This is not a jest. If Miss Gideon had not been there to help fend off the assailant, or to nurse you back to health, you may very well have been killed."

Julius glanced away. He was well aware of how much he owed the remarkable young woman. He was still trying to work out his thoughts so he could inform Audrey of his intentions. His proposal must be done so as to not raise false hopes. The notion of hurting her was more than he could bear, but his vow to never marry was at war with his honor. Subsequently, he had not settled on his precise offer to save her. The scandal she would encounter the moment they left

Aunty Gertrude's to return to the real world would be great. His sense of loyalty rang strong in his veins, and offering a marriage in name only while he gallivanted around London did not sit right somehow. He needed to find a compromise that addressed all ramifications so that Audrey was well taken care of.

Seeking a distraction from these uncomfortable issues, Julius endeavored to change the subject.

"Has anything happened since we last met? Sunday, was it not?" It was hard to believe it was less than a week since the baroness had been startled by the intruder in the Ridleys' library.

Brendan cleared his throat but did not respond.

Abbott interjected from across the room. "An intruder broke into Filminster's study. Michaels fought him off but was injured."

Julius straightened in alarm. He had known Brendan's cantankerous butler for years, and often teased him into rousing arguments to break Michaels out of his belligerent moods. In other words ... Julius was fond of the old man.

"Is he ... well?" He tensed, bracing himself for the worst of news. Michaels was not young, and a hired thug could well wreak some damage.

"Michaels is recovering. He was back on his feet despite doctor's orders by the next morning. I have one of the footmen reporting to me, and I have ordered him to take it easy."

Julius exhaled in relief at this news. "So he is to work ten hours rather than twenty?"

Brendan grinned. "Most likely. I told him he could work four or five hours at most, so ten would be a good guess by my estimation. He is determined to prepare Ridley House for the renovations we plan with Barclay Thompson when he returns to London. Not to mention the new staff we hired that must be trained in the ways of *his* household." The last was laced with irony.

"He is serious about his work." Julius snorted. *Unlike moi.*

"He is serious about the Ridley family. I always thought the old goat was critical of me, but it turns out that it is just his personality. He is loyal."

A man I can respect.

Julius paced up and down, thinking about this revelation and the lack of progress he had made over the last few days. They now knew the killer must be Stone, Montague, or Scott. But beyond that, no further evidence had come to light.

"This is so frustrating. There must be a way to force progress in this investigation!"

Abbott snapped back, "Not if it gets you killed!"

Julius stopped, arms akimbo, as he tried to find a path forward. "I will remain low, in the hopes that it keeps the killer on the hook. If he believes there is a possibility he will remain unaccused—that he can still walk away from this crime as long as he can silence me—perhaps he will make a mistake in his desperation to keep me quiet."

Brendan nodded. "Agreed. You remain hidden."

"But," Julius continued, "we must come up with a plan to draw him out."

Abbott scowled. "You are not to go off and do something foolish!"

Julius was not accustomed to answering to anyone, but considering Audrey was with him, he would have to act with more discretion than the clumsy attempt earlier this week. He had no wish to meet his death, but, more than that, he could not drag Audrey into unnecessary danger.

"Agreed."

* * *

AUDREY HEARD footsteps on the stairs. She watched the two men departing from the alley, vigilant to her duties as guard, while she waited for Julius to join her.

"This situation is so frustrating," commented Julius as he entered the room and took a seat on one of the cots that the grooms slept on. "I feel I am so close to uncovering the killer, yet we make no progress. Three days of following these men has brought nothing to light other than ... well ... they all seem to go about their daily business with no cares about the murder."

Audrey moved away from the window after ensuring there were no signs of movement. His friends had disappeared from sight several moments earlier, and the alley was still clear, so her work was done for now. She walked over to take a seat on the opposite cot, watching Julius with sympathy.

"I would agree that none of these men appear to have dire emergencies pressing on their thoughts. On the other hand, the guilty party is a stone-cold killer, so we cannot expect him to behave as we would under similar circumstances. The baron may have been killed during the heat of passion, but that ruffian attacking you in the street was calculated."

Julius heaved a deep sigh. "There must be something we can do to draw him out."

Audrey felt selfish, falling silent while she struggled with her desire to remain on this adventure with Julius. Struggled with the notion that the longer it took to solve their dilemma, the longer she could spend time with him and enjoy herself.

A very cold reception awaited her when she returned home. Or a very hot one. Who knew how these upper-class types would react when riled? As long as she remained at Lady Hays's home, she could pretend all was well. She had not had so many interesting challenges since her father had passed away. Their time together was drawing to a close, and Audrey admitted knowing this filled her with a feeling of desolation.

"Perhaps ... now that the killer knows where you live ..." Audrey stopped, reluctant to propose the end to their excursions. She had enjoyed unfamiliar sights and sounds, discovered parts of London she would never revisit on her own, eaten dodgy food bought on the street, and savored strawberries all the more sweet because of the handsome beau who had purchased them for her. One could almost pretend he was courting her. Almost.

She fidgeted with the skirts of her mourning gown while her conscience fought with her desires.

Julius leaned forward, arching an eyebrow in question. She stared at his handsome face, taking in the dark brows and lashes at odds with his blond mop, and slipped her hands under her buttocks. Leaping into his arms for a third time seemed unreasonable. The sort of wanton behavior that Lady Astley would be gossiping about at this very instant, somewhere in London. Over a cup of tea with other matrons of the *ton*, perhaps.

A snake coiled and uncoiled in her belly at the thought of facing the world. She had never been considered scandalous until now. Perhaps eccentric by high society standards, because she had apprenticed with her father, but the *ton* was not aware of her routines in Stirling.

"... we could try the blackmail letters again, and perhaps some runners can watch the locations you specify, but I think we should focus on Lord Stirling's home."

He straightened up, his expression intrigued. "The killer sent his man to find out where I lived and then kill me once they could identify me from my address."

She nodded. "Why wait until you reached home, unless it was to learn where you reside?"

Julius blanched, pale beneath his tanned skin as he seemed to consider the hazards of his incomplete planning. "What I did was so reckless! What if my father had been at home? He may have become a target. He could still become a target when he returns home, if the killer believes he is involved in my scheme."

Audrey did not answer. It had, indeed, been a foolish move. His idea had been a stroke of brilliance, but the execution had demonstrated a lack of thoughtful prediction. If Julius had informed his friends of his intentions, they might have been able to hodgepodge a plan that would have been less risky and more effective.

"I must resolve this muddle!" he announced, waving his hands about. Julius was attired in plain buckskins, and a rather conservative green coat from his wardrobe. It was a far cry from the foppish attire he favored, but Audrey had been appreciating the sight of his lean, but muscular thighs encased in pale leather. The colorful garments he wore distracted from his unique features and athletic form, in her opinion.

She turned her thoughts back to the conversation at hand. It was painful to suggest that they end their mutual venture, but she could not be so self-absorbed as to withhold the inspiration that had struck her while she stood watch for the meeting downstairs.

"Precisely. If you return home, the killer's man might show up to silence you. If you attempt the blackmail again, he should appear. We could focus our attention on Lord Stirling's home, but with the proper preparations."

Julius sprang to his feet, pacing the alley formed by the two lines of cots. For a man of his height, he was light on his feet, barely making a sound on the wooden flooring, shoed in his Hessians. "I shall have to post men inside the house to protect the household."

Audrey's smile was tight, pleased that Julius was thinking through the plan to any unintended repercussions. She was of the opinion that the young lord was something of a genius, but he needed to employ a little more discipline to his schemes. When he did so, he would achieve his goals on a much larger scale. He needed to mature his cunning intelligence to discover his full potential.

"And placed along the street, including here in your aunt's home," she suggested.

Dejection twisted in her gut. She would not be present to see Julius come into his own. Nay, she would be living in Stirling, unable to return to London because of her damaged reputation. They were days, maybe hours from parting, and Audrey was not yet ready to say goodbye.

"I shall discuss it in the morning with Ridley and Abbott. They are returning after dawn."

"Is that wise?"

"I told them to walk up separately a good fifteen minutes apart so they do not arrive together as they did today."

There it was, confirmation that Julius was thinking his plans through to the end. He would be a magnificent lord for Stirling when the day came for him to fulfill the role.

She supposed she should be gladdened she had contributed to that distant future, but she could not shake off the dismal sensation that she could not share the journey. Her own path was yet to be determined now that she had scandal dogging her heels.

CHAPTER 11

"I am bound to add that the excess in too little has ever proved in me more dangerous than the excess in too much; the last may cause indigestion, but the first causes death."

Giacomo Casanova

* * *

SEPTEMBER 1, 1821

"*A*bsolutely not! It will not work, and if it does, you could be slain!"

Abbott's outrage was plain. He had been the last to arrive, dressed as a footman rather than a groom, with a great overcoat, buckled shoes, and a powdered wig to conceal his identity. A footman to which household, Julius wondered, not recognizing the livery.

"It might work," cajoled Julius.

Brendan shook his head, clearly of the same mind as Abbott. "We do not know that, and you are a valued friend."

Julius felt frustration rising from his gut. This was why he worked alone. Or with Audrey. She tempered his plans, but did not try to stop him from pursuing his intentions. The young woman had buckets of courage, not to mention she was a useful companion when things went awry. Although ... the fact that he now counted a female as one of his closest chums still served to disorient him.

Not just any female, a beguiling one at that!

"It is time we take the knowledge we have gathered to the Home Office. There have been far too many incidents where one of us could have been hurt or killed. Lily ..." Abbott swallowed hard, evidently overcome by the recollection of the day his sister had been attacked.

Brendan's face tensed, clearly reliving that terrible day. "I would never forgive myself if something happened to you, Julius."

Well ... I suppose I should appreciate that!

Indeed, it warmed the cockles of his heart. Julius valued his friendships above all else. However, that could not be allowed to dissuade him from his commitment. His chums had suffered egregious offenses, and he had it within his grasp to solve their dilemma once and for all.

"We cannot give up our advantage when we are so close to unmasking the murderer."

"We must! I demand we end this investigation and turn it over to the Home Secretary."

Julius narrowed his lids, approaching the taller Abbott with a menacing mien, his temper roused. "Considering I cleared your father-in-law of a heinous crime, and ruined one of my favorite coats with a bloodied slash in a spot that can never be mended ..." Julius shook his head in regret. He had loved that coat. "This is my call, Abbott. And I do not care to be told what to do!"

"Easy, gentlemen. Quarreling amongst ourselves will solve nothing," Brendan called from across the room. Julius inhaled to calm himself, before spinning on his heel to retreat before he did something foolhardy, such as hit a larger man while he was recovering from a knife wound.

The baron paced, a thoughtful expression forming on his face. "The clubs are buzzing with talk about your disappearance with Miss Gideon."

Julius's resolve dimmed. The longer they were absent, the more her reputation was being decimated. He hoped that providing her the protection of his name would be sufficient to mitigate the scandal because it had now been six days since she had helped him flee to Aunty Gertrude's.

"What is your point?" His bark belied the nonchalant front he preferred to portray, his belligerence unrestrained with Audrey's welfare on his mind.

Brendan came to a stop, peering at him through the shadows of the dim tack room. "We could plant a story that you are terrified of your father's reaction when he returns, certain that he will cut off your allowance for your dastardly behavior. The earl is healthy, so it will be years before you inherit and access funds from the estate."

Abbott growled from the corner where he was standing. "No!"

Julius grinned. "I am a desperate man, willing to resort to blackmail to secure emergency funds."

"Did you hear me? I said no!" Abbott's tone was both adamant and pleading.

Brendan nodded. "Then, you return home and send the letters to inform the three suspects that you have obtained an interesting letter, which the late baron wrote. A letter you intend on delivering to the Home Office unless someone persuades you to do otherwise, but your time is limited, so a deadline looms."

Folding his arms to think, Julius stared down at the hard-packed earth beneath his feet. "It is a good plan. The murderer might be wary of a trap, but we might incite him if we can trigger his emotions into making a rash move. Or … he may attend the meeting and reveal himself if he believes I can be paid off."

Abbott strode between them, bristling with disagreement.

"Have either of you considered how vexed the earl will be when he returns home to find the family reputation destroyed with rumors? Or how this will affect Miss Gideon?"

Silence fell as they contemplated the questions.

Encouraged that he had caught their attention, Abbott inhaled deeply as if to calm himself. "This is as rash as anything you hope to provoke the killer into doing. We must calculate a better strategy than this. Each time we attempt to uncover the killer, we have made things worse. It is time to take what we know to the Home Office. If the killer makes a run for it, so be it. It is not worth risking anyone's safety."

The reaction Julius felt was visceral. To allow the murderous fiend to escape? After all they had been through, all the work they had done to uncover the facts they now possessed? He would not stand for it.

"I am not ready to give up. Once the killer knows a public investigation has been opened, he will disappear. He must pay for killing the baron, and for hurting the baroness. And what of Michaels? Does he have a say in this since he, too, has been assaulted? Do you forget he was forced to kill another servant to save your sister?"

Abbott stared back at him, a helpless expression on his face. "Do you think that does not keep me up at night? I think of nothing else!"

Brendan raked his hand through his hair, staring into space as he considered the arguments. "What of your father, Trafford? When does he return?"

"I do not know. He left for the Continent but did not provide any details, so he could be gone a few days or a few weeks."

"We shall discuss all these options with the duke. If we agree to proceed, when will you return home?" Brendan's response was a reasonable one. Halmesbury and Lord Saunton had proved reliable allies in the past, and Halmesbury knew the Home Secretary well. Considering the duke's father-in-law had been the murder victim, it seemed ill-advised to exclude him from the decision.

"Miss Gideon wishes me another day or two of rest before I put myself in any danger. Even with runners hiding in the house and here at Aunty Gertrude's, she does not advise physical exertion."

"That is excellent because we need a day or two to put men in place if we proceed with the plan. But ... what of Miss Gideon? Abbott is right that the damage to her reputation will be much worse if we fan the flames of rumor doing the rounds."

Julius did not wish to discuss his intentions. He would take care of Audrey, but the details were undetermined, and she deserved to hear from him before his friends did.

"That is my concern," he replied.

Abbott scowled, keeping his distance but his ire on display. "That young lady saved your life!"

Being berated did not sit well, but Julius understood he was debating with two men who had recently chosen to do the honorable thing. Brendan had married Abbott's sister in July under a cloud of controversy because of the drama created by providing him with an alibi, and Abbott had taken his vows just a week ago to abate a similar crisis.

"I am aware … and I will take care of her."

"Blast this intrigue!" Abbott cursed, his face flushed. "I am not made for underhanded ploys!"

Julius was tempted to mock the younger man, to resort to his customary glibness, but he chose the course of logic instead.

"We have all been through great ordeals these past weeks. The two of you were forced to marry under duress." Julius grimaced. *As I will soon be.* "But all we have been through, all the trials we have endured for the sake of justice, will be for naught if this fiend escapes unpunished. All three of the suspects have their own funds and can slip away to never be heard of again, and I will not stand for it."

Brendan straightened, his expression turning to one of resolve. "I shall discuss the options with the other parties. Mayhap there will be a better plan if we put our heads together."

"I, for one, vehemently refute any plan that damages Miss Gideon's reputation any further. She is an innocent young lady and deserves to be considered in this … this … foolishness!"

The inference that Julius was unconcerned about Audrey aggravated him worse than anything Abbott had ever said to him. "It was Miss Gideon's idea!"

Abbott blinked, his expression dismayed at this revelation.

"Ahem." The feminine throat clearing made the men flinch in surprise. They turned in unison to find Audrey standing in the doorway. Her dainty slippers had muted the sound of her approach, which was rather galling, considering they were meant to have their wits about them in the event of someone attempting to invade the premises.

"There is too much activity out in the alley. A delivery wagon is blocking the way, and a groom is loitering on the other side. I came to alert you gentlemen that at least one of you must remain in here for a little while yet."

Julius nodded in acknowledgment. Audrey bobbed her head, turning on her heel to hurry back to her post and leaving all three of them to watch her departure.

"She is lovely," Brendan finally commented when she was out of earshot. "She seems like quite a catch, Julius. Are you to do the right thing?"

Again with the pressure. Did his friends think him a veritable scoundrel who would desert a gently bred young woman to the feckless judgment of polite society? Did they not trust him to take care of his Audrey?

"Of course I will do the right thing … as soon as I figure out what that is."

Three heavy sighs ensued, all three of them walking over to slump on a bench against the wall to stretch out their legs.

"This has been a hell of a summer," Brendan declared, contemplating the work boots of his disguise.

"That it has been," agreed Abbott. "I am just thankful to have straightened out my botch-up with Gwen. Turns out attempting to unmask a killer has unexpected ramifications and is rather trying on one's nerves. I confess I may have caused some chaos myself with one or two poorly judged decisions."

Julius snickered, his mind racing through the recent bedlam the late Lord Filminster had instigated when he had chosen to attend the coronation back in July.

"If the baron only knew that his death would result in new unions. It is rather ironic considering his insistence that Brendan marry this year. He achieved his goal, if not in the way he might have hoped for."

Abbott scratched around his ear. "Deuce it! The late baron has much to answer for. I am wearing a powdered wig, for the love of heaven!"

They burst out laughing, and Julius acknowledged that if nothing else, he had acquired new chums on his quest to help Brendan with his troubles. It was a comfort, considering there was much melodrama ahead of them.

"I propose we win the day, gentlemen, and not allow a tragedy to unfold. Much has been sacrificed to uncover the truth, and I want to see this scoundrel brought to justice."

"Aye," replied his companions.

* * *

Julius's friends left, and Audrey watched from her post, thinking about what she had overheard. That the idea she had proposed would worsen her own situation. A cloying feeling of dread rose each time she thought of returning to the earl's home to face the consequences.

The needs of the patient outweigh any other considerations.

However, now that Julius was on the mend, the other concerns had inevitably made themselves known. Audrey stroked her thumb over the pads of her other fingers in a repetitive motion while she tried to imagine what would happen when she returned across the street. Would she have to face anyone other than the earl? How would the earl react? Would he be furious?

Surely not if I saved his son?

She was not close to Lord Stirling, who was as solemn as Julius had pointed out, but he had always been generous to her. Discovering that he was her guardian had been a surprise, but not overly so. And he had been kind enough when he came to attend Papa's funeral and escort her to London.

Audrey had been grateful to leave Stirling while she recovered from her father's abrupt death. He had been delivering a baby and returned home alone in his curricle in heavy rain. Best they could tell, something had startled his horses, perhaps booming thunder or lightning striking too close, and the curricle had been overturned in their panic, crushing her father. Papa had been instantly killed, a fact for which she was grateful. It was a comfort to know he had not suffered, but … she had. Her entire life had altered in the course of a few hours, and soon after, she had arrived in London, dressed in the black garments of mourning.

At first, she had been relieved to leave Stirling while she was grieving. Audrey knew that the process of healing from her father's death would have been all the worse if she had woken in the familiarity of their home each morning, only to remember he was gone. To go about her day in their home or to visit the village without his presence nearby would have been more than she could have borne.

Instead, she had spent her time walking about the earl's palatial townhouse, enjoying the art of centuries displayed in ornate gilt frames, perusing his fabulous library and, when she had been ready, planning her future without Papa. He had been her parent, her mentor, and her tutor. They had assumed she would continue working at his side for years to come, but she knew wherever her father was now, he was gratified that she had not accompanied him that night.

Unfortunately, they had never discussed how she would succeed as a healer without him. Her first patient and she had immediately been compromised. There were logistics to her being an unmarried young woman that they had not discussed.

Despite the looming controversy, Audrey did not regret what she had done. If there had been time to think, to plan, perhaps they could have conceived an alternate action, but in the heat of the moment, she had made the right decision.

The rules of polite society did not supersede life and

death, after all. However, polite society would not concur with her point of view.

"Are you coming?"

Audrey spun around to find Julius standing in the door with a quizzical expression. She had been so absorbed in her thoughts, she had failed to hear him climbing the creaking steps. She nodded, walking over to join him. They descended to the lower level, and Audrey realized her companion was rather more subdued than usual.

"What was the outcome?" she asked as they crossed to exit the mews, curious about what occupied his thoughts.

"Hmm … they wish to discuss it with the other men. The duke, and his cousin Saunton, who is husband to Abbott's cousin. Abbott wishes to determine less risky alternatives, so … I suppose I shall rest until they return. I cannot proceed without their agreement—at least, not without great risk. I must consider your involvement."

Julius paused midway in the garden, turning to gaze at her. "I want to thank you."

He shook his head, his wheat mop glowing in the morning light. Audrey ached with the desire to comb her fingers through the wild tangle, to stand on tiptoes and press a kiss to the firm lips that had claimed her own over the previous days.

She nibbled at her lip, remonstrating herself for her maudlin sentimentality. She was behaving like returning home, parting ways with Julius … she was behaving as if she had been condemned to the gallows.

Julius moistened his lips, clearly wanting to say more but struggling to find the words. Audrey took pity, interjecting when he continued to search for what to say. "It was my pleasure, Julius Trafford."

He was wearing the forest green coat from the day before, which picked out the color in his fascinating two-toned eyes.

Some would consider the strange brown spots a flaw, but she thought it was endearing. It was a visible mark of his eccentric character. The character that accepted her credibility as a physician without question, and thought nothing of her donning masculine clothing to join him in the domains of men. Those eyes were staring deep into her soul, emotions coiling in their depths that she could not decipher.

At that moment, her stomach emitted a mortifying grumble and Julius's buoyant spirits were restored, his face breaking into a wide grin. "Shall we eat?"

Audrey could feel the heat that was climbing her neck at the embarrassing bodily function choosing to interrupt so rudely. Her chuckle was rueful as she nodded. Whatever he had wanted to say would have to wait.

CHAPTER 12

⚜

"I don't conquer, I submit."

Giacomo Casanova

* * *

*A*fter enjoying a hearty breakfast in the kitchen, freshly baked bread and eggs, they went to the library. Patrick had removed the dust sheets from a couple rooms at Julius's request so that they might make use of them, and Audrey had mentioned she had explored little of the stacks on earlier visits, unable to decipher how it was organized. Julius was excited to show her Lord Hays's fine selection.

Leading her through the stacks, he showed her novels and poetry, pulling out a copy of Lord Byron's poems.

"I noticed Casanova's memoirs in your chamber. Does it belong to your uncle's library?"

Julius grinned, shaking his head. "I own multiple copies. Anywhere I lay my head, you will find his memoirs. When I have trouble sleeping, I read about Giacomo's brazen antics."

Audrey smiled up at him, a mischievous twinkle in her eyes. "Do they serve as inspiration?"

"Indubitably, I like to be unpredictable." He laughed.

Audrey gave a little snort. Her eyes fell to his lips before skittering away. "More like incorrigible."

He smiled in response before changing the subject. "Have you seen the portrait gallery?"

Audrey shook her head. "I mostly spent time in the drawing rooms and library on my previous stays, although I have wandered the halls."

Julius offered an arm. "Shall we?"

He led her to the gallery where Audrey exclaimed with delight over the portrait of his aunt displayed directly by the entry.

"She is so young!"

Indeed, Aunt Gertrude was dressed in the fashion of forty or fifty years earlier, her hair powdered and lifted with whatever odd contraptions they had used in the last century. Her moss-green eyes stared down, her face perfectly austere as was characteristic of aristocratic portraiture.

Julius preferred the real-life version, being rather fond of his maternal great-aunt. Countless times as a youth, he had escaped Lord Snarling's grim lectures by sneaking into her home. Rose, who helped in the kitchens when the family was in residence, made the best biscuits, warm from the oven, and, despite being a traditional lady of the *ton*, Aunty Gertrude had always been kind to her unhappy nephew.

They walked together down the length of the gallery, stopping to view each of the family portraits that recorded the history of the Hays family until they reached the far end.

"What is this?" asked Audrey, pausing at the end of the gallery. Julius sauntered after her, finding she was staring up at a recent portrait of Lord Hays mounted above a display case covered with a dust sheet. His great-uncle was attired in the style that had been adopted in London of late, that of a Highland lord with a box-pleated kilt of red, green, and yellow. The artist had been generous, filling out Lord Hays's aged figure to make him appear far more robust than he was at the time of sitting for the painting.

"Lord Hays holds a minor title in Scotland that he inherited through his mother, which is why he belongs to the Highland Society of London. They took it into their heads to collect the patterns of tartans. Something about preserving the clan histories. I think they might be deluded about the whole thing, but it has become quite fashionable amongst those who hold Scottish titles to claim these ... vanity tartans, if you will."

Audrey pointed up at the kilt. "So this is meant to be the tartan of the clan that he is from?"

"That is the theory. My valet has family from Scotland, and he tells me it is all a bit of fanciful propaganda, and that there were no official clan tartans until this recent obsession took hold." Julius leaned down to grab the edge of the sheet, yanking it back to reveal the ornate enamel and glass display case beneath.

Julius tapped a fingernail on the glass, his hands still bare from eating. Below the glass was a catalogue. "See, there is Bannockburn's key pattern book, published a few years ago, which is a collection of tartans that the lairds have submitted as belonging to their clans."

Audrey peered down, tilting her head and pursing her lips in thought. "May I look at the pattern book?"

Julius raised a brow in surprise, but acquiesced, feeling about for the latch to the case and swinging the lid up. He reached in and pulled it out, then closed the lid to place the book atop it.

Audrey leafed through, nibbling on her lip, which was a sure sign that she was worried about something. She stopped on a page featuring a green and blue tartan pattern. Audrey leaned forward, then back, viewing it from different angles while Julius waited for her to reveal her interest in the book.

"I have seen this worn by a Scottish regiment," he finally proffered, hoping to prompt her into conversing.

Her eyes found his, clouded with some emotion he could not quite place. "The blackguard who attacked you in the street … I glimpsed this pattern. What does that mean? That he is part of a regiment?"

Julius frowned, shifting his gaze to the illustration and to read the words beside it. "Perhaps. Or he might be connected to Clan Campbell."

"Does that mean something?"

Julius's forefinger and thumb found their way to his signet ring, which he twisted. Somewhere in the recesses of his mind, a memory had been tickled, but he could not quite grasp onto it. "I do not know."

"Is it a clue?"

He closed the book, replacing it under the glass lid. "It might be. If Campbells are connected to one of the suspects. Or it could be nothing, merely that the attacker himself has Campbell blood. Or simply liked the pattern and purchased it. Do you know what it was you saw?"

Audrey shook her head. "It could have been a scarf, or lining, even a coat. I just saw a great overcoat and a hat, but when he moved, I caught sight of this somewhere in the vicinity of his collar."

Julius pulled the sheet back into place. "I will inform the others when they return. For now, I cannot say what it means, but it is more than we knew until now. It is shameful that I missed it."

She laughed, her blonde eyelashes fanning down to the

curve of her cheek. "That may have had something to do with fighting off a knife attack with only a walking stick to protect you."

Julius did not hear what she said, for he was caught, a wave of lust surging through his veins while his fingers itched to reach up and remove the pins from her flaxen hair. It was coming loose, as it often did, and the urge to complete the task, to see the locks flowing down her back, made him salivate with desire. Audrey looked up, alerted by his silence that something was amiss. Her eyes locked with his, and time slowed down as he considered the morals of peeling the mourning gown from her curved body. The one which did not require stays, he recollected. She had been drenched in the rain, revealing the outline of her nipples through the wet fabric.

I have to wed the girl. Can I not …

He licked his lips, Audrey's gaze dropping to trace the motion, which was when he noticed that her breathing was frayed, ragged, as was his.

Do not get attached! A proper marriage will destroy the friendship we have formed.

His thoughts were scrambled and all he could think of was how he wanted to drag her to the floor and—

Out in the hall, the sounds of footsteps interrupted the moment, and they both blinked as if waking from a dream.

She swallowed hard before speaking. "Patrick, I think."

"Aye." Julius rubbed his neck, relieved that in this one instance he had not savaged her like a beast. Audrey had a terrible effect on his self-control, but the knowledge that the servant was nearby was sufficient deterrent to quell the ravening beast within.

* * *

LATER THAT EVENING, Audrey was once again seated by Julius's bed. She tucked the end of the fresh bandage, her eyes on the hard angles and curving muscles of his chest. Sensation tingling low in her loins as her pale hand reached out to hover over him.

She dared not look up to see what Julius was doing. Abruptly, she made her decision, and lowered her fingertips to trail them down his chest. He felt at once hard, as she scraped over the curling chest hair, and soft.

Julius hissed, and her gaze flew up to meet his. His lids were heavy, and she was gratified to find languid heat reflected in his eyes. "Are you seducing me, Audrey Gideon?" His voice was rough, as if he struggled to focus.

Audrey hesitated, then nodded. All afternoon she had been thinking of their imminent parting, about the unknown future awaiting her, and she had discovered something about herself. Licking her lips, she replied, "I find that … I think I will regret … if I do not …"

Flames flared in the depths of his green-brown irises when he reached up to grasp her by the wrist. Gently, he brought her hand up to his mouth to kiss the vulnerable spot on her inner wrist. Audrey was riveted, gasping when she felt the flicker of his tongue where his lips were pressed.

They stared at each other, scarcely moving—scarcely breathing.

Julius's lids came down, concealing his molten eyes. "This time, we are alone in my room. I have resisted the temptation thus far, but—Audrey, I do not have the strength to stop if we begin. You must walk away now. Until we … Until we have an understanding."

She did not know what that meant, but she knew she had considered her options and she refused a lifetime of regret that she had never lain with the man … the man she …

The man I love!

Audrey blinked at the revelation, somehow surprised at her dismay. It was not so astonishing. Julius Trafford was a handsome and unique gentleman. Surely dozens of women over the years had fallen for the intriguing glib charm, but it was his loyalty and his acceptance of her which had drawn her in as a moth to the flame.

His light grip, and the warmth of his breath teasing over her wrist like a lover's caress, made her ever more certain that she wanted to divest herself of clothing, to feel his naked body pressed against her. Just the once. Just so she could know his touch. This might be their last night together—the last time they were alone. The coming days were going to be hard for her. She would be found guilty of doing … *this* … even if she had not.

Nervous, she placed the forbidden envelope on his abdomen. "I … brought prevention. It is a condom."

His eyes flew open, and he emitted a despairing groan. "I know what an English frock coat is. And you should not have —" Julius's gaze shifted to her leather valise on the dressing table. "Your magic bag?"

Audrey nodded, biting her lip and wondering if she had made a mistake, but, if she had, it did not prevent the desire to lean down and lick the flat disc of his nipple to taste if it was salty. She stared at the tawny skin, sorely tempted. "Papa kept a supply in case someone needed them."

"Are you … sure?"

She tugged her hand loose, lowering it to rest on his chest and marveling at the heat emanating against her palm. With far more confidence than she possessed, she ran it down, over the bandage, to pause over his midriff where the sheath rested and feel the ripple of his muscles as he tensed.

Julius shook his head, his hand coming over hers to hold it in place. "My father always said one should honor the requests of a lady."

With that, he put the French letter aside. Sitting up, he swung his legs over the side of the bed to rise. Still holding her hand, he pulled her to her feet and lowered his mouth to hers. Their lips were hungry when they met, fusing together as if they were one. His arms came up to lash her to his half-naked body, and he coaxed her lips to part. Her head was pushed back, but his fingers threaded through her hair to provide support. He tasted of honey and tea, with a hint of spice, the satin warmth of his tongue exploring her mouth causing her crave him with feverish need.

Audrey squeezed her thighs together to relieve the agitated pulsating between her legs, enjoying the crush of her breasts against his bare pectorals. She squirmed, moaning in ecstasy, when his free hand reached down to cup her buttock and press her to his pelvis where she could feel the rigid evidence of his desire against her belly. She brought her own hands up to marvel at the hard muscle and youthful strength of his broad shoulders, kneading his warm skin with curious fingers as their kiss deepened.

She growled—*growled!*—in protest when his lips left hers, but then gasped at the swirling headiness of feeling his mouth trail across her jaw to find her earlobe and suckle it with a light nip of teeth.

Audrey bucked in astonishment, thrilling excitement cascading through her veins to pool and quiver between her thighs. There was a muffled laugh from Julius as his hands bracketed her hips, tugging her gown up to hitch her up against his hips, her skirts bunching around her thighs.

Understanding his intent, she brought her knees up to brace against him, a weightless feather in his powerful embrace. Sensation pooled at the apex of her core as his erection pressed against her most intimate of areas and she undulated against him to relieve the accumulating pleasure discomfort, discovering that his heated length ratcheted it ever higher.

The tantalizing scrape of his stubble against the tender skin of her neck thrilled her to new heights of pulsing desire, as he plumped her breast through the cotton of her gown and shift beneath. Her nipples puckered to painful points as instinct drove her to grind her pelvis against his loins, to chase some sort of release to the exquisite agony gathering between her legs.

Julius growled in the back of his throat, striding forward to pin her up against the wall. Her head fell back, and she keened when her pelvis pushed ever harder against his. Grabbing her hand from his shoulder, he raised it above her head, threading his fingers through hers while his mouth found hers in a hungry, drugging kiss. Lips, tongue, and teeth clashed as they sought a mutual fusion of bodies, her thoughts swirling with him. His scent, his taste, the feel of his hard body against hers, the contact of his rough palm against hers.

Audrey moaned in distress when Julius yanked his head back, panting as his blazing gaze seared a path into her heart. "We must slow down, Audrey. You are too inexperienced for where we are heading."

She could barely hear him over the rushing, pounding blood in her ears, overcome by a riot of new feelings in places she had never paid mind to. He waited for her to comprehend his words until she swallowed and blinked in acknowledgment.

Julius turned back toward the bed, Audrey clinging to him like creeping ivy while his lips nuzzled against the sensitive skin at the base of her throat. His deft fingers worked the fabric-covered buttons of her bodice. Soon, its tight embrace sagged while he turned to lower her onto the mattress. He tugged the gown down to her waist, and she obligingly raised her hips so he could yank it off.

Once he removed it, his sartorial nature got the better of him—he straightened the garment out and hung it over the back of the armchair next to the bed. Audrey grinned at his meticulous care. He returned to stand over her, his gaze caressing over her bosom with keen appreciation. Her breathing was labored with her frustrated passion, but she eyed him back, admiring his tall form and the ripple of muscle beneath his bronzed skin as she watched him watching her.

Julius rubbed his jaw. "I find I am not as disciplined in this as I might be. Having a maiden in my bed is something of a novel experience," he admitted in a hoarse voice, a flush rising up his neck and cheeks.

"I am not a maiden," she responded simply. "I am Audrey."

His face gradually split into a wide grin, his humor restored. "That you are."

With that, he leaned over her to work off the shift that was the last remaining item of clothing on her quivering, aroused figure.

He threw the shift aside with far less attention than he had given her gown, returning his gaze to the swell of her breasts before falling to the shadowed cleft between her legs. Audrey blushed, raising a hand to cover herself, but he leaned over to capture it against her thigh and continued to look, skimming gentle fingertips over the length of her stomach. Then even lower with ragged control, dipping a single finger to flicker along her crease. She tossed her head back, gasping at the searing escalation of pleasure.

* * *

JULIUS WATCHED in raptures as Audrey writhed at his touch. Just a week ago, he had provided instruction to his new chum, Abbott, on bedding a maiden. Turned out it was easy to dispense the advice when one had no stake in the game. To deflower a virgin, as Audrey had requested he do, was more daunting than he had thought.

But …

I am up for a challenge.

Audrey was a delight. Responsive. Untamed. He almost wished they could be a proper man and wife so he might school her in the art of love over the coming months, reveal new heights of thrilling enjoyment as he savored the task of indulging her in the numerous forms of bedding.

What a complicated situation they were heading into. He would wed her to protect her, but he had no intention of staying by her side, so what did that mean? Would she enjoy this and perhaps a wedding night, and then never be bedded again? That seemed a great pity and unfair somehow.

Julius shoved the thought aside. It was not his usual inclination to overthink things in the heat of passion. Right now, he had a beautiful woman displayed on the bed. Who desired him, and it was his duty to please her.

Tossing the rest of his considerations to the floor to fall beside her shift, Julius leaned a knee between Audrey's parted legs so he might take care of those unbound orbs, tipped with pink nipples that made his mouth water in anticipation. His palm came up to cup her full breast, plumping it up so he could run his tongue on the hardened tip. He groaned, her sweet, feminine fragrance over-whelming his senses more than any perfume could. She tasted of honey, and herbs, and fresh country air, and he wanted all of it.

Audrey bucked her hips in response. She bore little resemblance to a naïve maiden. The problem was, she did share one important aspect with other maidens … her maidenhead.

Julius moved to the neglected bud, tipping the other creamy globe, chastising himself to be gentle. Each time they came into proximity, it was as if a siren's call had been sounded. Except it was not he who would be beaten on the rocks, but Audrey who would be hurt if he kept losing his head. He caressed the breast, brushing strokes against the sensitive side while he tried to think how to bring her to her peak without smothering her with his lust.

She moaned, pushing up against him to send a fresh wave of lust sparking into his groin. By Jupiter, he took pride in his finesse bedding a woman, but Audrey crept under his skin and fractured his self-control.

Rolling off Audrey, he pulled his body away to regain command over their coupling. His hand slid down, teasing her with a languid pace that made her hips rock in protest. Licking his lips, he continued his path to the silky curls that shielded her, teasing his fingertip fleetingly over her slick crease. Audrey cried out, and he repeated the vexatious stroke, willing his ardor into retreat when he dipped in to trace the honeyed petals of her sex.

Audrey gyrated up in pleading response, but Julius retreated then returned until, with torturous discipline, he nudged his fingertip into her tight, slick channel. He pulsed his finger in and out while his Audrey keened and wailed, biting down on her forearm to muffle the threatening scream. Julius fought his urge to possess her, push her down into the mattress with his weight and take his pleasure. Instead, with infinite patience he did not feel, he continued his teasing touch until he found her pleasure building. Rhythmically, he stroked her to her climax, nearly spending when she cried out, her intimate muscles spasming around his finger.

He rode out the waves of her pleasure with thin resolve until she relaxed from her arched position. Julius rose from the bed, struggling out of his buckskins in clumsy impatience. His cock was harder than it had ever been, the desire to possess the goddess in his sheets fueling his lust to hitherto unknown heights. Desperate to sink into her inviting heat, he fumbled around for the French letter she had brought to his bed. Barking in triumph, he sheathed his length in the animal gut before rolling back to settle between her legs.

Drawing a fortifying breath, he reached up to run a trembling finger over the curve of her cheek. Audrey slowly opened her eyes, the liquid silver causing his heart to hitch.

My God, she is beautiful.

The sight of Audrey flushed with her sated pleasures, the creamy curves cradling his hard body, her pink lips, and nipples tightened into sharp points. He could not recollect a moment when he was so enraptured. Mayhap because they were chums, perhaps because he admired the content of her soul, or mayhap it was her innocent curiosity. He shifted his hips in discomfort, the desire to thrust into her overwhelming as he fought for his control. She was tight and inexperienced, he berated to himself.

"It will hurt."

Audrey pulled a face as if to tell him he was daft, rolling her pelvis up to coax him into motion. Julius swallowed, lowering himself to the cradle of her hips. Guiding his length, he teased over the swollen folds, again and again, unhurried, until Audrey's eyes flickered shut and she began her arousing undulation. Soon he had her heated, panting for him, and he gradually nudged into her then retreated, building her pleasure anew now that she was more prepared to receive his invading thrust after her initial peak.

Her eyelids flew open, an expression of impatient outrage

on her features, when she surprised him by bucking her hips into a high arch to sheath him to the hilt with a gasping sob.

Julius froze, surprised by her ferocious thrust and watching her with shock as he struggled to remain still in the warmth of her tight embrace. He took hold of her hip, delicately lowering them both to the mattress.

Julius waited, stunned by what she had done, anguished—*terrified*—that he had injured her when she remained silent and taut. Just as he considered saying something, Audrey relaxed around him. To his great relief, she gyrated her hips. Sweet relief flooded into his head and, needing no further invitation, he withdrew to plunge in. He tossed his head back, overcome by the sensation of her wrapped around him, startled by the depth of his pleasure.

Reaching down, he stroked his finger over the tender nub that wrought her climax, a rhythmic sweeping the way she liked until she was flushed and keening, her head arching back into the pillow. Thrusting into her, he enjoyed the waves of her pleasure building until she cried out and her pulsing response rushed over him, then his hips thrust forward in a final plunge as he spilled his seed within her throbbing channel.

Once he had caught his breath, Julius rolled off her and pulled her into his embrace to bury his face in the sweet, blonde hair that had come undone to lie in disarray over the pillows and sheets.

CHAPTER 13

"My errors will point to thinking men the various roads, and will teach them the great art of treading on the brink of the precipice without falling into it."

Giacomo Casanova

* * *

*J*ulius was confused. Utterly baffled. His desire to embrace Audrey close against him, to sniff her herbal scent, savor her warm skin, bury his face in her hair, were all fresh impulses.

This is what comes of bedding a woman I admire.

He had assisted her to clean up, and himself, before drawing her back into his bed. Patrick and Rose were discreet, but for sure, they knew that he and Audrey were up to inappropriate activities with the amount of time they had spent alone. It was inevitable they would tumble into bed.

Holding her close to his pounding heart, Julius listened to her breathing as she slipped into a satiated sleep. The desire to nibble on her shoulder for another round of lovemaking was stomped with ruthless determination. She might be a brave warrior of a delicate girl, but even so, she needed to recover from her deflowering.

Deflowering?

Julius wanted to howl. He had always made a point of pursuing experienced women—widows, for the most part—not chosen for their intellectual abilities or strength of character. Women adept in bed and willing to experiment with a variety of positions. He could not recollect bedding a single woman whom he had ardently admired or desired to spend time conversing with. The dangers of love were an ever-present horror, his parents a cautionary tale of which he was frequently reminded.

Audrey let out a small, bleating snort in her sleep, shifting closer so her buttocks rubbed against his groin in an intoxicating caress. Julius shivered in aroused despair.

This is a bleeding disaster.

He had known intuitively it would be a mistake to engage in carnal relations with Audrey. He liked her too much. Not only had he dragged her into a dangerous intrigue, he had destroyed her reputation. Her presentation of the French letter at least assured him she did not have unreasonable expectations regarding him, but he had yet to break the news that they would marry.

Audrey was not a typical female. He believed she would be displeased. That she would resist a marriage in name only. If she had not been ruined, she might have moved back to Stirling and eventually met a gentleman. Settled down and had babes of her own. That was an impossibility, considering she had disappeared with a man for a week. Not just any man—him. No one would believe that he had not had his way with her multiple times during their absence.

Nay, there is no alternative.

Truth was, he did not care for the image of Audrey married to another. As selfish as it might be for him to want her to himself while maintaining his distance, he could not help the possessiveness. Audrey was his—dash it!

Julius was not accustomed to feeling such a riot of conflicting emotions in the wake of one of his escapades, but he was forced to admit that his daft plan had led to terrible consequences for the young lady sleeping in his arms. Yet … somehow … he could not find an iota of regret that he was holding her naked body.

Perhaps they could spend a few weeks together at the start of their marriage? Perhaps he could ensure she had a babe in her belly before he escorted her home to Stirling? Perhaps she would be less angry with him if she had a child to take care of?

Julius groaned into his pillow. What a bloody tangle. He was not accustomed to dealing with consequences, nor to the obligation to consider the needs of another. Audrey had slipped under his skin and—heaven forfend—he now cared about her and desired a happy future for her.

This is a bleeding disaster!

Carefully removing his arm from under her, he rolled out of bed to don his small clothes and buckskins. None of his ideas about their shared future were sitting right. He needed to find a better resolution but, in his experience, it needed to be set aside until later. The situation would work itself out, he concluded.

Holding the oil lamp from beside his bed, Julius padded barefoot out of the chamber, careful not to disturb the sleeping beauty in his bed. He strode down the hall to find the stairs, descending with the inkling of a memory niggling in his brain. Heading into the library with the outline of an idea forming. It would not assist him with the predicament he faced with Audrey, but it might be progress in the investigation. There was danger lurking in the shadows, and it was time to resolve the minor matter of murder. He had to secure Audrey's safety. It was premature to concern himself with the rest.

Julius put the lamp down on a library table, the light revealing a more recent portrait of Aunt Gertrude than the one that hung in the portrait gallery. She wore her hair in a more recent fashion, and a jaunty turban added a splash of color to the ensemble.

Aunty Gertrude peered down her nose with an expression of reproach.

Julius winced. He was supposed to put aside the dilemma he faced with the physician's daughter, not be fighting off a stabbing guilt over his despicable behavior.

"We will wed. I will provide her the protection of my name, Aunty."

Lady Hays continued to stare.

"I swear it! I will take care of the young lady. She will not want for anything."

It might have been his imagination, but Lady Hays sniffed in disgust. Egad, he hated disappointing his great-aunt. She would flail him alive if she knew he had deflowered Audrey under her own roof without even a betrothal contract in place. He was the worst kind of rascal for not securing an agreement to wed before engaging in carnal relations.

Julius shook his head, determined to set the matter aside. Walking over to a nearby shelf, he found an older copy of Debrett's *Peerage* and brought it back to the table, thunking it down hard on the surface to help focus his attention.

Taking his seat, he bent over its pages, leafing through to look up the heritage of the three men he had been investigating. He and Abbott had attended a myriad of dinners, soirées, even a musicale and a ball to learn what they could about their suspects. Julius had a vague memory of attending a soirée at one of the homes of the suspects. At the time he had noted the old style of the livery uniforms—deep blue and gold-braided coats with shoulder knots, knee breeches and, more important, he seemed to recollect that the servants' uniforms had possessed a unique feature. When one of the footmen had turned a corner, the tails of his coat had flittered up and Julius had caught sight of a patterned lining. A brief impression of green and blue.

Leafing through the book, he flipped to the entry he wished to read. Julius whistled through his teeth, realizing that the mystery was falling into place.

I think we found our man!

* * *

AUDREY WOKE UP, stretching her limbs out, and gradually noted the coolness of the sheets. She frowned, reaching out to where Julius had lain behind her and finding an empty space.

The room was dark, and she realized he must have extinguished the lamp. Sitting up, she pushed her hair back and clutched the sheet to her bosom with a befuddled head and a disappointed heart.

She knew their time was ending, but she had been savoring her one night in his arms. There had been a vague hope that perhaps they might make love one more time before she faced her fate. Something a little less ignominious than her initial deflowering. Something to remember when she returned alone to Stirling to the house she had inherited from her father.

Audrey's throat thickened, and she blinked away the tears forming. She had known the risks of accompanying Julius to take care of him the day he had been stabbed. And she had known that Julius was a free spirit. She was not so conceited to believe that she could tame one like him. It still stung to wake up alone.

Had he enjoyed their time together?

Had she satisfied him as a man?

Would there be one last opportunity to feel his firm lips on hers?

Audrey jumped out of her skin when the door swung open, revealing Julius in the light of the oil lamp in his hand. Her hungry gaze devoured his half-naked form, his wide shoulders and narrow hips in silhouette, and she found she was both pleased he had returned and shy.

"I think I know who did it!" he announced, swinging the door shut behind him and striding over to the bed. "Now we just need to confirm it!"

Audrey pushed her hair from her face as Julius sat on the bed next to her, the mattress sagging under his weight. He put the oil lamp down on the table beside the bed, holding up a leather-bound book for her to see.

"Simon Scott!"

She tried to focus her thoughts. "Scott?"

"Simon Scott is the younger brother of Lord Blackwood, but they do not share the same mother. Lord Blackwood and his second brother Peter were issue from their Sussex-born mother, who appears to have died in childbirth based on the dates in Debrett's. Their father, John Scott, went on to marry another woman who died without children before he married his third wife who is a wealthy peeress from Scotland—Lady Isla Scott was Lady Isla Campbell and she is a Scottish viscountess!"

Audrey leaned forward to peer to where he was pointing at the page. "So Simon Scott is descended from Campbells, but, as you said, there are infinite Campbells."

Julius threw her a triumphant grin. "But few who have a household of liveried servants whose coats are lined with

Campbell tartan. This is a new fashion, to flaunt one's clan-ship amongst the *beau monde*, only begun within the last few years and only by a few. If the footmen's coats are lined with the pattern, they might have been provided overcoats with the same lining. The scoundrel who attempted to kill me might not have been dressed in livery in an attempt to hide his identity, but he might have used the only overcoat he possessed."

Audrey's mouth fell open. "Truly?"

"I saw the pattern myself at an event at Scott's home. Abbott and I latched onto a friend who was attending, and the tartan intrigued me. The name Scott should have been a clue, but I saw the tartan myself. Scott's mother runs his household, so she must have ordered the livery. I thought their whole appearance rather out of date, and Scott does not seem a man stuck in the last century, but his mother would have been young when this type of livery was in fashion. If Scott is a member of the Highland Society, she could have ordered the tartan as part of the design."

She nibbled on her lip, considering the revelation. "When you say his mother is a viscountess …"

Julius nodded, his lean face in profile. Audrey appreciated the straight nose, sculpted chin, and firm jaw before flickering down to … appreciate … the muscled shoulders she had gripped earlier when Julius had picked her up.

"I know it is odd, but many of the titles in Scotland are granted a remainder which allows females to inherit if there are no males to take the title. Isla is the oldest of four sisters."

Audrey blinked. "Stirling is far from the Scottish border, so I know little about our northern neighbors, but you seem to know quite a bit about a family so far from London."

"There was another volume." Julius pulled a second book from under his arm. "See, I found Isla's family in here."

"It is solved?"

Julius hesitated, pondering her question. "I suppose we need some sort of confirmation, but I think this points to the resolution. It is him. I feel it in my bones."

Which meant this was their final evening together, as she had suspected.

"So ... there is nothing to be done this evening?" She was taken aback by the seductive tone of her question. Lud, she sounded like a fallen woman, but she was damned if she would waste a second of the time she had left with the outrageous Lord Trafford. This was her one night with him, and she would not waste it.

Julius must have noted the purring quality, licking his lips and tilting his head toward her. "I suppose not," he echoed in a suggestive tone.

"Good."

Audrey reached over to press her mouth to his, the fire in her belly reigniting. She brushed her palm down the slope of his back, letting the sheet drop to press her breasts against his arm. Julius groaned, biting at her lower lip to tug at it as he turned to lower her back on the bed.

CHAPTER 14

"Real love is the love that sometimes arises after sensual pleasure: if it does, it is immortal; the other kind inevitably goes stale, for it lies in mere fantasy."

Giacomo Casanova

* * *

SEPTEMBER 2, 1821

*A*udrey savored the kiss Julius pressed to her forehead, reluctant to open her eyes and admit their night was over. He had made slow and passionate love to her one more time before pulling her into his arms to sleep. Audrey had lain awake for an hour, enjoying the unity of his heart beating against her cheek as he had drifted off. She had recorded how he felt, the warmth of his bare skin against her body, the shape of his torso with her hand. Every ticking second had been bittersweet while she had resolved not to think of what came next but just be present.

She had a dreadful feeling that she would be ever so lonely when she left for Stirling. Separating from Julius after the wonderful time they had shared left her heart hollow.

At least she had gotten her one perfect night.

Audrey's eyes flickered open to find Julius peering down at her in the morning light, his green-brown eyes reflecting the glow of sunrise.

"Good morning," he whispered.

She realized this was what it would be like to be married to Julius. Waking up with the sunrise to greet him before embarking on the adventure of the day. Yearning pierced her very soul. "Good morning."

"Filminster and Abbott will be here soon."

Audrey nodded, accepting this aberration of a week was ending and it was time to return to Lord Stirling's home. Swallowing hard, she sat up with a sheet draped over her front.

"What of Patrick and Rose?"

Julius paused mid-rising, his blond hair lit up by sunlight from the window. "I will speak with them, but they are far too fond of me to gossip. That we were here will never be shared. You witnessed their joy that you had rescued me from the brink."

"That is a relief." Her response was tense. Anguish at confronting the scandal back in the real world was tying her stomach in knots.

He cocked his head back to glance at her, his expression indecipherable. "I will protect you, Audrey. Your reputation will be restored."

She averted her gaze, her eyes misting with trepidation over the coming days. "There is nothing to be done. I ... do not regret ... anything."

Julius reached out a hand, cupping her cheek and coaxing her to look at him. "I have a plan to take care of you. I ..." He halted, staring at her as if he wished to say something. Audrey waited, wondering what he could have in mind that would save her from ruin, but he released her to rise from the bed. "I have a plan, which we will discuss. Do not distress yourself over Lady Astley."

He walked over to the washstand to clean himself. Audrey sighed, getting out of bed to search for her crumpled shift. She pulled it on before finding a robe in Julius's wardrobe. Picking up her mourning gown, she silently left the room.

Returning to her own room down the hall, Audrey washed up while her thoughts remained on what was to come. Despite Julius's assurances, she did not think there was anything he could do to mitigate the approaching crisis. Certainly he could not plan to wed her. She was a mere doctor's daughter from Stirling, a wholly unsuitable match for the heir to an important earl, if Julius were inclined to wed at all.

Failing a wedding, she was ruined beyond redemption. Despite his assurances, Audrey knew she was in deep trouble, and she hoped the earl would support her in planning a future. She still held hope that they could prevent word from reaching Stirling and she could resume her life in the village with no one the wiser about her London adventures.

Flapper chirruped from his cage, as if to provide solace to her maudlin thoughts, making her heart squeeze even tighter as she dressed. She had succeeded as a physician, it would seem, but lost her heart along the way.

Crossing the room to collect his cage, she placed it on the dressing table before taking her seat. Opening the cage, Audrey reached in to lift the little starling. She unraveled the dressing on his wing, placing it aside to inspect the wing with gentle fingertips.

Tears sprang into her eyes as she placed the unbound bird back in the cage. As expected, Flapper was ready to take flight, not unlike the buck down the hall. For just a second, Audrey considered keeping the bird in the cage.

The needs of the patient outweigh any other considerations.

Audrey sniffed, wiping the moisture from her lashes. "I know, Papa, but who will mend my heart? Is there no remedy for me? Is the physician not a patient, too?"

She chided herself for being selfish. It was time for the bird to fly free.

Gazing up at her mournful reflection, Audrey brushed out her hair and pinned it up before jumping to her feet. Taking hold of the cage, she departed her bedchamber to go to the garden, lest she convince herself to keep the bird against its will. Flapper could not serve as a memento of her time with Julius. He deserved his freedom. She had not rescued him to break his spirit and turn him into a pet.

The garden was still cast with shadows as the sun made its way across the deep blue sky. It was a perfect day for a little bird to find its way home. Setting the cage on a bench, Audrey sat down by a neat box hedge and swung the little door open. To her dismay, tears threatened again as she reached to take hold of the trembling bird. It was as if Flapper knew his time had come.

She set him down on the grass. Audrey wanted him to test his flight nice and low so he was not injured yet again. The bird hesitated in a mild state of confusion, waddling forward with shrill chirps. Then Flapper extended his wings in the manner of a newly birthed lamb attempting to stand.

Audrey watched, nibbling on her lip and hoping that her assessment had been correct. She was sure the wing had healed, but the wild creature had been caught in a cage and binding for three weeks. Did Flapper recall what he was to do?

The bird peered around, cocking his head back and forth, before turning to stare at Audrey herself. For the briefest moment, she thought the creature was going to return to her, but the wings extended once more and, without warning, the bird took flight. Wheeling through the air, Flapper took a few dips, and then he was gone.

Audrey stared in the direction he had flown for endless minutes, the ever-threatening tears finally streaming down her face. They dripped off her chin to run down her neck, and work their way into the fabric of her gown. She was a complete ninny for weeping over a tiny bird but, somehow, his departure symbolized the end of her adventure in Town. Soon, she and Julius would gather their things and head home to Lord Stirling's. The townhouse might be just across the street, but it felt more like a journey of hundreds of miles. A journey from a beautiful fantasy land back to grimy London.

Soon her single night with the handsome lord who had stolen her heart would be a distant memory, and Audrey cried for all she wished could be. She wished she could remain by his side. She wished Julius could be her husband and escort her on more visits to the places of men. Taverns, perhaps. Dance halls, certainly. She wished she could visit those places with him, share conversations with him over meals, return home to join him in his bed. That they might have babes with his strange blond and brown hair running about their home, dressed in unexpected colors selected by the odd gentleman who had sired them. That he would make her smile when she was sad, and laugh when she was happy, and that she could take care of him. Provide him counsel, keep him and their children out of the hands of quacks, perhaps together choose a new crusade to pursue.

She supposed one day there would be a woman who

tamed the wild spirit barely contained within his earthly form. Audrey just wished it could have been her.

* * *

JULIUS WAS STILL MULLING over his proposal to Audrey when he reached the door to the alley to await his friends. He could tell she was tense this morning, anticipating her return home and the awaiting controversy. Opening his mouth to inform her of his intent, he had realized he still did not know what he was offering her.

A marriage in name only would allow her to pursue her goals in medicine. In fact, as a married woman, she would be far more acceptable as a healer than an unwed girl. Not from his personal standpoint, but most people were rather unyielding in their social expectations.

But, somehow, sending her off to Stirling as his estranged wife was not sitting well.

And, to make matters worse, he was not ready to let her go. He had enjoyed holding her in his arms the night before.

Marriage leads to indifference.

He sighed. The thought of his delightful friendship with Audrey descending into ambivalence was unpalatable. Nay, if they stayed apart, they could maintain their mutual regard. Yet ... perhaps ... he could visit her from time to time to take care of their mutual needs. She was a passionate lover, and he had little interest in returning to his prior carnal arrangements.

Making love to a female he considered a friend had been a new experience, and he had never envisioned being the sort to marry and keep a mistress. He recalled being rather appalled when he had attended a house party in Somerset the year before and a scoundrel of the upper classes had set his sights on a debutante connected to Lord Saunton's family.

Both he and his chum Brendan had warned the beef-witted boor that Lord Saunton would not tolerate such behavior toward a young lady under his protection.

Julius was still reeling at the idea of marriage. He had sworn it would never happen, but it was the honorable thing to do since Audrey had discarded her reputation to see to his longevity. Considering her assertive behavior in bed the night before, he could not make a muddle of his proposal. She would hardly be passive with her words if he botched it. Which was why he needed to be concise and clear about what he was offering. Unfortunately, he was still vacillating about what the offer was precisely.

Checking his timepiece, he leaned against the wall, drumming his fingers while he tried to think about what to do about Audrey. Soon they would leave, and he should settle the matter with her before they departed from Aunty Gertrude's.

Julius was not accustomed to such indecision. Under normal circumstances, he got a notion in his head and concluded if he was interested or not in pursuing it. This state of affairs with Audrey was different. Her welfare notwithstanding, Julius was having difficulty grasping what his own desires were when it came to the unusual female.

He did not want a marriage, but he wanted to marry her. He did not wish to answer to anyone, but Audrey had proven an excellent chum who tempered but did not attempt to curtail his objectives. Not to mention, it would be terrible to cause misery for a dear chum. A chum who had saved his life a week ago.

His wound ached in reminder of what he owed Audrey. Is that what plagued him? A sense of obligation to the avenging angel who had chased his would-be assassin away? Mayhap his debt of honor to protect her from salacious gossip obfuscated his thoughts so. Perhaps the best thing was to offer to wed her with the provision they live apart. Then the sense of duty would dispel so he would have a clear head.

A brief rap on the door alerted him that Abbott had arrived. Julius swung the door open, stepping aside to let the other heir in, and shutting them in with a brisk click of a lock latching.

They waited for Brendan, the rustle of leaves in the morning breeze the only sound. Neither dared discuss anything where they might be overheard out in the alley. Julius took the interlude to settle his worries. Proximity to Audrey and his friendship with her were clouding his mind. They would wed. He would escort her to Stirling to settle her in and then … he would return to London to sort through his thoughts.

He could abstain from women for a while. When he knew how he wished to conduct himself in the future, he and his bride would concede to an acceptable compromise. His future activities need not shame him if they agreed on the terms of their marriage.

Julius's anxieties molded into a decision. He just needed some time to restore his equilibrium before he amended their arrangement.

"Are you going to let Filminster in?" hissed Abbott in reproach. Julius blinked, glancing up to find Abbott waving with irritation toward the door. His eyes flared in dismay, recognizing that he had missed the muted knock. He gestured to Abbott to move out of sight and opened the door to reveal Brendan disguised as a groom. The baron scowled at him in rebuke, stalking in without a word.

After the door was secured, the three men headed into the mews to find the tack room. Brendan spun on his heel as soon as they entered, throwing up his hands as an irritated question.

"My apologies. I was woolgathering," Julius mumbled.

Brendan's chestnut eyebrows rose to his hairline in surprise as he shot a look at Abbott.

"About a certain young woman?" he proffered.

A surge of umbrage made Julius straighten up in defense. "Certainly not! I just ... have news to impart!"

That Brendan had guessed where his thoughts lay was galling. He was not some insipid youth pining over a female. Just because these two buffoons were besotted with their brides did not mean he was following suit. Nay, he was cut from a different cloth than most.

The fact that he had sated his lust, yet still desired Audrey, still felt the impression of her beneath him—that was neither here nor there. Once he put things right, life would return to normal.

"We need to finish this. I believe I know who murdered the baron!"

This proclamation had the desired effect. Brendan and Abbott inhaled in a surprised chorus.

"How? I thought you were resting yesterday?"

"I was. That is when Aud—Miss Gideon recalled a detail from the day of my attack." Julius pulled the leather-bound books from his coat pockets. "She recalled that the hound who attacked me had a pattern lining his coat. Tartan. From the Campbell Clan."

Brendan frowned, combing his fingers through his hair with a thoughtful expression as he appeared to search for a memory. "One of the men had a mother—"

"Scott! His mother is a Campbell. A Scottish peeress, in fact!"

Abbott balked, ever the voice of dissent. "It could be a coincidence."

Julius tutted. "I observed that the servants in the Scott household have uniforms lined with the same tartan. Aud—Miss Gideon identified them from a pattern book."

Brendan whistled through his teeth. "This could be it!"

"I think it is."

Abbott stalked over. "There must be a way to confirm it."

Julius nodded. "I agree. I think we should question Stone and Montague as to their whereabouts on the night of the coronation. If they possess alibis, we can rule them out to focus our attentions on finding evidence against Scott. Unearth Peter Scott's marriage to a woman from the Continent in whatever parish records are relevant to his family."

Brendan rubbed his neck, staring at the ground beneath their boots. "You are that confident?"

Julius grinned, spreading his arms out in exuberant emphasis. "Gentlemen, I am coming home."

* * *

MUCH LATER, after the sun had set and London was in darkness, Audrey and Julius sat in the large drawing room at the top of the stairs—the one that faced the street and over-looked the entrance to Lord Stirling's townhouse.

Neither of them had spoken since entering the room ten minutes earlier. Audrey would have paid more attention to the fact that Julius was more subdued than she had ever seen him, but she was subdued herself. Outright melancholy, in fact.

Her valise sat at her feet, along with the empty birdcage that reminded her that her first patient was gone. Flying free through the skies of London while Audrey contemplated her lonely future. She crossed her fingers within the folds of her skirts.

Please allow me to return to Stirling unscathed.

It was her last chance to escape. She needed to leave London as soon as possible to avoid the agony of parting from Julius. When they walked across the street, their unusual friendship would be over. She would never be alone with him again after they left Lady Hays's. It would be agonizing to brush past him in the hall from time to time, or perhaps sit across from him at the dinner table, but pretend they shared no relationship. That he did not hold her heart from this day. That he had not woken her from the slumber of mourning, the endless melancholy of grief, to reveal a new world of exciting adventure.

Audrey swallowed the lump in her throat, staring out at the shadowed street while they waited for the guards who would protect them.

She wanted to savor her last time alone with Julius, but her stomach coiled with dread. There was no knowing what crisis she would face come morning when news of their return got around. Audrey picked at her skirts in agitation.

"Audrey?"

Looking away from the window, she found Julius staring at her with a strange expression.

"I … wish to inform you—"

The sound of carriage wheels interrupted what he wished to say, both of them spinning back to the window to see who had arrived. Two carriages stood out on the roadway, several servants disembarking from the dark interiors. As they approached Lord Stirling's front door, passing under the street lamp, Audrey noted they were unusual choices for footmen. Their heights were disparate for one, several of them shorter than the rest when they were usually hired to be similar in appearance.

"The Johns are here."

Her brow wrinkled as she threw Julius a questioning look.

"The guards from Markham House. They each call themselves John for some reason. I suppose they wish to hide their identities," he explained.

Audrey drew a deep breath, rising from the settee. Leaning down, she picked up her valise and birdcage. "It would seem we are ready to leave."

"We need to discuss the future. The plan I mentioned."

Audrey nodded, but she had to admit she was rather overwrought at that moment. She wanted to get this parting over with, and deal with the scandal as a separate issue. The truth was, she was feeling rather fragile, and discussing the looming gossip was not foremost on her mind. Right now, she wanted to return to her room and nurse her breaking heart.

"In the morning, perhaps. It … has been a long day." It was all she could offer in the way of explanation.

Julius reached out, attempting to take the cage from her hand. "In the morning, then. May I … assist you with that?"

Audrey shook her head, drawing back. She needed to get accustomed to fending for herself. Papa was gone, and Julius would be off on his adventures without her. "I can manage. Shall we?"

Julius nodded, reaching up to tuck a lock of hair behind her ear. The sweetness of his gesture pierced her heart with longing, but she squared her shoulders, determined not to stray into wishful thinking. They left the drawing room, descending the main staircase. The mood was gloomy. Neither of them appeared to be thrilled about their return home. Audrey wondered briefly about the cause of Julius's pensive tone, but she was struggling with her own despair, so did not pay it much mind.

They reached the front door, and Patrick was there to open it.

As Audrey stood in the doorway contemplating the house on the other side of the street, she fought back a black cloud of depression. She welcomed the weight of the cage and the valise tugging on her arms. They helped her focus on the here. She did not want to think about how this was so much like the night she had arrived in London as a grieving daughter, only to return a dejected female who had lost her heart to the gentleman standing at her side.

It had been a glorious few days, but now she was waking from the strange dream she had been caught in. Audrey just hoped she could leave for Stirling soon, and that the scandal would not follow her there. She needed time to grieve anew while she picked up the pieces of her life and tried to work out what would make her happy.

CHAPTER 15

"It is only necessary to have courage, for strength without self-confidence is useless."

Giacomo Casanova

* * *

SEPTEMBER 3, 1821

*A*udrey went down to breakfast, nursing a headache. She had lain awake all night considering her future, and regretted not speaking with Julius about whatever plan he had mentioned to rescue her from scandal. Perhaps she could have slept if she had a solution to the future, but instead she had tossed and turned, unable to stop worrying about it.

When she had awakened and rung for the maid to assist her, a different maid had arrived. Audrey had been nonplussed, questioning the young servant to learn that the other maid had quit a few days earlier. This had been jarring news. Had she quit to distance herself from Audrey's situation, or perhaps as a direct indictment of Audrey's continued disappearance?

Belowstairs must be rife with gossip over her, especially now that she had returned. It was not uncommon to lose servants over disreputable occurrences, and she hoped she had not created too much chaos for Lord Stirling when he ultimately returned.

Approaching the breakfast room, she noticed a footman standing sentry in the hall. She noted it must be one of the new Johns that arrived the previous night, because she did not recognize him. The guardsmen had arrived while it was dark, so she had not gotten a proper look at most of them. The servant in question was a little too short, a little too worn around the edges, and his livery was askew. Especially the stock around his throat. Not to mention that his sleeves were too long. However, he had a glint in his eye that suggested a fierce nature—someone who could hold his ground in a fight.

Passing him to enter the room, Audrey found a footman she did recognize standing in wait at the sideboard where the breakfast trays were laid out. Taking up a plate, she served up eggs and fruit and dropped into a seat with a heavy sigh. She had been hoping to find Julius—or rather, Lord Trafford, she supposed, since they were back in polite society. If he had thoughts on how to mitigate this disaster, she would like to hear them. The logistics of her situation were what had plagued her all night.

Did she need to wait for the Earl of Stirling to return before she could leave London? There did not appear to be an alternative.

Must she alert someone she was home?

Send a letter to Lady Astley with some contrived explanation for her disappearance?

She was loath to announce she was home. It might serve as an invitation for Lady Astley to show up and scold Audrey. The old bat might insist that Audrey leave with her so she could chaperone her moving forward. A prospect that was unappealing. And pointless.

The earl's footman, the one she knew, cleared his throat, having approached while she had been staring at her plate. "You have correspondence, Miss Gideon."

He proffered a small tray with a single letter set out.

With acute reluctance, Audrey picked it up just as Julius appeared in the doorway.

"Aud—Miss Gideon!" he exclaimed with buoyancy.

Despite her thudding head and the dread of the letter in her hand, her spirits were lifted to see Julius. He was handsome in his purple silk, even if it was a foppish choice. Or, perhaps, she was just hungry to spend time with him.

Lud, I need to leave London.

"We are to speak this morning about"—Julius's gaze flickered over to the servant—"the situation ..."

Audrey smiled, her headache relieving mildly at his presence. "Please, Lord Trafford, have you eaten?"

Julius shook his head, crossing to the sideboard. He spoke in a low voice with the servant, who departed the room and shut the door while he gathered a plate for himself.

Audrey unfolded the letter. Now that Julius was here, she wanted to learn who had written as quickly as possible. She had a friend to discuss the contents with, whatever they might be, so she did not want to waste the opportunity to have his support if it was bad news.

As soon as the letter was revealed, her eyes darted down

to confirm it was from Lady Astley. Then she read the contents, her stomach clenching into a knot as her worst fears were manifested.

"That ... that ... that interfering shrew!" she cried out, throwing the page away from her onto the table in distress.

Julius spun around in alarm, following her gaze to the letter.

She sprang to her feet, her hands trembling with the force of her emotions. Audrey could feel herself spiraling into fear, her lungs tightening as she gasped for air, and her hopes of a quiet retreat to the village lay dashed in smithereens on the table from where Lady Astley's poisonous ink taunted her.

"What is it?" Julius demanded, setting his plate down to stride over.

"That noxious old biddy, Lady Astley, informs me she has written to the vicar in Stirling so he will know I am a scandalous baggage!"

She could not breathe. Any hopes of returning to Stirling unscathed were obliterated. She could not remain in London, but she could not return home.

Audrey buried her face in her hands, breaking into hysterical laughter. She was doomed. Her plans were destroyed. She would have to start anew somewhere she was unknown.

Was Scotland in need of healers?

Was Edinburgh far enough away?

Lawk—must she brave the seas for the New World?

How far did she have to travel to outrun the damage to her reputation?

Her laughter turned to weeping, tears gushing down her face as she sobbed in horror.

She was vaguely aware of Julius snatching up the letter to read it as she collapsed back into her chair to bury her face in her arms. Her life as she knew it was over. There was nowhere to go! She would have to start over in a new country!

"Audrey!"

She had not thought her day could get any worse. No one would accept treatment from her if she was a fallen woman. No one respectable, that was. She would face lewd suggestions from uncouth men. Decent women would shun her. Children would be ushered away from her presence as if she were a contagious leper. Her only choice was to find somewhere far, far away.

Her mind raced through possibilities, each seeming worse than the last.

"Cornwall?"

Would that be far enough?

"Audrey?"

She did not respond. Could not respond. Instead, she continued weeping, her shoulders heaving as her lungs fought for air. Exhausted from her sleepless night, grieving that she must part with Julius, mourning that she could not talk with her dear papa. She wanted to be brave, but the ground was collapsing beneath her feet.

"Audrey!" Julius tugged at her arm. "You must calm down! I have a solution, I swear it!"

Audrey attempted to calm herself from the blind panic. The tears slowed down as she sucked air into her lungs until she finally raised her face to look at him.

Julius was kneeling beside her.

"We are to wed," he announced, taking her hand up in his.

Audrey stopped breathing, staring at him in shock. Hope trickled in as she took in the sincerity of his expression. Did Julius feel about her the way she did about him? Was he professing his regard?

"You can return to Stirling to treat patients as a married woman," he continued.

She frowned, confused by the declaration.

"It will be a ... marriage of convenience. You will have the protection of my name so you can pursue your goals."

The fledgling hopes that had just begun to gather scattered like leaves in a sharp gust of wind. Audrey slumped back in her chair in numb despair. She supposed it was a resolution but, just for a moment, she had thought that maybe he was inviting her to be his partner. Perhaps all along she had hoped he would fall in love with her, but dared not think about it lest she raised her hopes. The unsuspected disappointment was ashes threatening to choke her.

Lud, it was a mistake to not discuss this last night.

If she had, perhaps she could have kept her wits about her instead of having the man she loved witness this mortifying display of emotion. This was not the pragmatic character she strived for as a practitioner of medicine.

Audrey swallowed hard, dabbing her face with a napkin from the table, pausing until she was sure her words would be steady.

"So ... not a real marriage?"

* * *

"THAT IS CORRECT."

Julius knew he was an awful cad, but he had resolved to make his offer thus, so he was going to stick to his decision. He could not offer more. Marriage was the death of regard. It trapped wonderful people like his mother in a cage. It made children miserable and turned fathers into distant strangers.

He would not become his father. He would not make Audrey despise him. They would wed, then remain apart.

Once she was settled in Stirling, pursuing her dreams as a healer, Julius could recover his peace of mind.

"So we are to wed and ... what? You will remain in London?"

Julius did not like the dull quality of Audrey's sweet voice. It made him feel like a dog. But he was one for not settling this with her the previous night. The sight of her devastation brought on by Lady Astley's foul attack had wrenched his very heart from his chest. He had, in fact, found himself examining his ribs as if to seek confirmation that they were yet intact and pressing around his sutures to ensure they, too, were still in place.

"Yes. You will be free to follow your dreams. I venture that being a married woman will make it easier to be accepted by the villagers as a healer."

Audrey's face was grim, her silver eyes clouded as she stared at him. Julius felt terribly uncomfortable.

"I do not wish to inconvenience you so. It is not your responsibility," she finally replied.

Laying her hand back onto the table, he rose to his feet. "I have no plans to marry, so this is not a hardship, I assure you. You can continue your life the way you had planned."

She did not appear to be convinced, her face remaining set in unhappy lines. He tried to think what to say, but she beat him to it.

"Julius, it is unnecessary. My father left me an income. I shall leave England. Perhaps I can move to Paris, even make up a dead husband."

Paris? What was with the women in his life? What was their obsession with living in France! It was a conspiracy to keep him at bay, as if they somehow knew he could not tolerate the vigors of sea travel and it was their assurance they need never tolerate his presence again.

"No!" Hearing his terse tone, Julius grimaced. He was

considered charming, unflappable even. Since setting off with Audrey last week, he appeared to have misplaced his very character. "I wish to do this. As a married woman, you will have your independence. You shall never want for funds. As my wife, you will be a future countess. None dare disrespect you. Even vile Lady Astley will be forced to retract her claims to the vicar when word is out that we are wed. I ... want to do this, Audrey."

Audrey turned away to contemplate her fingernails. "So you wish to wed me ... but you do not wish to be my husband."

Gadzooks, that sounds terrible!

But it was true. He was a childish clot who resisted maturity. Any of his friends would concur without hesitation.

"Yes."

Audrey flexed her jaw as if she had been punched. But, even if it was difficult, Julius was determined to be forthright. He liked Audrey far too much to manipulate her.

"What of ... bedding? Do you plan to ... bed other women?"

It seemed unlikely, considering he could not stop thinking of her in his bed, but ... "I do not know. I would discuss it with you if I wish to alter the terms of our agreement."

Audrey's face grew grimmer.

"The ... terms of our agreement." She stated it out loud, as if exploring the words.

Julius grew nervous. She was going to turn him down. For some reason he could not quite name, it was imperative she agree to the marriage. The notion of her leaving England to get away from the scandal was inconceivable. It was—he sought for a reason—his duty to protect her. She would be safer if she remained here, he reasoned. Her goals would be attainable. She could pursue her dreams and remain in the village where she had been born, surrounded by friends who admired her and her father. Lord Snarling could keep her under his protection, so no harm would ever befall her. Travel was rife with risks.

Therefore, he had to persuade her that this was her best option. He had the sense that she was going to refuse him, and he found himself rather invested in the outcome because … because … What explanation could there be? Because she had saved his life and it was his duty to keep her safe?

"Perhaps … a babe would be possible?"

Audrey's face softened at the suggestion. Julius twisted his signet ring, trying to think what to say next to clinch the deal. He was not quite sure what he wanted from Audrey, and he needed some time and distance from her to sort it out, but it was essential that she be near when he was ready to address this in a more permanent manner. If she left, he would not have that opportunity to do so, and he was sure it would cause regrets. And what of the terrible guilt if he was responsible for her being chased from the only home she had ever known?

"I shall escort you to Stirling, and we will ensure that there is a babe." It was all he could think to say. He waited, hoping she would accept those terms.

A babe? How do I feel about that?

That was an impossible question to answer, because he had never considered it. He was to never marry, ergo there was never to be issue to consider.

Issue?

Julius curled his lips in disgust. He had been reading far too much of Debrett's if he was referring to children as *issue*. It was more of that ghastly appropriate language that polite society subscribed to. This was precisely the type of maturing he was attempting to avoid by remaining unmarried, yet here he was applying himself to the persuasion of a woman to marry him.

Audrey was deep in thought, nibbling on that plump lower lip she loved to abuse, until she exhaled. "I shall accept those terms, but I do not agree to you parading around London with your paramours without my approval. You will inform me if the terms are to change. If they do ... I shall not want to see you again. If you find the need to pursue other women, I will raise our child without your interference and you will remain far from Stirling."

Julius's relief was profound, another oddity to be set aside and considered when a clearer head prevailed. He was aware of the despicable nature of his proposal, but he could not reconcile his long-held goal of avoiding marriage with his desire to take care of Audrey.

Perhaps it would become clearer over time. He hoped so. This was a temporary reprieve at best because the entire situation was causing him acute discomfort. The one thing he was certain of was that Audrey must be protected ... and she must remain close to hand.

"What do I do about ... this?" She gestured to the letter as if it were a snake poised to sink its fangs into her.

"Brendan has asked the duke to organize a special license. We should be married before the week is out, at which time I will ensure that announcements are made in the news sheets. As for Lady Astley ... ignore her. We remain here with the guards while the matter with Scott is determined, and then we leave for Stirling. I shall visit your vicar to address his concerns."

"As you wish," she replied, but Julius found he did not like their current terseness. He wished he had spoken with her before leaving Aunty Gertrude's. Audrey was unhappy, it was plain to see, and he hated he could not offer her something more. She deserved to have a husband at her side, but the idea of settling down and over time turning into his father left him cold.

Perhaps when they were wed, he could find a better resolution to all this, but each time he tried to solve it, his emotions grew tumultuous and murky.

It did not help that he had been stabbed, lost his wits to a fever, and had yet a murder to finish solving.

Julius almost wished that Lord Snarling would return, so he might argue with his father over the specifics. That was sure to rouse him from his muddled thoughts and settle his mind on how he wished to continue with Audrey. Quarreling with his father about appropriate behavior had always been something of a palate cleanser that had helped clarify his position on the argument at hand.

Failing that, he would have discussed the problem with his excellent new chum, who had been assisting him. Audrey was a remarkably fine partner to have along—more in tune with him than any of his male friends had ever been. It was the first time he had spent such a considerable time with one person without the desire to brain them. Nay, he wished to do altogether other things with his sweet Audrey.

Unfortunately, his current problem *was* the selfsame chum. Bedding her had been a terrible idea, muddying his thoughts in the worst way. If he had been uncertain of what he wanted to do about Audrey, it was far more perplexing since sharing a passionate night with her in the sheets. How was he to seek perspective when he kept recalling how warm and soft she had been beneath him, or how her moans of desire had thrilled him to hitherto unknown heights of sensual pleasure?

The lines between obligation for his part in her ruin, and genuine regard for her as a person, were blurred into an amorphous muddle.

Nevertheless, Julius reflected, it was a heady relief that

she had agreed to their wedding. What he was certain of was that Audrey must not disappear. Or cross the Channel to France. He was very much afraid if she did, he would be forced to follow her, and the thought of standing on deck as it swayed back and forth made bile rise in his throat. Returning from his Grand Tour had been a terrible ordeal, and he had no plans to leave their little island again. Which was why Audrey must stay.

CHAPTER 16

"The mind of a human being is formed only of comparisons made in order to examine analogies, and therefore cannot precede the existence of memory."

Giacomo Casanova

* * *

*A*udrey battled mixed emotions, watching from the drawing room window. Julius was to be driven off in Lord Filminster's carriage to visit the vicar Stone, along with two of the Johns disguised as footmen.

She had been awaiting his departure for some time, pacing alone in the room that faced the street below while she tried to sort through her feelings.

On the one hand, it was an immense relief that she did not need to flee the country under a cloud of controversy. Journeying alone to foreign lands was not enticing.

She was a little flattered Julius had sufficient appreciation for her to give up any aspect of his freedoms to offer her marriage. It had been unexpected, to say the least.

Acknowledging these truths did not change the fact that she was seething with unspoken resentments. Audrey had no desire for the type of marriage Julius had proposed. The offer of a babe was appreciated, but the rest!

Nay! It will not do at all!

If they were to be married, she wanted it to be a genuine partnership. The kind of partnership she had envisioned he would one day share with a wife by his side. She wanted to accompany him on his adventures, visit hitherto unplanned places, and build a family of wayward souls like that of her future husband.

She would not be discarded to rusticate in Stirling while her husband decided whether he could forgo other women!

It was sort of laudable that he intended to be candid about the whole thing, but ... but ... he wanted to have his wife *and* unfettered freedom. That was untenable! Did Julius have no notion what a marriage was?

That brought her to a sudden halt.

It was possible he had some odd ideas on the subject. Audrey was herself, by society standards, considered of the lower gentry. Her father had been a physician and landowner, and they resided in the countryside, where the values of a husband and wife differed from these high society types. She believed Lord and Lady Stirling might be estranged. Audrey had not seen the countess or her daughter in some time—a minimum of three or four years since either of them had visited Stirling.

Perhaps this outrageous plan to inform her of his possible intent to wander off with paramours had something to do with whatever arrangement his parents had? She could not be certain, but Julius had implied strained relations between him and his father. She had overheard them quarrel since arriving in London.

Audrey leaned a knee on a settee beneath one of the street-facing windows, nibbling on her lip as she craned her neck forward to see if the carriage had yet left. Two cloaked figures exited below, crossing to mount the waiting steps. The Johns unhooked the steps to put them away, then shut the door to take their places. Their demeanor was watchful, observing the surrounding street with sharp concentration while they went about their duties.

The carriage rolled forward and soon turned the corner to disappear. It was all the cue Audrey needed.

She and Julius had reached a temporary agreement at best. If they were to marry, Audrey had the chance to seduce Julius into a genuine marriage like the one she had imagined for him during their time at Lady Hays's.

But Audrey was not a skilled temptress who knew the art of beguiling men. She was a young country lass from a small village. Until very recently, she had been a maiden. This did not prepare her for what lay ahead—seducing her future husband into loving her.

The one skill she possessed was her ability to study and diagnose the ills that plagued a person. In order to do that, she needed to understand Julius.

Rising from the settee, she made for the door. Asking Julius what he was about would not reveal much. He would prevaricate if she tried to pry his justifications from him. One thing was evident about the unique individual he was— Julius was intensely private about himself. He showed one face to the world with his foppish garments and glib charms, but she knew there was a keen and calculating intelligence behind the mask he presented.

Julius had his reasons to evade a true meeting of the

minds, but she would not be so easily cast aside. The past few days had proven the gentleman was loyal to his friends whom he must love dearly. She needed to tap into that loyalty if she wished to maneuver him into a happy marriage. Since he had proposed, she had concluded, he was now hers and hers alone. Audrey had every intention of holding on to him.

She knew of one person who might be privy to his guarded thoughts. The man whom Julius had implied he admired above all others. And Audrey knew of one place she might find that man—Casanova's memoirs would be in his bedchamber, and she was going to read them. Within those pages would be the clue to persuading her betrothed. It was time to employ strategy to forge the path she wished to walk with him.

* * *

JULIUS DRUMMED his fingers on his knee, watching through the carriage window as they drove through the busy London streets. His thoughts were on Audrey—again.

He did not wish to be the sort who wed and kept mistresses. Such behavior had always been repulsive to him. For all the faults of his parents' marriage, they had never engaged in such contemptible activities. He knew this because he had investigated it for himself. If Lord Snarling had kept a mistress, Julius would have found out about it by now.

For some reason Julius could not fathom, the situation with Audrey had brought up memories he did not wish to recall.

He had returned from his Grand Tour three years earlier, feeling worse for wear from his Channel crossing. Reaching his father's townhouse, Julius had been looking forward to reuniting with his mother and sister. He had always had a close relationship with Lady Smiling, and being gone for such an extended time from his family had been difficult. Letters from his mother had kept him informed of developments over the years, and he had kept all of them in his trunk, rereading them when homesickness had occupied his mind.

Little Penelope would be more grown than the little girl he had left behind to complete his education.

Lord Snarling would be ever more distant than he had been when Julius had left.

Lady Smiling would be vivacious and welcome him home with a cup of tea and conversation.

Except ... Julius had reached home, bursting in to seek his mother and sister only to find that Lord Snarling was off to the Continent on Crown business. Nothing unexpected there. What had been a surprise was to learn from the butler, whom Julius had not previously met, that his mother and his sister had left for Paris two months earlier and not returned.

Julius had been flabbergasted, writing to his mother at his uncle's home to clarify why she was still in Paris. He had received a cheerful note in response that she would be remaining for a while yet. She was enjoying her time with her brother, who was attached to the embassy there, and Penelope's French was improving. Julius was not fooled. The note did not ring true, and he had known his mother was deflecting.

Subsequently, he had written frequent letters to urge his mother to come home. After several months, it became clear that Lady Smiling was not returning, and so Julius had buried himself in his pursuits. The gradual decline of his parents' marriage over the years had always been frustrating to witness, something which had infuriated him as a youth, but this development had affected him more than he cared to admit. It had been the final straw, leading to his vow to never wed.

Marriage is naught but an unhappy trap.

It was ridiculous that he could not board a ship to visit with his family, and he had attempted to do so twice, but his stomach had roiled at even the mild sway in the docks and he had quickly disembarked. Another crossing was an impossibility. He had cast up his accounts too many times before. The mere idea of boarding made him feel nauseated in the pit of his stomach.

Perhaps Audrey knows of a remedy?

Julius growled at the errant thought.

"Have you offered to marry her?" Brendan was watching him from across the vehicle.

"What?"

"Miss Gideon. That is what you are chewing on, is it not?"

Julius frowned. He did not wish to have his mind read. In fact, he had always gone to great lengths to be inscrutable.

"Why do you say that?"

Brendan shrugged. "I know of one subject that stirs my emotions to that degree. My wife. Her happiness. Her safety. How she will react to something I have done. Your expression was not typical."

"I informed her we will wed."

Brendan made a snorting sound. "And how did she respond to that?"

"Uh … she initially turned me down."

Brendan's lips quivered with suppressed laughter. "You were forced to persuade her?"

Julius shifted, uncomfortable to admit what had happened. "I was. And I did."

The baron leaned forward, his eyes narrowed with suspicion. "What precisely did you offer the young lady?"

Julius dropped his gaze to his gloved hand, his fingers still drumming on his knee. Looking back up, he realized he was revealing his tension. Julius was not someone who shared his problems with his friends, preferring to distract rather than expose his vulnerabilities. He rolled his shoulders and decided to try a fresh approach.

"Miss Gideon received a letter from that ghastly Lady Astley and was distraught, so I offered to marry her, which she declined. She did not wish to trap me and was thinking of leaving the realm to escape the gossip!"

Julius clenched his teeth, realizing he had given away much with the frantic tone of the last words.

Brendan cleared his throat. "And leaving the realm—that would be a bad thing?"

Julius raised his head to glare at his friend. "Yes!"

"Why?"

He continued to glare while trying to find an explanation. "Because …" An explanation did not arrive.

Brendan arched an eyebrow, awaiting his reply.

"Because I am responsible for the damage to her reputation."

His friend gave a hollow laugh, averting his gaze to the front window of the carriage. "I recall being a complete arse when I proposed to Lily. I even accused her of providing me with an alibi to trap me in marriage. It was not my finest hour."

Julius could not help himself—he winced. Brendan must have noticed within his peripheral vision, snapping his gaze back. "What did you do?" he demanded.

Julius squirmed like an errant schoolboy in his seat. "I may have … told her it was a marriage in name only."

"Which means what, exactly?"

Julius found the signet ring on his finger, awkwardly twisting it through the fabric of his glove in determined agitation. "I told her I could not promise I would not pursue other women in the future."

Brendan groaned, dropping his head into his hands. "You fool!"

"I do not know! I might. It was best to be direct and leave my options open."

His friend groaned again. "Julius … it is time for you to grow up!"

"I never planned to marry! At least I am offering her the protection of my name. She will have her independence to pursue her goals." Julius defended himself, even while appalled at how he was handling the situation. But Brendan did not understand how the idea of marriage made him cold with dread. It was futile to attempt an explanation.

The carriage drew to a halt, and Julius peered out to find they had stopped in front of the vicarage. Flinging the door open, he jumped down to the roadway without waiting for the steps to be put in place. He needed to walk away before he confessed his reservations about the arrangement he had suggested. There was nothing to be gained by discussing his muddle, and discussing any of it had been a mistake.

Leaping from the carriage had been dramatic, but impractical. He was forced to wait on the street for Brendan to disembark. Neither of them spoke. Brendan appeared to have something he wished to say, but his lips remained sealed while they approached the vicarage door.

Julius used the knocker to announce them. After a minute or two, the door swung open to reveal a buxom housekeeper of advanced years.

"May I help you?"

Brendan gave a bow, presenting his card. "Please inform Mr. Stone that Lord Filminster and Lord Trafford wish to meet with him."

The housekeeper's watery vision flickered with surprise,

and she dropped into a hasty curtsy, clearly not used to such esteemed guests. "Milords."

She scurried down the hall, returning a few minutes later. "Please, milords, come this way."

They were shown into the study, which was packed with books and overstuffed chairs. Vestments were hanging behind the door, while Stone's weighty form was dressed in a dark gray coat with long tails. His breeches were an even darker gray, and his calves were covered in black stockings. The vestments were favorable, in Julius's estimation, in that they would forgive the rounded form they concealed. In his early fifties, Stone had a wide face, bulbous nose, and a full shock of white hair.

Julius watched him carefully, but Stone did not seem alarmed by their presence. The killer would know who Julius and Brendan were, so would be guarded if surprised by a visit from them.

Stone bobbed his head in quick bows, his expression amiable if perplexed. "Lord Filminster, Lord Trafford, welcome."

"Mr. Stone, it is a pleasure to meet you."

Julius considered the vicar while they took their seats at his desk. He was hearty and had enjoyed too many biscuits and cake visiting his parish, but there were no signs of strain regarding their visit. After a few minutes of preamble, Julius leaned forward.

"We have been most impressed with what we hear about your parish. Lord Filminster and I are here to make a donation to your church."

Brendan smiled. "Indeed. I have instructed my man of business to do so."

Stone blinked in surprise before clapping his hands in gratitude. "That is wonderful news, milords. The church is always in need of repairs."

Julius nodded, observing with attention. "We hear that you have a most esteemed connection. Is it true that your brother is Lord Harlyn?"

Stone smiled, revealing a full set of slightly yellowed teeth. "Indeed, Lord Harlyn is a patron of our little church here in London."

Brendan chatted about Harlyn and the Stone family roots in Cornwall for several minutes until steering to the purpose of their visit. "Were you so fortunate as to attend the coronation in July with your brother?"

The vicar shook his head. "Oh, no! That would have been a fine event to attend, but my brother could not procure an additional invitation. No, I am afraid we had a bereaved family in our parish that day. My wife and I attended them well into the night. Sad business."

Julius set his face into sympathetic lines, despite the triumph he felt. Now that they were confident in approaching Stone and Montague directly, it was going to be short work ruling them out so the investigation could focus on Simon Scott.

"That is terrible news. Is there something we can do to assist?"

Stone gave them an account of the merchant who had passed, and the wife and children he had left behind. It was, as he had stated, a sad affair. Brendan was quick to state that they would like to visit and deliver their condolences. Having secured the name and address of the alibi, Brendan and Julius bade Stone farewell with a promise that the donation would be delivered to the church within the coming days. It would be simple to confirm the vicar's presence the night of the coronation with the family he provided solace to.

They returned to the carriage, setting off to pay a call to Montague. Brendan placed his beaver on the bench seat beside him, pulling off a glove to rake his hair, a sure sign he was uncomfortable about what he wished to say.

"Julius ... are you certain about this arrangement with Miss Gideon? She is a beautiful and competent young lady. Considering you will be wed, would she not make a good wife?"

Julius stared out the window at the passing traffic. He had been afraid Brendan might return to the subject. It was rare that he and his friends discussed such private issues, but Brendan was besotted with the delicate Lily since they had wed. "I do not wish to be wed."

Brendan sighed. "Why are you marrying her? You must care about what happens to her?"

He could not answer that question, even to himself. The idea of marriage filled him with dread. The thought of Audrey leaving England made him want to howl. Reconciling these conflicting emotions was proving impossible.

"I must protect her," was the reply Julius could give. They fell into a deep silence; the sounds of people and vehicles in the street outside, wheels hitting the beaten earth, filled in for any further conversation until they reached their destination.

Montague was fortuitously in, and they made their excuses for meeting. This time it was not quite so easy to ascertain where he had been on the night of the coronation, Montague being rather evasive, so they left without settling it. Discussing it on the way back to the Stirling townhouse, they agreed the man appeared to be more embarrassed than defensive about it. Brendan suggested that two runners working on the investigation might pay a visit to the physician's surgery. One could distract the doctor while the other took a peek at the accounts book which would list the specifics of Montague's visits for billing.

Perhaps Montague had received the same barbaric blistering treatment that Audrey had declared would incapacitate him. It would account for his unwillingness to discuss it. If that was the case, they could rule him out. It was unlikely Montague would have visited Ridley House at midnight to bludgeon the late baron if he were covered in painful blisters.

Now that matters were almost settled, and it was days until they confronted Simon Scott with his murderous deeds, Julius had nothing to distract him from the problem of his wretched betrothal. He wished he and Audrey could return to Aunty Gertrude's. Their time together had been genuinely diverting—the most fun he had in years. It had been far simpler when expectations and scandal had not imposed on their intriguing new alliance. He wished he could seek Audrey out to kiss her soft mouth, but he doubted such advances would be welcome after his dreadful proposal.

CHAPTER 17

"By recollecting the pleasures I have had formerly, I renew them, I enjoy them a second time, while I laugh at the remembrance of troubles now past, and which I no longer feel."

Giacomo Casanova

* * *

rendan's guards escorted Julius to the front door, waiting for him to enter before departing. As the door shut behind him, Julius cocked his head, his senses telling him something had changed in the few hours he had been gone. His eyes fell on a pile of trunks stacked in the hall.

A vibration of tension ran through him, and Julius exhaled in an effort to relieve it. Striding down the hall, he found the door to his father's study was open. Julius groaned in dismay, taunting himself for the butterflies fluttering in his gut.

Lord Snarling was back.

Rolling his shoulders, Julius stepped into the doorway.

"What is the meaning of this, Julius!" Lord Snarling stood near his fireplace, holding a letter with a frown on his face. It must be another poison letter from the vicious Lady Astley. Perhaps Julius should have anticipated a second message and searched the study to remove it, but he supposed he had been distracted.

"It is a letter." Julius smirked with deliberation as he gathered his thoughts. "As to its meaning—I hazard that is subjective to the reader."

His father looked up, his face set in angry lines. "You ruined Miss Gideon?"

Julius tensed, despite his prediction of its contents. "Ruined is such a … indeterminable concept, is it not?"

Lord Snarling clenched his jaw before responding. "Did you disappear with Audrey Gideon for over a week, when a narrow-minded chaperone with a penchant for gossip was to collect her?"

Julius stared back, wordless. How the bloody hell was he to explain the myriad of details that had led to compromising Audrey's reputation beyond repair? Or that he was now betrothed to the young lady?

"There were mitigating factors," he finally replied, no ready quip in the recesses of his mind.

"What could justify … this?" The earl shook the page, clearly on the verge of losing his temper altogether.

Julius considered a facetious remark but, somehow, he understood his father's point of view on this. They both cared about Audrey, and his outrage was understandable.

"She accompanied me in a bid to save my life. My … circulation was compromised at the time."

His father dropped his hand to his side, the letter crumpling as he scowled at Julius in perplexment. Then Lord Snarling shifted his gaze to over Julius's shoulder and did the damndest thing—he smiled!

Julius squinted in amazement, unable to credit the pleased expression painted across his father's face. He appeared ... happy?

"I hate to hear two of my favorite men quarrel so."

That voice!

Julius's spirits soared in startled joy. Spinning on his heel, he found someone unexpected framed in the doorway. She was even lovelier than the last time he had seen her, wearing a colorful Parisian gown. Her hair was twisted into a fashionable coif that displayed the blonde and concealed the brown. As ever, she had a broad smile upon her lips. Julius grabbed the back of an armchair in shock, his knees inexplicably weak.

"Mother!"

Lady Smiling tilted her head, her moss eyes sparkling in the afternoon light. Julius could not believe it—his mother was home.

* * *

AUDREY WAS ENSCONCED in the library, battling through the second chapter of the memoirs. Her lack of sleep, her limited German, and the unfamiliar nature of the subject had made for painful progress through the printed words. She had just woken from a doze, patting her hair to ensure it was still pinned, when a footman knocked and opened the door.

"His lordship has requested an audience in his study, Miss Gideon."

Audrey blinked in bewilderment, bobbing a nod. The manservant left, and Audrey dropped her head into her folded arms, moaning in agonized denial. Lord Stirling was back? How was she to explain what had happened? It turned out there was something worse than facing that fusty lug,

Lady Astley. And that was facing someone she respected to explain her mortifying behavior!

Was Lord Stirling aware that Julius had proposed marriage? How was the earl going to react to his heir marrying a nobody from Stirling? No one would defend that she was prepared for the role of a future countess!

Anxiety writhed in her gut. Analytically, Audrey knew it was physiologically impossible for her gut to be tied in a knot, but the empirical sensation of it belied such logic. The scandal had caught up with her, and she must face the first criticism.

Audrey rose, shaking out her shoulders and arms in a bid to gather her courage before heading out the door. Until the footman had announced the earl's return, she had not even thought about the earl and what he would have to say about all that happened during his absence. Lord Stirling had been a proper guardian, so even after months under his roof, Audrey did not know how he would react.

It was a short walk from the library to the earl's study, but even so, Audrey noted the signs of occupation. Footmen were carrying a trunk away, which seemed oddly large for the quick trip that the earl had been on. And the servants seemed on high alert—because his lordship was home?

She knocked on the study door, waiting for a command to enter and taking hold of the handle. Squaring her shoulders as if to prepare for battle, she entered.

* * *

JULIUS and his mother had departed Lord Snarling's study to talk in private. Sitting on the terrace overlooking the garden, they had a tray of tea between them, Julius still finding his feet after her unexpected appearance.

"It is good to see you, Mother." It was. Julius was still rather overcome about their reunion.

"It has been too long. Over six years since I saw you off at the docks."

Julius could not recall much about that day, other than having his head buried in a bucket. It had been such a sweet blessing to plant his boots on French soil. The winds had blustered something fierce that day as if to mock his propensity for seasickness.

"Is … Penelope …"

"She is upstairs. Exhausted from traveling, but she will be down for dinner."

Julius stared at the hedges, trying to think what to say. The timing of his mother's return was rather awkward. He had yet to explain to his father what the letter from Lady Astley meant, or the macabre circumstances that had prompted Audrey to go into hiding with him. The prospect of explaining any of it to his mother, whom he well liked, was mortifying. Especially when he considered the terrible proposal he had made—that he might pursue other women in the future? Sitting beside his mother was highlighting the despicable nature of it. Brendan had been correct. Why was he not doing the honorable thing? Not for appearances, but from genuine intent.

His mother's presence was making him face an uncomfortable truth. The reason Audrey could not be permitted to leave England was …

He cut the thought off.

"How …"

Lady Smiling sipped her tea, then put her cup and saucer down to gaze at him. "I have to thank you for bringing me home."

Julius stared at her blankly for several seconds, light-headed with the joy of seeing his mother after such a lengthy time apart, while horribly embarrassed that she would learn about his Audrey. Not to mention befuddled by the words she had just uttered.

He swallowed and tried to find words to sort through the morass. "I brought you home?"

His mother smiled and nodded. "You did. You stated the words your father needed to hear. It brings me to an understanding about the pitfalls of being raised in high society."

"Which are?"

"We are raised to not speak our minds. I was unhappy with the state of affairs with your father. I hated he worked so much, and had so little time or energy to spare for me, for our family. So I left for Paris, hoping he would change his ways. Months turned into years, but he did nothing. After a while, I gave up and resigned myself to remaining estranged. The problem was … I never attempted the direct route."

Julius struggled with his mother's intimate confession about her relationship with his father. He had suspected all that she had revealed, but it had never been spoken. His mother was not a typical member of the *ton*. She was lighter of spirit, less likely to criticize, and pleasant company. Lady Stirling was well-liked amongst the *beau monde*, despite her colorful fashion and irreverent manners, but she was still a very private person who did not discuss her problems with others. At least, never in Julius's presence.

He licked his lips, which had gone dry, raising his tea to take a sip. "The direct route?"

She smiled. "It was brave of you to speak your mind to your father. I could have saved our family a great deal of trouble if I had done so instead of haring off to Paris. It seemed at the time to be the right move, but in retrospect I was being rather dramatic to avoid"— his mother shook her head, as if to remonstrate her past self—"all in an effort to avoid being dramatic."

"Dramatic?" It was the one word he could get out of his mouth.

His mother laughed, the tinkling quality reminding him of the happiness of his youth. Long before the stilted interactions that were characteristic of the Trafford family. "Melodramatic is more like it. I never told your father that I wished for things to change. How was he to know my wishes if I never informed him?"

Julius was struggling with their conversation. His view of the world had been formed, set in stone, but currently he was back at sea. The decks were tilting beneath his feet, his head was swimming, and he was fighting back a wave of nausea. His mother's proximity, the sentiments she was vocalizing, were forcing him out of kilter as he reconsidered the conclusions he had formed over the years.

"But ... do you not ... regret being trapped in a marriage with Lord Snarli—Father?"

His mother pursed her lips, the moss hue of her eyes clouding with regret. Julius did not notice the tiny brown spots within the bands of her irises—but hers had always been harder to make out than his. "Is that what you think of your father? That he is a snarling beast?"

"He is a beast!" Julius asserted, but he was not as certain as he had been.

"Your father shoulders a great number of responsibilities. More than is fair for one man to shoulder. Your remonstrations over our family affairs have made him re-evaluate his priorities. Which is why he has informed the King that he cannot continue with his duties on behalf of the Crown. He is to make time for his other affairs. Us."

Julius frowned, dropping his gaze to the teacup and feeling a little like a boy who had been caught sneaking into the pantry. It was uncomfortable to reveal his criticism.

"Father has neglected you for years. It is untenable how he abandoned you."

He glanced up to gauge her reaction and discovered his mother's lean face reflected regret. Her fingertips stroked over the rings on her fingers as she contemplated Julius. "Son, I do not regret my marriage. I wish I had spoken with your father and attempted to assist him with his burdens. The mistakes were just as much mine as they were his. Instead of insisting he pay more mind to his duties at home, I added to his burdens. A simple conversation would have accomplished much. Your words to him were taken to heart, and I regret … I should have been more sincere in my communication with him. I cannot expect him to guess my grievances, which is why I appreciate you stated your thoughts more openly than I."

Hearing his mother accept her role in the decline of her marriage was the last thing he wished to hear. He had put his mother on a pedestal and laid all the blame on his father. Blamed it on marriage when the truth was far more compli-cated. Lord Stirling was a great man who had made mistakes. His mother was a wonderful woman who was flawed.

It had been easy to witness the stern countenance of his father and the merry mien of his mother and assume who was at fault but, if he understood her correctly, marriage was a cooperation that required efforts from both parties to succeed.

Julius dropped his face into his hands, groaning his despair as the hypothetical deck tilted to throw him off his feet, his head dizzy with the revelation he had been trying to conceal from himself.

He was in love!

There was not another on earth like his sweet Audrey!

He could not pursue his usual women, bed any widows, when all he could think about was the incredible creature who had stolen his heart. His horrible proposal was a total muck! Audrey must feel so unappreciated after his contemptible assertions that he did not know his mind and might wander off like a grubby child distracted by sweets!

Of course, he knew.

He knew that each day with her, his ardor would increase. She was bold and courageous, and he admired her more than any other he had ever met. Even Lady Smiling could not compete with such magnificent perfection. It was as if the gods themselves had forged the perfect female and presented her to his ignorant self.

Which meant he had gravely insulted the one woman who could challenge him into being a better man. A woman who could act as his true partner. Who did not attempt to chain him down, but rather tempered him into more thoughtful action.

Brendan was right. I am a fool.

* * *

AUDREY WAS the most nervous she had ever been as she walked into the earl's study. Perhaps if she had not invited Julius to deflower her two nights earlier, she would have felt more confident meeting with Lord Stirling. She would have had the confidence of one who had done no wrong.

But she had, and they had engaged in carnal relations, which meant Audrey was mortified to speak with the father of her lover about the terrible cloud of scandal she had visited upon the Stirling household.

Lord Stirling was standing by the fireplace, his hands clasped behind his back as he stared into the hearth. Audrey waited in nervous anticipation for him to turn, but after a prolonged pause, she decided to speak.

"Lord Stirling?"

He glanced over his shoulder, not quite looking at her directly, before turning his gaze back to the hearth. "I am afraid I have let you down, Miss Gideon."

Audrey fidgeted, confused about what was unfolding. "I am afraid it is me who let you down, Lord Stirling."

His shoulders tensed. Heaving a sigh, he spun on his heel to face her. He still did not make eye contact, gesturing for her to take a seat on one of the plump navy-blue armchairs facing the fireplace.

Audrey hesitated, moving forward to perch on the edge of the seat while the earl sank into the other and then picked at the pristine lapels of his coat as if to divest them of some invisible lint, as if he were ashamed to face her.

"Your father entrusted me with your welfare, and I believed I was up to the task. I never considered that my son would … Lord Trafford has never dallied with maidens before now, or I would have kept you apart."

Audrey swallowed. It would seem that the earl had not yet spoken with Julius and was unaware of the details.

"Jul—" She stopped, stricken that she had used his Christian name.

The earl tensed in alert surprise.

Audrey blew out in distress. "Lord Trafford has not informed you of the circumstances?"

"He has not. Julius made some jest about his circulation being compromised. My son is a law unto himself, and I fail to understand him at the best of times."

"I see … um … well … Lord Trafford was attacked right out in the street." Audrey gestured toward the front hall. "When I saw the knife, I had to help. I grabbed one of your swords from the display to frighten the scoundrel off. Jul—Lord Trafford sustained a laceration to his torso, he was losing a lot of blood, so I was compelled to treat him … but he insisted we were in danger so … we dashed over to Lady Hays's so I might … clean and stitch the wound—"

Lord Stirling leapt to his feet with an expression of alarm. As he was a gentleman in his fifties, with a solid build, Audrey had not been aware he could move so fast. She supposed he was rather fit, so it should not have been astonishing, but still she stared at him in consternation.

"Are you telling me Julius could have been killed?"

Audrey nibbled on her lip, giving a slight nod.

"What the blazes is going on?"

She licked her lips, trying to think how to respond. It felt disloyal to reveal what Julius had been doing without his approval. "Perhaps Jul—Lord Trafford should explain the situation himself," she proffered with a hopeful tone.

Lord Stirling shook his head as if to clear his thoughts. "I shall speak with him. Nevertheless, we have your reputation to consider. The specifics notwithstanding, I will impress on Julius that he must do the honorable thing. His outspoken objections to proper behavior matter not—he will be required to marry you. If that is what you wish?"

That was a relief. Audrey had been worried the earl would disapprove of a wedding. It was rather heartening that he held her in sufficient regard to accept her into his family. She was not a high-born lady of the *ton*—the kind of daughter-in-law that Lord Stirling would have intended to be the future countess of his people. For him to accept her despite her lower status was a considerable compliment.

"Lord Trafford has offered me the protection of his name. He informed me that a special license is being obtained by the Duke of Halmesbury in order that we wed by the end of the week."

The earl's brows drew together in a perplexed frown. "Julius offered you marriage?"

"He did."

Lord Stirling scrutinized her, cocking his head as if seeing her for the first time. He was a busy man, frequently tied up with his duties to the Crown. Audrey had no complaints; he had collected her from Stirling and taken her into his home with no indication of impatience. She understood he had had little time to take note of her, and they did not know each other all that well. But he seemed to notice her now with a studied interest. He raised a hand to rub his clean-shaven chin, his blue eyes intrigued.

"Then there is no doubting that you are unique, Miss Gideon. I was prepared for him to put up a great resistance to being wed. That he will marry you willingly … You may have done me a great favor by bringing him up to scratch. I thought … Well, never mind that."

Guilt and remorse flashed through her mind. Julius had made the offer to salvage her reputation. She still had to prove herself by winning his regard as a wife, or they would be forced to part when he pursued other more enticing paramours. The thought of losing him was enough to make her tear. Reading Casanova's memoirs was proving more difficult than she had anticipated, which meant she yet had no inkling how to win the heart of such a contrary buck.

"Thank you, my lord."

"Is this what you want? I feel I may have neglected my duties as a guardian. We should have discussed the future before now."

Audrey fortified her courage. This was her chance to make her wishes known, at least in this one subject, and she did not know when she might be granted another opportunity to do so. It was imperative she forge her path, or she would continue to be bandied back and forth by the determination of others.

"I wish to be a healer. My father taught me much over the

years, and it is my earnest desire to care for the health of others."

The earl grew thoughtful, considering what she had declared while the ormolu clock on the mantel announced the passing of seconds. "It is remiss of me to not have known this. As a future countess, you cannot engage in paid work, but it is customary for ladies of the household to care for the tenants' needs. Your father a skilled physician, and I would be gratified to have his apprentice help me with the welfare of the servants and tenants on my many estates. There are issues that you can assist me with in the coming days."

Audrey beamed, pleased to hear the earl would support her contribution. She knew that the apothecaries' guild might never allow her into their ranks, but she could forge an alternate path for herself with his patronage, which would make it much easier to be accepted by the villagers in Stirling. Through the earl, she could reach thousands of people with her knowledge.

Now if she only knew how to impose her wishes on her betrothed. She hoped she did not disappoint Lord Stirling's hopes that she could manage his son. Not only would failing break her heart, but it would prove humiliating within her new family, too.

CHAPTER 18

"I leave to others the decision as to the good or evil tendencies of my character."

Giacomo Casanova

* * *

"You ou are my heir, Julius! You could have been killed!"

"You have Pierce if something happens to me! No need to fret about heirs," Julius barked back.

Lord Stirling paused his pacing to glare at Julius with a pained expression. His features eased. "I meant to say … you are my *son*, and your loss would have been a terrible tragedy."

Julius frowned, perplexed by this strange version of his father, who had returned home with his mother. "Never say you would mourn my death? I thought I was an incorrigible lout?"

"Both can be true," snarled Lord Stirling in irritation.

Julius grinned. "I am gladdened to hear you have not

completely lost your character, Father. For a moment there, I thought your trip to Paris had tamed you into a domesticated pet."

The earl stared at him, tensing his jaw while clearly searching for a rebuke. His father was excellent at concealing his thoughts, which was why it was up to Julius to press him into genuine reactions. He did not wish for his father to harden into a cold marble statue, after all. It was, Julius theorized, important to the earl's flexibility that he be provoked with frequency.

This time, however, instead of breaking into a scathing rant about Julius's deplorable behavior, the earl continued to glare at him until, suddenly, he burst into a gale of laughter.

Julius flinched, taken aback by the echo of his youth, when his father had been more exuberant.

His father caught his breath. "I believe it is *you* who has been tamed, son."

Julius grimaced. Nauseatingly so. If his father had not insisted on this audience, he would be making reparations to Audrey for his much-lamented offer of non-marriage. He had yet to speak with her since his revelation on the terrace, but his father had caught him heading inside, so he was unfortunate to be entrenched in the study for a scolding. He supposed he must get this out of the way, so he could focus his energies on recovering his romance with his Audrey.

He made a sound that was something between a growl and a groan. What if Audrey did not love *him*? Perhaps she wished for the marriage in name only?

That was a dreadful thought to consider. He had still to reconcile himself to being besotted with his betrothed, and building a future with her. If it turned out to be for naught, and Audrey did not wish for something more, he would be sorely disappointed. They had not spoken since breakfast, and he was worried about her. He hoped her unexpected meeting with his father had not traumatized her.

His father arched a flaxen eyebrow in question.

Julius gritted his teeth, put out that he was revealing his emotions thus. "It is true! I am ... partially ... tamed."

The earl's lips spread into a smug smile. "It is more difficult than it appears to be."

Julius gave a reluctant nod.

"I approve. Miss Gideon will make an excellent wife."

He snorted. "*Miss Gideon will make an excellent wife*," Julius repeated back in mocking mimicry. "Audrey has lived under your roof for five months and you still address her as Miss Gideon. Dash it! I hate the formality of the peerage! You are such a stuffy lot."

Lord Stirling soughed heavily, dropping his gaze to contemplate the intricate navy blue and red Aubusson rug upon which he was standing.

"We could stand to be less stuffy. At least amongst family." He drew a deep breath. "*Audrey* will make an excellent wife. You have chosen well."

Julius huffed. "There was not much choosing."

His father smirked in response. "I do not believe that is true. The gods themselves may have created her because I think she may just be the perfect match to moderate my rebellious offspring. Minimally, she can patch you up in case of future punctures."

Julius twisted the ring on his finger in seething resentment. This new rendition of his father was amused by Julius's troubles. Lord Stirling probably considered the unforeseen betrothal to Audrey as comeuppance for his heir's prior mutinies. Worse, it might be true.

He just hoped the gods were kind when he presented a new offer to the lady who possessed his heart.

"What of this murder investigation? Is there a risk to your

mother and sister?" The earl's abrupt change in subject was to be expected.

Julius nodded. "There might be. We have guards in the house, but Mother and Penelope should remain home for the next few days until this danger is resolved."

His father's face hardened into stern lines. "This is untenable. I expect to meet with the other men, so we may bring this to a quick resolution."

"Agreed." Julius hoped his father might assist him with another problem, so this was not the time to resist Lord Stirling's wishes.

* * *

AUDREY HAD dinner with the family, enjoying a conversation with the lively Lady Stirling and delightful Penelope, who was a younger version of the countess. After warm congratulations on the forthcoming nuptials, along with the European custom of kisses to both cheeks, the countess talked about their adventures in Paris. It sounded like a wonderful place to visit but made Audrey yearn for the simple life she had enjoyed in Stirling. The long nights and endless social events were daunting to hear about.

After dinner, the earl asked Lady Stirling to play the pianoforte, and they adjourned to the music room which Audrey had never visited. It was an intimate room that matched the countess in style, who was wearing an exquisite sea-green dress with froths of white lace which gave the appearance of foam tipping the edges of crashing waves. The walls of the music room were covered in bronze-green wallpaper, and the floor was adorned with a rich rug woven in an elaborate radial design of red, ivory, and gold.

Penelope and Audrey crossed the room to sit on red silk chairs with gilded frames while Lady Stirling headed toward the fortepiano by the windows overlooking the shadowed gardens. The instrument was a work of art—elegant casework in mahogany with a flame maple interior and fine ormolu mounts.

Gathering up her music sheets, the countess took her seat on the bench, and Lord Stirling followed her to lean against the instrument in a relaxed pose of a man satisfied to spend the evening with his wife. Soon she began to play a popular Irish aria while Lord Stirling moved the pages, his expression one of fascination as Lady Stirling sang in a clear, perfect pitch.

The two young women listened with raptured attention. The countess was accomplished at both the instrument and singing, befitting the talent to be found in an opera house.

Audrey's thoughts drifted to her impending nuptials with Julius and her hopes of securing his attentions, entering a dreamlike state that must be ascribed to her lack of sleep as the beautiful music swept over the room like emotional recollection of times gone by.

After a few minutes, she noticed that Julius's sister was staring out the window at the setting sun with what appeared to be yearning. Audrey realized that soon she and Penelope would be sisters, so mayhap she should make an effort to build a relationship with her.

"It must have been interesting to come out in Paris?"

Penelope smiled. "Paris is a beautiful city, and the fashions there are so sophisticated compared to England. I believe Mama will be quite disappointed when she realizes she must return to London modistes for her attire."

Audrey nodded, thinking about the expression of longing she had seen on the young woman's face. "Did you meet any interesting gentlemen in Paris?"

Blinking as if returning from far-off thoughts, Penelope

hesitated. Audrey perceived she must be considering that they did not know each other well. Perhaps reaching a similar conclusion to Audrey's regarding their new relationship, she finally responded. "There was one. I was hopeful he might announce his intentions, but when I told him I was returning to London ... he did not appear moved in the least. He wished me a safe journey and ..." She stopped mid-sentence, her eyes falling to her lap where her gloved fingers toyed together.

"You hoped for a match?"

Penelope gave a short nod, her expression sad, and Audrey wished she could think of something comforting to say. She felt a tormented understanding because Penelope had lost her gentleman and been parted by hundreds of miles, while Audrey was to marry the gentleman who held her heart. They could not be more different, yet in the same predicament. Apparently, they were both lovesick for gentlemen who were all too willing to forget them.

Watching the earl in his blissful reunion with Lady Stirling, it made her want to cry. The couple were overjoyed to be together, their love evident. She wished Julius would look at her with the expression of boundless affection the earl displayed as he moved the music sheet for his wife so she could continue to play.

"Perhaps he will follow you to London," Audrey proffered, knowing her optimism was prompted by her own hopes to win Julius. Yet, she supposed, if she could not win Julius's heart, at least she was gaining a new family. It was strange but comforting to consider she would no longer be alone.

Penelope sighed. "Perhaps."

The countess played several arias, then announced it was time for their beds after such long travels. Rising to walk with her new kin into the hall and up the stairs, Audrey parted ways in the family hall and made for her bedchamber with a heavy heart.

Julius had not appeared, and she wondered where he was yet did not feel comfortable enough to question his family. She had not seen him since the morning, when they had reached their unsatisfactory agreement, and it had been a long day. What with having to meet with the earl, trying to finish reading chapter two of the curst German memoirs, and fighting with exhaustion from her sleepless night.

Despite her wish to speak with Julius, she was relieved to head to bed so she might lay her weary head on her pillow.

Sleep claimed her quickly, pulling her into its dark embrace. Sadly, it was as belligerent in its affection as Julius had been. It presented her with disturbing outcomes to her future. Her alone in Stirling, searching through the empty rooms. Before flittering to her as a silent witness in Lady Astley's home, overhearing the latest *on dits* about that disgraceful bit of muslin, Miss Gideon. Audrey had just found herself standing in the earl's study preparing to be lambasted for the social crisis she had created, when the one person never physically present in her dreams called her name.

"Audrey?"

She looked about the study in her dreams, but she could not find Julius anywhere. It was a common theme in all the dreams—that he was absent while she yearned to find him. To hold him and find out where he had been, all the while struggling with the impending doom that when she located him, he would be in the seductive arms of a trollop who had stolen his adoration.

"Audrey?"

She walked out of the study amid the earl's stern lecture to look about the hall outside, but still she could not find him.

Hesitating for a second, Audrey set off down the hall, racing up the staircase to fling open doors in the family hall. He must be here somewhere! Surely he would have informed her if he was to abandon her to her fate?

"Audrey?"

Slowly, Audrey's eyelids flickered open to discover she was in her bed and a candle must have been lit because the room was not shrouded in the shadows of the night. She blinked in a daze, her eyeballs dry and grainy. Rolling to lie on her back, she turned her head to find the source of the light, letting out a low shriek when she found Julius's face peering at hers from mere inches away.

"Good! You are awake." He rose to his feet, still dressed as she had seen him for breakfast.

"I am now. What are you doing in my room?"

He pressed his lips together, frowning. "You do not wish to see me?"

Audrey scrambled into a seated position, pressing the covers against her night rail in the manner of a proper miss. Realizing what she was doing, she released the bedding. "I … wish to see you. I am just surprised."

"I know the hour is late, but I wish to speak with you without anyone about. I have news."

Audrey's spirits plummeted. He had found some other solution than to wed her! He was here to cancel their betrothal! How she wished they had never left Aunty Gertrude's. She had been so happy there.

Her eyes misted. She needed time to read Casanova so she might work out a strategy to win him! It was horribly unfair to spring this on her—

"Your father's journals. I have found a solution."

It was as she thought! He was here to inform her—

"My father's journals?" she echoed in bewilderment. Julius did not wish to retract their arrangement?

"The guild would not budge. I used leverage on several members, but I could not make them agree."

"A-agree?" Audrey wondered if perhaps she was still asleep and this was some new hellish dream.

"To approve your membership."

She ran her hands over her plaited hair, trying to make sense of what he was saying. "Are you trying to get rid of me?"

Julius had been pacing, but he froze at her question before hastily returning to the side of the bed and sinking to his knees. "Never! I was thinking about how much you wanted to publish your father's works to help people better understand their health. I was hoping I could help, but it was to no avail. Father says he will see what he can do on your behalf, but he does not know anyone at the guild, so he must find a connection that can help."

"I … see." She did not understand, but it seemed Julius wished to help her with her goals. Perhaps he wished to balance the scales after what she had done for him? But she did not want his gratitude. She wanted his love.

"When I failed to make progress, I reconsidered the problem. You can treat people if you wish. No one will stop you from doing so. But that did not solve the problem of your father's journals—that you wish to publish his works. Father gave me the names of physicians he had been researching. Men who share similar philosophies on treatment with your father. He wishes to tempt one of them to reside in Stirling in your father's place. I met with all four men this evening and found one!"

Audrey nibbled on her lip, attempting to follow what he was saying, but she was still half asleep. With a bleary head, she noted that Julius was no longer referring to the earl as Lord Snarling. Did that mean they had reconciled some of their differences?

"One of the doctors is willing to move to Stirling?"

"No! That is up to Father to sort out. I found someone willing to add their name to your father's research!"

Audrey straightened up, sleepiness tossed aside as her mouth fell open. "What?"

"Dr. Hawley. I showed him one of your father's journals, and it turns out he has dabbled with some similar research. He said if you can assist him in organizing your father's notes along with his, he will publish the works and he agreed to credit your father."

Alarmed, she sprang from the bed to run over to her dressing table. There lay her valise along with her father's collection. Indeed, a single volume of her father's journals was missing. Spinning around to face Julius, she cried out, "Where is it?"

His face was tense at her distress. He pulled the leather-bound notebook from his pocket and held it up for her to see. "It is here. Did I make a mistake?"

Audrey stared at the notebook, befuddled. She had panicked when she had thought it was gone, but now that she knew it was safe, she was gathering the threads of what Julius was trying to tell her. He was usually more lucid, but she supposed the hour was late and he must be weary after such a long day.

"Thank you."

Julius's face relaxed in relief. "You will like Dr. Hawley. He reminded me of Dr. Gideon … actually, he reminded me of you. We spoke about the barbaric practices rife within the field. I told him about what you had done, and he was most impressed. He examined my sutures and said it was some of the neatest work he had seen. He thought my wound had healed well in such a short time."

She licked her lips, tentatively excited to meet this Dr. Hawley. An informed discussion with a fellow healer was a tempting prospect, and securing her father's legacy was welcome news. That the doctor had not been contemptuous of her skills was a promising sign. "Why did you do this?"

Julius walked over to where she was standing, returning the journal to its place and shifting to gaze down at her. He tucked an errant lock of hair behind her ear with gentle fingers. "It is my apology."

His proximity distracted Audrey. She had yearned to see him all day, and now they were alone in her room. If she moved ever so slightly, she could put her arms around him in a hug so she might hear the comforting sound of his heart beating against her cheek. Yet ... it seemed ill-advised to appear needy, even if she was feeling so. Instead, she drew a thready breath.

"What are you apologizing for?"

"For being a complete arse."

She tilted her head back so she might look at his face, and was rather amazed by what she saw there. Julius was gazing at her with a deep affection, and Audrey could not help feeling hopeful about what he was here to tell her.

"And why do you think you have been an ... arse?"

"This morning, I proposed to the most ravishing woman in London ... and had the temerity to suggest that I could ever consider bedding any of the mere mortals treading the earth when I am to marry a veritable goddess."

The damn tears threatened yet again, and Audrey was overcome by a wave of hope. "Am I dreaming?"

"You are not. I deeply regret my proposal this morning. It bothered me to have made such an ignoble offer. After speaking with Ridley and my parents, I concluded I was fighting my very destiny."

"Why?" Audrey realized the question was poorly worded, but she was enthralled by the implication they were destined to be together. "Why were you fighting destiny?"

"I suppose … I was enjoying our time together and I feared what would happen if I committed to something more. I did not wish to be trapped in a terse marriage. My parents have been unhappy for many years, so I thought it was inevitable that we, too, would grow apart." He took hold of her hand, raising it to press a kiss to her knuckles. "But I remembered what you said about me being my own man. I am not my father, and you are not my mother. We can forge our own path. Together. Which is why I would like an opportunity to restate my esteem."

Audrey swallowed. "Esteem?"

"It would be my great privilege to wed you, Audrey Gideon. Not because of the scandal, or because it is the honorable thing to do, but because I want to. You are the truest soul I ever met and I wish to wake up by your side for the rest of my days." He reached up to tuck another lock behind her other ear. "Fixing your hair, listening to you rant about the follies of ignorant medical professionals, and kissing that poor abused lip of yours better after you have nibbled it without mercy."

She winced, realizing she had been doing just that when his gaze fell to her mouth. "I … would like that very much."

It was a weak response, but Audrey was too overcome to think of words to express her joy that her dreams were coming true.

"We have much to consider. I do not wish to live in Stirling all year round, but I thought perhaps that your work with Dr. Hawley would occupy some of your time?"

Audrey grinned. "We can work something out that is mutually acceptable as long as you are by my side."

Julius smiled in agreement, lowering his head.

"Always, my love," he promised before their mouths fused together.

CHAPTER 19

"The Herbs ought to be distilled when they are in their greatest vigor, and so ought the Flowers also."

Nicholas Culpeper

* * *

Their kiss deepened, with a slow hunger of seeking tongues and breathless awe, before she slowly pulled away.

"You said … the other night—" Audrey halted, embarrassed to bring it up, but she had thought of it often. She needed to know. "—I was too inexperienced for where we were heading …?"

Julius said nothing, staring at her before reaching out to drag a solitary fingertip over her lower lip. The riot of tingling sensation he set off would have been fascinating if she had not been enthralled by the glow of his eyes which peered deep into her own.

"You liked that?" His whisper skimmed over her flushed

skin, his lips quirking into a naughty smile as he studied her intently.

She bit her lip, drunk with longing, and nodded while a blush crept up her neck. "I did."

"What the lady asks for ..." Julius toyed with the edge of her rail and trailed his fingertips over her collarbone with great concentration. Then he lowered one hand to rest it on the flare of her hip, using his restless fingers to gather her shift inch by inch so that her hem dragged up her thighs. Audrey grew agitated as he teased her with patient delibera-tion, before dropping his other hand. Taking hold of both sides, he drew the rail up, as his gaze found hers. He disap-peared from sight as the garment was pulled up and over her head to be tossed aside.

She shivered, exposed to his gaze as he stepped back to look her over, flickering over her breasts before dipping to the shadowed cleft between her legs. Heat fired a path from her moistening folds and up through her belly as she pressed her thighs together to relieve the throbbing discomfort.

Julius licked his lips, stepping back again to shrug off his coat. To her amazement, he cast it aside without his usual scrupulous attention to his wardrobe's protection. He unwound the cravat from its elegant knot, dropping it, too, without heed. Next, his jacquard waistcoat hit the floor, his blazing eyes never leaving her as she watched him disrobe. With practiced ease, his boots and stockings were discarded and his hands went to the falls of his straining breeches.

Audrey watched as he undid the buttons with his long, blunt fingers. Trembling anticipation hitched her breath when Julius tugged the buckskins and small clothes off to reveal his length standing at rigid attention. There was just enough light in the room for her to observe what she had not the other night.

She gasped in pleased revelation as her gaze flew up to

meet his. He quirked an eyebrow in curiosity. "Your … the … it *is* a different color from the …" She waved toward the crisp blond curls over his chest.

Julius chuckled, revealing a white slash of teeth in the dimness as he shook his head at her. "Ever the inquisitive physician. Perhaps I am not tempting you sufficiently if you are paying mind to my physiological … eccentricities?"

He flexed his shoulders, and she watched the muscles ripple beneath his bronzed skin, ratcheting the relentless pulsation at her core to searing heights. Noting the agitated shift of her hips, he strode back into her arms. She moaned as their naked skin came into contact, her head falling back in invitation.

Julius grazed a hand up to her breast, cupping it to flick his thumb over the turgid tip. His free hand grazed up higher, tipping her chin to steal a kiss. As his mouth brushed against hers, she panted with impatience, pressing closer so that her breasts were flattened against his hard form as she sought a deeper kiss. She could feel his hardened shaft against her, and she yearned for the sensation of him filling her aching emptiness. With great relief, she felt his large hands scraping down, down, down over her waist, her hips, until cupping her buttocks in a firm, kneading grip as he relented to her kiss. Their tongues melded together as he walked her back until she felt the bump of the cool wall against her heated skin.

She caressed with rough franticness over his back to his own firm buttocks until he turned his mouth to growl against her cheek. "Careful of the bandage, my sweet."

Audrey giggled, surprised at her ardor, hissing when his hands dipped lower, to just below the lower curve of her buttocks. He pulled her up, and Audrey raised her knees to straddle his hips as he pushed her up against the wall. His erection made contact with her swelling cleft to slide against her and brush over the throbbing pearl at the center of her pleasure. Her eyes flew up to meet his, at eye level because of how she was leveraged against the wall.

Julius pressed butterfly kisses across her cheek until he was whispering in her ear. "You have laid waste to my defenses, Audrey Gideon. Infiltrated my heart and soul, so there be not a solitary inch of me you have not pervaded with your bewitching presence."

She inhaled in tormented delight, the combination of his lean, muscled body against her, the union of their loins, and the beautiful words he whispered overwhelming her senses as she leaned her head against the painted surface. Gyrating her hips to feel the slide of his shaft again, she almost swooned from the heady delight.

A scholar of anatomy, Audrey knew it was her clitoris scraping over his penis that solicited such shooting excitement, but her academic knowledge had not prepared her for the exhilaration of the activity. Her hips bucked as she attempted to replicate the skimming contact.

"Easy," Julius purred, his face still pressed against her cheek. One of his hands slid from her buttock over the curve of her thigh to slide between her legs. A fingertip flicked over the pleading nub she attempted to assuage, circling in practiced undulation while she panted and cried in dismay at the escalation of feeling. Gyrating in rhythm with his motion, she scaled the dizzying heights until she buried her face into his neck to muffle her scream of white-hot release.

They both eased off their frantic pressures, Julius leaning down to take a hardened nipple into his warm mouth to lather the yearning tip.

* * *

JULIUS WAS RAVENOUS, his manhood rigid and impatient as he lathered Audrey's spiked nipple with his questing tongue. He wanted to drive his cock deep into her honeyed sheath, but his pride made him wait until he could wrestle his lust under control. Audrey was curious, responsive, and bold. A heady combination as he savored the scent of her womanly essence and the silky hair near to where his face was pressed. He harnessed control over his rampaging passion; the seconds ticked by until he knew he had hold of the reins.

Shifting the hand that had brought her to climax, he took hold of his member to guide it to her dripping entrance. Tensing, he plunged into her tight channel with a growl. Her naked thighs wrapped around his hips in a tight embrace, and her soft breasts pushed against him so that the turgid points of her flushed nipples dug into his chest as if to provoke him to new highs.

The sensation of her tight channel clenching his cock was overpowering. Even more so because he did not have one of those damn frock coats on to spoil the fun. Now that they were betrothed, they could dispense with such annoyances and enjoy the full experience.

Lowering his hand back to her rounded derrière, he hoisted her back up the wall to seek the right angle, then withdrew to lunge back into her sweet warmth. He wanted to howl, but they had to be mindful that the sound of their passion did not escape the recesses of her room.

Audrey was right—he could be his own man. Flippant, adventurous, and averse to traveling. He simply had a lovely new companion, and he was growing fond of that prospect.

He had not planned to make love to her tonight, willing to wait until the nuptials, but her shy invitation had been too much to resist. That as her husband he could bed her frequently was exciting beyond words. He would enjoy introducing her to many facets of carnal relations.

The thought of her beneath him, or on her knees, riding him from above, was almost too much. He was forced to pause the rush of sensation, letting his passion recede until he took up the rhythmic thrusting again. He wanted to bring her to her peak in order to feel her pulsing her release around his length.

Grabbing hold of her hands, he raised them above her head to press them to the wall, causing her back to arch so that her pelvis tilted just so. It would allow for the delicious rubbing of her tender nub against his loins as he buried his face in her neck to stroke his tongue over the elegant length, Audrey bucking her hips as a fresh wave of sensation hit her from the new position. Nipping gently at the taut flesh, he growled in satisfaction when she keened her raptures. Julius was relentless, his throbbing length driving into her again and again as his mouth explored her throat and her delicate shoulder hungrily.

Using one hand to clasp hers, he lowered the free one to cup a rounded buttock to drive into her with wild abandon as sweat beaded on his skin. He knew she was close from the frantic pull of her lungs; her face contorted and her eyes shut tight as he brought her ever closer to the brink with driving ambition until she cried out and he could feel her pulsing as she summited to her second climax.

Groaning in triumph, he continued his lunging, pleasure accumulating at the base of his spine as he drove into her, his passion thrusting her ever higher against the wall behind her back. She was glorious, and hot, and soft, and his!

Julius was mindless with craving, pounding his ravishing companion until he peaked, arching with one deep plunge forward as he spilled his seed into her tight hug with a growl of primal passion.

They remained wrapped around each other, both panting from the vigors of their lovemaking as they gradually recovered their senses. Julius backed up so she could slide down his length onto her dainty feet, but he did not let her go. He held her head to his shoulder, and her arms found their way around his waist as they leaned into each other.

"You were right," she commented, tickling him with the exhalation of her whisper.

Julius did not respond for several seconds, just enjoying the feel of her soft curves pressed to him. "About what?"

"I was too inexperienced to do that the first night," Audrey replied in an awed tone.

Julius huffed a half laugh, leaning down to lift her into his arms and walk over to her rumpled bed. "Give me a few minutes and I might show you … more."

Her silver eyes flared in wonder. "There is more?"

Julius grinned. "There is much, much more," he purred, thinking of all the positions they could try and which she might enjoy the most based on their previous encounters. He was going to enjoy schooling her far more in the practical applications of carnal relations than the theoretical tutelage he had provided his other chum for his wedding night.

Which made him think of their wedding night, and what he might do to make it special.

After another bout of lovemaking, Julius had mercy on his tender betrothed. He held her in his arms in what he supposed was a cuddle—an activity he was not well familiar with—listening to the sound of her sleeping. Their athletic endeavors had exhausted Audrey. She dozed off in the crook of his arm with her head resting on his shoulder. He should leave, but he wanted to stay a little longer to appreciate this night the way he should.

That she had welcomed him back with little complaint, and was amenable to arranging a future together, was the sweetest relief. He had not wished to approach her empty-handed, but he had reached a point earlier in the evening when he thought he might be required to. The first three physicians on his list had been, in his opinion, disappointing. They had some merits, but they were not as adamant in their beliefs as Audrey had been. His perception was they were afraid to rock the boat and would not stick to their principles, so he had not even offered them a peek at Dr. Gideon's notes.

Frustrated, he had driven himself to do one last visit despite believing it would be a waste. But meeting Dr. Hawley had been perfection. The physician had left his family dinner to take a meeting with Julius, and it had been instantly clear he differed from the others. Hawley had been intrigued by what he had to say, asking permission to inspect his injury and reading through the journal with fervent interest. Julius looked forward to introducing Hawley to Audrey so she could converse with someone who understood her passions. He himself would learn about her interests, but he could never be an expert like she was, and he wanted her to fulfill her goals.

One aggravation which needed to be dealt with was the need to have the Johns accompany him everywhere he went. Julius was willing to share his adventures with Audrey but not sullen guards, who were the leering grotesques mounted on the eaves of an ominous château in the woods. He was feeling like a fated hero from a melodramatic gothic novel, and he wanted his freedoms to be returned.

The mere thought of his current restrictions made him roll his eyes.

Shifting his head, he buried his face in the flaxen locks of Audrey's hair to inhale deeply of her herbal scent. It cleared his mind to recall what he was gaining by letting go of a few of his frivolous liberties.

Eventually, with reluctance, Julius rolled her onto her back. Gathering his clothes with a grimace—he should have folded them properly, but his desire to bury himself in Audrey's soft heat had overtaken his usual impeccable habits —he quietly left the room.

Soon they would be wed, and he would no longer need to keep up appearances for the servants or his family. He would spend every night in her bed. Would they live here, in his father's townhouse? He supposed that would be something for him and Audrey to discuss. They had numerous details to discuss about their mutual future, but he was rather excited at the prospect.

It was time he embarked on a new chapter in his life, and Audrey was his cure to the ennui that had overtaken him these past few years and the key to his future interests.

* * *

SEPTEMBER 4, 1821

Audrey rose before dawn to inspect her room before any servants appeared. She tidied away the evidence of her night of passion with Julius. Then, noting she was still fatigued from the activities of the night before, she pulled her crumpled night rail back on and climbed back into bed to fall asleep once more.

Much later, she woke again. Checking the timepiece beside her bed, she learned it was nearly noon. Not the habits of the country girl she was at heart, but she would repeat the night a thousand times and never weary of hearing Julius declare his esteem. She stretched out and turned to sniff the pillow where he had lain. It smelled like spice and leather and … man.

Rolling out of bed, she began to prepare for the day,

standing by the washstand to clean herself with the cold water when she heard a low knock on her door. She located her robe, and pattered in her bare feet to see who it was.

When she swung the door open, she found Julius leaning against the opposite wall. He grinned when he saw her, waving up a folded document in a teasing gesture. "Would you care to say your vows?"

Her mouth fell open in pleased amazement. "The license?"

"It is. Are you ready?"

Audrey snorted, gesturing at the night things she was wearing. "I think not."

He dropped his gaze to skim over her form, a lustful expression on his face. "I do not see the problem, but if you wish to change, do you have something pretty in that wardrobe of yours?"

Audrey looked back at the mahogany wardrobe and pulled a face. "There is nothing but mourning garments in there," she admitted.

"Then my mother will be along to assist you. Between her and Penelope there should be a French gown that will suit."

She nodded her agreement. "What of a vicar?"

Julius smiled. "The Reverend E. Stone is enjoying a repast in the breakfast room while we dawdle upstairs."

"Mr. Stone! You confirmed he had an alibi, then?"

"We did. He is in the clear and was most flattered to be invited to conduct the nuptials for such an illustrious family. He was the first person I thought of when the special license was delivered this morning."

Audrey found she was pleased. The vicar seemed a jovial sort. "Then send your mother!"

She shut the door and raced back to complete her ablutions before dressing in her stockings and shift. Then she took a seat at the dressing table to brush out her hair. Soon Lady

Stirling arrived with her lady's maid who had several gowns folded over her arm. They chattered with good cheer while helping Audrey into her stays and one of the gowns which seemed most likely to fit, with its relaxed bodice to hug her full bosom and flowing skirts. It was a soft azure with indigo braiding at the waist and neck, with a froth of ivory lace down the bodice. Peering in the mirror, Audrey was pleased with her appearance. The lady's maid twisted her hair into a soft coif that allowed her blonde locks to billow and frame her face, and the dress accentuated the color of her eyes.

"You look beautiful, my dear." Lady Stirling was staring at her in the mirror, dabbing at tears with a lace handkerchief as she considered Audrey's reflection. She was unaccustomed to a motherly presence, but it was nice to share this with the countess.

Audrey grinned. It would do.

Shortly after, they left her room, Lady Stirling accompanying her to the drawing room that overlooked the street where they found several people gathered. Lord Stirling was sartorial perfection in dark blue. Penelope was by his side, more cheerful than the night before.

Julius was chatting with Stone. In addition, Lord Filminster was in attendance with a diminutive young lady who must be the baroness. Her coloring was the same as her much taller brother, Lord Abbott who stood at a window with his bride—the lovely Lady Abbott who towered over the other women in the room. Julius came forward, offering his arm so he could walk her around for introductions.

Another couple entered while she and Stone conversed over the coming ceremony, and Julius drew them over.

"Miss Gideon, I would like to introduce my sometimes chum, Lord Saunton. Although it is his brother with whom I am closest."

Lord Saunton, a handsome nobleman, shook his head in grinning rebuke before dipping a bow to Audrey. "Pay Trafford no mind, Miss Gideon. We are never friends. I merely tolerate him for my brother's sake."

Audrey smiled, dropping a curtsy. "The honor is mine, my lord."

Julius turned to the earl's wife. "Lady Saunton, may I present my bride, Miss Audrey Gideon?"

Lady Saunton's expression was warm as she gave a nod of her head. "Miss Gideon, my cousins are most pleased that you saved Lord Trafford from himself. They have spoken of nothing else in days!"

The countess gestured to the tiny Lady Filminster and her towering brother, Lord Abbott. Audrey was relieved to have the connection clarified to help her recollect that Julius had mentioned the Sauntons before.

"Unfortunately, the duke is meeting with the Home Secretary this morning to discuss what has happened, so he and the duchess will not be joining us for the nuptials."

Audrey blinked in surprise, not having considered that a duke would feel the need to make his excuses. She had not known the duke even knew who she was, but she recollected that Julius had mentioned something in regard to the special license. It must have been His Grace who had had the documents delivered this morning. It was daunting to consider that she was marrying into such lofty circles and she had several peers in the room to witness her vows.

Soon she and Julius were standing in front of the vicar, and the ceremony was underway. Until their vows drew to a close and she was Lady Trafford, an honorary viscountess with an earl for a father-in-law and a beloved husband who had her arm tucked around his.

She peered up at Julius to see how he was responding to

the loss of his bachelorhood, and he returned her gaze with a joyful smile before dropping his head to buss her cheek.

Much later, after a hearty wedding breakfast with their exuberant guests, Audrey pulled him aside as the ladies made their departures but the men remained behind.

"What of the investigation?"

"Montague is confirmed to have been at the physician for that terrible blistering treatment on the afternoon of the coronation. We are satisfied that he could not have been visiting the baron within a few hours, so the entire investigation has turned to unearthing evidence against Scott. That is what the duke is about this morning. He is having an informal discussion with Sir Robert about what we know without providing any names or details. The men will meet with my father later when the duke returns from the Home Office so we may determine how to move forward."

"So this matter is almost done?"

Julius leaned down, speaking in a low voice that sent shivers racing down her spine. "It is. And matters between us are just beginning."

Audrey was unable to respond, her heart overflowing with the knowledge that the elusive Julius Trafford was now her true husband, and best of all, he seemed more than content to assume the role.

His whisper skated over her cheek as he asked an unexpected question.

"Do you wish to visit my tailor with me in the morning?"

She squinted in confusion. "Do you mean a modiste?"

Julius grinned, a mischievous twinkle in his green-brown eyes. "Nay. My mother can accompany you to a modiste. I was thinking you might like some gentlemen's garments made to fit so we might visit some new places. Would you like to see the horse auctions at Tattersall's?"

Audrey's mouth fell open. "Yes!"

"You shall need clothing that conceals ..." His hand brushed over her hip, his gaze growing heated as it fell to caress over her curves.

She licked her lips, recalling their previous evening in her bed and hoping that he would be free to join her soon. Very, very soon.

EPILOGUE

"Hatred, in the course of time, kills the unhappy wretch who delights in nursing it in his bosom."

Giacomo Casanova

* * *

*T*he men gathered in the earl's study, waiting for the duke, who had not yet made an appearance. The afternoon was warm, and the windows and doors stood open to facilitate a draught through the room. Julius checked his timepiece with impatience. He wished to join Audrey upstairs, but they needed to bring this investigation to a conclusion.

The duke was to come by after the Home Office, having heard the Home Secretary's thoughts on the information he was presenting about the baron's murder. Julius moved to stand in the breeze from one of the windows, leaning an arm against the window frame.

A tap at the door had all the men turning their heads to

see if the duke had arrived, only to find a footman. The servant hurried in to speak with Lord Stirling in a low voice, before exiting. Soon he returned with a familiar figure accompanying him.

"Mr. Briggs," announced the footman, bowing in departure.

Brendan and Saunton had risen to their feet with surprised expressions. "Briggs!"

The runner was the first authority to have been summoned on the morning Brendan had found the baron lying dead in his study weeks ago. The investigator was a wiry man in his forties, with a crumpled overcoat, a beaten-up hat he was carrying under his arm, and scuffed leather shoes that had seen better days. But the true evidence of the risks his occupation posed was the scar over one of his beetling brows, which gave his lean face a menacing appearance.

Briggs had believed Brendan was innocent from the first meeting, and once he had been cleared, Brendan had hired the runner to head a private investigation into the murder. Julius had not seen the runner since that time because the runners had been occupied with the hunt for information.

"Milords, Lady Filminster said I would find you here and that I ought not hesitate to join you."

"Have you news?"

Julius could hear the tension in Brendan's voice. The runners had been searching parish records across the country to find a record of one of the Peters marrying a woman from the Continent.

Briggs nodded, stroking his mustache to look about in question.

Brendan grimaced. "Lord Stirling, this is the runner who is heading the investigation."

Briggs turned toward him to give a bow, but Julius's

father waved a hand. "Please do not concern yourself with formalities. Let us hear what Briggs has to say."

The runner gave a nod. "We found something. When we received word that Simon Scott was likely the killer, we concentrated our efforts on the parishes near the Blackwood family estate, where we found a record of a Peter Scott marrying a—" Briggs pulled out a notebook and consulted it. "—Bianca Romano. They wed in 1794. We believe she might have been from Florence, where Peter Scott spent considerable time."

Brendan appeared shocked, sinking back into his seat. "It is true, then. Simon Scott murdered my ... father?"

Julius caught the glimpse toward Lord Stirling and the hesitation in his question. Brendan had recollected that the earl was unaware of the peculiarities of Brendan's parentage.

Briggs gave a noncommittal shrug. "That is how it appears."

Saunton remained standing. "Any clues why the family is unaware of the nephew who is the true heir to Lord Blackwood?"

"What we could gather from speaking with some locals was that Peter Scott and his father had a terrible falling out when the son refused a commission in the army. It is not clear that anyone informed the late Lord Blackwood that his estranged son had married, and it appears Peter Scott left the area—possibly the country—soon after. Now that we have an accurate window of time, it will be easier to locate more information."

Julius whistled through his teeth, amazed to confirm they had narrowed down to one suspect after expending so much time and energy. Lady Filminster had been brutalized, three men forced to marry, and Simon Scott went about his day with the air of one who was carefree. It was beyond the pale, what the scoundrel had put them all through.

"I propose we confront the fiend with his crimes," Julius announced, faces swiveling in his direction as they contemplated his announcement. "It will end the risk to our families when there is no longer a secret to conceal."

* * *

Meet Simon Scott and his talented neighbor, Madeline Bigsby, in the next chapter of Inconvenient Scandals, *The Trouble With Titles.*

She has loved him for years. In his darkest hour, she is determined to save him by uncovering the real killer.

AFTERWORD

Sir Walter Scott convinced King George IV to visit Scotland, which he did in 1822. This rocketed the notion of clan tartans into widespread popularity which lives on to this day, but at the time of Julius's adventure with Audrey, it was already a fashion amongst members of the Highland Society of London.

Giacomo Casanova wrote his memoirs in the 18th century, completing them over twenty years before the year in which this story is set. Written in French, the first volume was published in German in 1822. Part memoir and part autobiography, his twelve volumes provided great insight into the customs of European social life.

The dates do not quite match up with my story, but I took the liberty of including the first volume in the story because it so encapsulated the adventurous and irreverent character of Julius Trafford. He is, after all, enterprising and may have received an early version of such auspicious work?

Nicholas Culpeper was a botanist and physician from the 1600s. His approach to utilizing herbs profoundly influenced medicine in the North American colonies and continues to impact modern medications. Notably, Culpeper detailed the medicinal benefits of the foxglove, which serves as the botanical precursor to digitalis, a treatment for heart conditions. He was among the pioneers in translating Latin documents that discussed the medicinal properties of plants, and his legacy endures through the presence of "Culpeper" herb and spice shops in North America, and beyond.

Audrey washes her hands before treating Julius's wound. Although not common medical practice in 1821, midwives did so which is believed, in hindsight, to be the primary reason they suffered fewer fatalities than medical personnel. Romans bathed frequently and gentlemen of ancient China washed their hands at least five times a day. These were all practices that Dr. Gideon could have been aware of as a healer who sought out traditional treatments.

Now that the missing heir is closer to being located, Simon Scott is about to have an uncomfortable confrontation with several powerful lords. With no alibi for the night of the coronation, and no defense to provide as the evidence mounts up, how can he prove it was not he who visited the baron on the night of the coronation to bludgeon him in a fit of murderous desperation?

Does he have an unknown nephew who will inherit what he believed was his birthright?

Other than he, who would have a motive to conceal evidence of a living heir?

As the stakes mount up, Simon will need someone by his side as he battles against the accusations. Can his childhood friend and neighbor, Madeline Bigsby, help him thwart the killer's plans to frame him for a murder he did not commit?

All will be revealed in *The Trouble With Titles*, the fourth book in the Inconvenient Scandals series of Regency mystery romances.

ABOUT THE AUTHOR

Nina started writing her own stories in her teens but got distracted when she finished school and moved on to non-profit work with recovering drug addicts. There she worked with people from every walk of life from privileged neighborhoods to the shanty towns of urban and rural South Africa.

One day she met a real-life romantic hero. She instantly married her fellow bibliophile and moved to the USA where she enjoyed a career as a sales coaching executive at an Inc 500 company before embarking on her new career as an author of Regency romances. She lives with her husband on the Florida Gulf Coast.

Nina believes in kindness and the indomitable power of the human spirit. She is fascinated by the amazing, funny people she has met across the world who dared to change their lives. She likes to tell mischievous tales of life-changing decisions and character transformations while drinking excellent coffee and avoiding cookies.

Join Nina's Newsletter at NinaJarrett.com for free books, fun Regency content, announcements, and exclusive discounts.

Follow Nina Jarrett on your favorite platform.

ALSO BY NINA JARRETT

INCONVENIENT BRIDES

Book 1: The Duke Wins a Bride

Book 2: To Redeem an Earl

Book 3: My Fair Bluestocking

Book 4: Sleepless in Saunton

Book 5: Caroline Saves the Blacksmith

INCONVENIENT SCANDALS

The Duke and Duchess of Halmesbury will return, along with the Balfours, Abbotts, and Lord Trafford in an all-new suspense romance series.

Book 1: Long Live the Baron

Book 2: Moonlight Encounter

Book 3: Lord Trafford's Folly

Book 4: The Trouble With Titles

Book 5: Lord of Intrigue

INCONVENIENT VENTURES

The duke's brother and his friends journey from Italy in a bid to right past wrongs through the pursuit of treasure.

Book 1: The Courtship Trap

* * *

BOOK 1: THE DUKE WINS A BRIDE

Her fiancé betrayed her. The duke steps in. Could a marriage of convenience transform into true love?

In this spicy historical romance, a sheltered baron's daughter and a celebrated duke agree on a marriage of convenience, but he has a secret that may ruin it all.

She is desperate to escape...

When Miss Annabel Ridley learns her betrothed has been unfaithful, she knows she must cancel the wedding. The problem is no one else seems to agree with her, least of all her father. With her wedding day approaching, she must find a way to escape her doomed marriage. She seeks out the Duke of Halmesbury to request he intercede with her rakish betrothed to break it off before the wedding day.

He is ready to try again...

Widower Philip Markham has decided it is time to search for a new wife. He hopes to find a bold bride to avoid the mistakes of his past. Fate seems to be favoring him when he finds a captivating young woman in his study begging for his help to disengage from a despised figure from his past. He astonishes her with a proposal of his own—a marriage of convenience to suit them both. If she accepts, he resolves to never reveal the truth of his past lest it ruin their chances of possibly finding love.

* * *

BOOK 2: TO REDEEM AN EARL

She planned to stay unmarried, but Lord Richard Balfour is determined to make her his countess.

In this steamy historical romance, a cynical debutante and a scandalous earl find themselves entangled in an undeniable attraction. Will they open their hearts to love or will his past destroy their future together?

She has vowed she will never marry...

Miss Sophia Hayward knows all about men and their immoral behavior. She has watched her father and older brother behave like reckless fools her entire life. All she wants is to avoid marriage to a lord until she reaches her majority because she has plans which do not include a husband. Until she meets the one peer who will not take a hint.

He must have her...

Lord Richard Balfour has engaged in many disgraceful activities with the women of his past. He had no regrets until he encounters a cheeky debutante who makes him want to be a better man. Only problem is, he has a lot of bad behavior to make amends for if he is ever going to persuade Sophia to take him seriously. Will he learn to be a better man before his mistakes catch up with him and ruin their chance at true love?

* * *

MY FAIR BLUESTOCKING: BOOK 3

A rebellious young woman. A spoilt buck. When passions ignite, will opposites attract?

She thinks he is arrogant and vain ...

The Davis family has ascended to the gentry due to their unusual connection to the Earl of Saunton. Now the earl wants Emma Davis and her sister to come to London for the Season. Emma relishes refusing, but her sister is excited to meet eligible gentlemen. Now she can't tell the earl's arrogant brother to go to hell when he shows up with the invitation. She will cooperate for her beloved sibling, but she is not allowing the handsome Perry to sway her mind ... or her heart.

He thinks she is disheveled, but intriguing ...

Peregrine Balfour cannot believe the errands his brother is making him do. Fetching a country mouse. Preparing her for polite society. Dancing lessons. He should be stealing into the beds of welcoming widows, not delivering finishing lessons to an unstylish shrew. Pity he can't help noticing the ravishing young woman that is being revealed by his tuition until the only schooling he wants to deliver is in the language of love.

Will these two conflicting personalities find a way to reconcile their unexpected attraction before Perry makes a grave mistake?

* * *

BOOK 4: SLEEPLESS IN SAUNTON

A sleepless debutante. A widowed architect. A lavish country house party might be perfect for new love to bloom.

In this steamy historical romance, a sleepless young woman yearns for love while a successful widower pines for his beloved wife. Hot summer nights at a lavish country house might be the perfect environment for new love to bloom.

She cannot sleep ...

Jane Davis went to London with her sister for a Season full of hope and excitement. Now her sister is married and Jane wanders the halls alone in the middle of the night. Disappointed with the gentlemen she has met, she misses her family and is desperate for a full night's sleep. Until she meets a sweet young girl who asks if Jane will be her new mother.

He misses his wife ...

It has been two years since Barclay Thompson's beloved wife passed away. Now the Earl of Saunton has claimed him as a brother and, for the sake of his young daughter, Barclay has acknowledged their relationship. But loneliness keeps him up at night until he encounters a young woman who might make his dead heart beat again. Honor demands he walk away rather than ruin the young lady's reputation. Associating with a by-blow like him will bar her from good society, no matter how badly his little girl wants him to make a match.

Can these three lonely souls take a chance on love and reconnect with the world together?

* * *

BOOK 5: CAROLINE SAVES THE BLACKSMITH

She helps injured the blacksmith on Christmas Eve, leading to a romantic attraction despite their aversion to love.

She has a dark past that she must keep a secret. He has a dark past he wishes to forget. The magic of the festive season might be the key to unlocking a fiery new passion.

She will not repeat her past mistakes ...

Caroline Brown once made an unforgivable mistake with a handsome earl, betraying a beloved friend in the process. Now she is rebuilding her life as the new owner of a dressmaker's shop in the busy town of Chatternwell. She is determined to guard her heart from all men, including the darkly handsome blacksmith, until the local doctor requests her help on the night before Christmas.

He can't stop thinking about her ...

William Jackson has avoided relationships since his battle wounds healed, but the new proprietress on his street is increasingly in his thoughts, which is why he is avoiding her at all costs. But an unexpected injury while his mother is away lays him up on Christmas Eve and now the chit is mothering him in the most irritating and delightful manner.

Can the magic of the holiday season help two broken souls overcome their dark pasts to form a blissful union?

* * *

BOOK 6: LONG LIVE THE BARON

After she clears his name of murder, a marriage of convenience

is the only way to save her reputation! Will their uneasy alliance spark a lasting passion?

A steamy historical suspense romance, about a young woman driven to do the right thing, a lord who does not quite appreciate the gesture, and a murder investigation that could end their new relationship before it begins.

Her conscience drives her to act ...

Miss Lily Abbott knows the new baron is innocent because she saw him entering the widow's home next door at the time of the crime. But when the widow refuses to assist him, this young woman who hoped to marry for love cannot stand idly by when she knows the truth. Lily risks everything to provide an alibi for the glib gentleman who barely remembers her name.

He can't believe he has to marry her ...

Lord Brendan Ridley stands accused of patricide to gain the title he now holds. Not even his close family connection to the powerful Duke of Halmesbury can help him. He prays his paramour will come forward to clear his name, but honor dictates he not reveal his whereabouts that night without her consent. When help comes from an unexpected quarter, he finds himself forced to marry an annoying chatterbox to save her from scandal.

When these two mismatched people are forced to marry, will they find a way to work together to reveal an enduring passion before the real murderer strikes again?

* * *

BOOK 7: MOONLIGHT ENCOUNTER

Lord Aidan Abbott investigates Mr. Smythe but compromises his daughter, Gwen, at a ball in front of a crowd of important guests.

In this steamy historical romance, the heir to a viscountcy is determined to protect his sister, accidentally ruining a young woman while searching her father's home. Now he will need to choose between his crusade and the growing love between them.

He feels guilty for failing his family ...

Lord Aidan Abbott neglected his duties as a chaperone when his parents left his little sister in his charge. Because of him, Lily was forced to wed under a cloud of scandal. Now Aidan must solve a murder to keep his sister and her new husband out of danger.

She is caught unawares ...

A mysterious lord interrupts Miss Gwendolyn Smythe while she is taking air on the terrace. Unfortunately, they are discovered together, so she is forced to marry a man she has never met before to quell the scandal. Now Gwen is determined to make the best of their new marriage, with or without his cooperation.

While Aidan continues to secretly investigate Gwendolyn's family, he realizes that the scholarly redhead now holds his heart in her hands. How can he reveal what he has been doing without shattering their only chance at love?

* * *

BOOK 8: LORD TRAFFORD'S FOLLY

A daring lord and a young woman find themselves in peril, igniting a possible romance as they escape to stay alive.

A steamy historical suspense romance, about a lord who agrees to help his friends with their quest to solve a murder. Now he must fend for himself while protecting the young lady he has endangered with his choices. Can he keep her safe from harm from both the enemy pursuing them, and his urge to kiss those plump lips?

He thought it would be a lark ...

When Lord Julius Trafford, the heir to an earl, agrees to help his friends in a quest to solve a murder, it was mostly because he was bored. Now he is in hot water, and he has dragged his father's delectable ward into danger with him. Together, they are forced on the run, and Lord Trafford must engage his wits before it's too late.

She is determined to keep him alive ...

Miss Audrey Gideon feels compelled to care for Lord Trafford when he is attacked by a murderous assailant. As they make their escape from London in search of safety, Julius begins to demonstrate his true potential and Audrey wonders if there is more to the foppish heir than meets the eye.

Can this unlikely pair rise to the challenge and discover true love along the way?

* * *

BOOK 9: THE TROUBLE WITH TITLES

She has loved him for years. In his darkest hour, she is determined to save him by uncovering the real killer.

In this steamy historical romance an heir stands to lose everything unless he can find the truth, and the girl next door is the only one standing by his side while danger lurks in the shadows.

He could lose his title and his life ...

Simon Scott is set to inherit a title and a fortune until powerful lords accuse him of murder. Now his betrothed has broken ties with him and he could be arrested at any moment. Trouble is he knows he is innocent, but who will believe him when all the evidence points to him?

She knows he is not a killer ...

Madeline Bigsby has been in love with Simon since they were children, but he was too self-absorbed to notice. In his darkest hour, she is determined to save him by uncovering the real killer.

The stakes are high and love has never been such a dangerous game. Can Simon accept help from the girl he left behind to discover who has framed him and perhaps learn the value of true love along the way?

* * *

BOOK 10: LORD OF INTRIGUE

A mysterious heir is on his way to England. Will Molly be able to find her place in his household, or will a tragic fate befall one of them within the week?

In this steamy mystery romance, two people are thrust together on the ashes of a disastrous murder plot. Now they must find a way to work together despite the unexpected attraction between them.

No one knows the new heir ...

Marco Scott has never been to England, but now he is next in line to a title. Surrounded by potential enemies, he must find his footing in this strange land. Learning he is to act as guardian to an enticing young woman only makes matters more complicated.

A ward stuck in a stranger's home ...

Molly Carter is handed over to the new heir, a man no one knew existed until it was revealed a peer was murdered to conceal his existence. To make matters worse, he might be the most beautiful man alive, which is making her blurt out the most embarrassing nonsense.

But someone is not happy that Marco will inherit. Danger lurks in the shadows, and he can't inherit if he's dead. Can Molly and Marco come to terms with their newfound passion to solve the mystery before one of them ends up in a grave?

Printed in Dunstable, United Kingdom